SEASIDE

Hearts

Seaside Summers
Love in Bloom Series

Melissa Foster

ISBN-13: 978-1-941480-03-8
ISBN-10: 1941480039

Cover Design: Natasha Brown

WORLD LITERARY PRESS
PRINTED IN THE UNITED STATES OF AMERICA

A NOTE TO READERS

As many of my readers know, I spend summers on the Cape, and the Seaside Summers books are born from my love of the area, the people, and my experiences. However, although friends might see pieces of themselves in the book, these characters are fictional. Pete Lacroux and Jenna Ward are two of my favorite Seaside friends, and longtime friends turned lovers are always so fun to write. I hope you enjoy Pete and Jenna's love story as much as I do. If this is your first Seaside novel, all of my books are written to stand alone, or to be enjoyed as part of the larger series, so dive right in and enjoy the fun, sexy ride! You'll find a recipe for Luscious Leanna's Sweet Treats jam in the back of this book.

The best way to keep up to date with new releases, sales, and exclusive content is to sign up for my newsletter. www.MelissaFoster.com/news

ABOUT THE LOVE IN BLOOM BIG-FAMILY ROMANCE COLLECTION

Seaside Summers is just one of the series in the Love in Bloom big-family romance collection. Characters from each series make appearances in future books, so you never miss an engagement, wedding, or birth. A complete list of series titles is included at the end of this book, along with a preview of the next book in this series.

You can download **free** first-in-series ebooks and see my current sales here:
www.MelissaFoster.com/LIBFree

Visit the Love in Bloom Reader Goodies page for downloadable checklists, family trees, and more!
www.MelissaFoster.com/RG

CHAPTER ONE

THERE SHOULD BE an unwritten rule about drooling over construction workers, but Jenna Ward was damn glad there wasn't. She sat on the porch of the Bookstore Restaurant, soaking up the deliciousness of the three bronzed males clad in nothing more than jeans and glistening muscles that flexed and bulged like an offering to the gods as they forced thick, sticky tar into submission. Their jeans hung low on strong hips, gripping their powerful thighs like second skins and ending in scuffed and tarred work boots. What red-blooded woman didn't get worked up over a gorgeous shirtless man in work boots?

God help her, because she needed this distraction to take away her desire for Peter Lacroux, which went hand in hand with summers on the Cape and consumed her in the nine months they were apart. She zeroed in on one particularly handsome blond construction worker. His hair was nearly white, his jaw square and manly. She wanted to march right out to the middle of the road that split the earth between the restaurant and the beach and be manhandled into submission. Right there on the tar. Wrestled and groped until all thoughts of Pete evaporated.

"Wipe the drool from your chin, *chica*." Amy Maples handed Jenna a margarita and, pointedly, a fresh napkin, as she settled into the chair across from her. "Good Lord, woman. What's up with you this summer? I swear you're in heat. I can practically smell your pheromones from over here."

Jenna gulped her drink and righted her red bikini top, which was trying its damnedest to relieve itself of her enormous breasts. Even her bikini top was ready for a man. A *real* man. A man who craved her as much as she craved him.

Jenna reluctantly turned away from Testosterone Road and faced her best friends. The women she had spent her summers with here in Wellfleet, Massachusetts, for as long as she could remember and the women she hoped would help her through her most important summer *ever*.

Okay, she'd self-defined it as such, and it was probably a poor excuse for *most important*, but that's how it felt. Huge. Momentous. Gargantuan. *Great.* Now she was thinking about other huge things...

"You've been here for a week, and you still haven't told us why you're all claws and hormones. Want to clue us in, or are we supposed to guess?" Bella Abbascia was a brazen blonde—and she, like Leanna Bray, the disorganized brunette of their bestie clan—had already found her true love. A feat Jenna only dreamed of. Ached for might be more accurate, and Bella was right; it was time to come clean.

Jenna downed the last of her drink and slapped her palms on the table.

"I don't care what it takes; this is *my* summer. I'm done pussyfooting around. I want a man. A *real* man." She slid her eyes to the construction workers again. *Yum!* She tried to convince herself to feel something more for the construction worker, but the only person her mind found yummy was Pete—and it didn't seem to want to make room for others.

She wasn't above faking it to pull herself through the charade. Maybe if she tried hard enough, she could talk herself into believing it.

"So, you're going after Pete?" Leanna sipped her margarita and arched a brow. "How is that any different from every single one of the last five summers?"

"Oh no. Peter Lacroux can kiss my big, sexy ass."

"Jenna!" Amy Maples's eyes widened. The sweetest of the group, she was perfectly petite, with kindness that sailed from her blue eyes like a summer breeze.

"You do have a mighty fine ass, Jen," Bella said. "But you've had a wicked crush on that man forever. If you're going to focus your attention on someone—" Bella bit her lower lip and shook her head as one of the construction workers wiped sweat from his brow, pecs in full, drool-inciting view. Bella raked her eyes down his sculpted abs. "Um...Okay, yeah. They're pretty damn hot. But why throw Pete away?"

Jenna had been over this in her mind a hundred times. She locked her eyes on her glass and exhaled. "Because I'm not going to spend another summer chasing a man who doesn't want me. And this is a tough summer for me. I have to break up with my mother, and that's enough heartache for a few short weeks."

"Break up with your mom? Can a person do that?" Amy glanced around the table.

"I gather she's not taking your dad getting remarried well?" Leanna asked. "I had such high hopes when she didn't fall apart during the divorce."

Jenna rolled her eyes. "So did I. You'd think that two years after her divorce, she'd be able to sort of compartmentalize it all, but, girls, you have no idea." Jenna shook her head and held up her glass, indicating to the bartender that she needed another drink. She could have gotten up and retrieved the drink herself, but Jenna wanted the diversion of the sexy waiter who would deliver it to their table. She'd take as many diversions as she could get to keep from thinking of Pete.

"She's gone…hmm…how do I say this respectfully? She's not gone cougar, but she's definitely acting different. She's dressing way too young for a fifty-seven-year-old woman, and I swear she thinks she's my new best friend. She wants to talk about guys and sex, and what's worse is that she suddenly wants to go dancing and to bars. I love my mom, but I don't need to go to bars with her, and talking about sex with her? *Please.*"

"I was wondering what was going on when she texted you a hundred times last night." Bella pulled her hair back and secured it with an elastic band. "She's going through a hard time, Jenna. Give her a break. She was married for thirty-four years. That's a long time. I'm not even married to Caden yet, and if we broke up and he married a younger chick, I'd be devastated." Bella and Caden met last year when Bella had been busy rearranging her own life. She'd started a work-study program for the local school district, fallen in love with Caden Grant, a cop on the Cape, and now she was as close as a mother to his almost-sixteen-year-old son, Evan. The Cape was a narrow stretch of land between the bay and the ocean. Bella and Caden lived on the bay side in a house that Caden had owned when they'd met, and they would be staying at Bella's Seaside cottage on and off this summer.

"I get it, okay? I just…God, it's just so hard to see her struggling with her looks, and honestly, you know I adore her, but she's sort of making a fool of herself. It's been two years since the divorce. She just needs to get over it and move on. I do feel bad because I had to take a firm stand and tell her that I wasn't going to come home until *after* the summer."

"Why do you feel bad? That's what you do every summer." Amy eyed one of the construction workers, a water bottle held above his mouth, a stream of wetness disappear-

5

ing down his throat. "Holy hotness." She fanned herself with her napkin.

Jenna watched the guy wipe his mouth with his heavily muscled forearm. "Yeah, but she wanted me to come home to *hang out* with her a few times." The sexy waiter brought Jenna her drink.

"Thank you, doll." She watched his fine ass as he walked away.

"Doll?" Amy giggled.

"See?" Jenna bonked her forehead on the table. "That's *her* word. Doll? Who says that? You have to help me. She'll ruin me, and I swear if I spend one more summer lusting after Pete, then I'll be empty on all accounts. My mother will hate me, my hoo-ha will be lonely, and I'll use words like *doll*. Jesus, do us all a favor and shoot me now."

"Yeah, well, about that whole Pete thing?" Leanna nodded toward the crosswalk, where Pete Lacroux was crossing the road carrying the cutest damn puppy.

Holy mother of God, he is fine. I want to be that puppy. Those construction workers couldn't hold a candle to Pete, and Jenna's body was proof as her pulse quickened and her mouth went dry. His shoulders were twice as broad as those of the boys on the pavement, his waist was trim, and—*holy hell*—he shifted the pup to the side, giving Jenna a clear view of the pronounced muscles that blazed a path south from his abs and disappeared into his snug jeans. Those damn muscles turned her mind to mush. Yup. She'd gone as dumb as a doorknob.

"Breathe, Jenna," Amy whispered. "You are so not over him."

Jenna couldn't tear her eyes from him. Years of lust and anticipation brewed deep in her belly. *Just one more summer? One more try?*

No. No. I can't do this anymore. "The man's one big tease. I'm moving on." She forced herself to tear her eyes away from him and guzzle her drink.

And then it happened.

She felt his presence behind her before he ever said a word. Jenna, the woman who could talk to anyone, anytime, had spent years fumbling for words and making atrocious attempts at flirting with the six-foot-two, dark-haired, mysterious specimen that was Peter Lacroux, but despite catching a few heated glances from him, she remained in the friend zone.

Regardless of how her body reacted to him, she didn't need to beg for a man she could barely talk to, or follow after him like that adorable puppy snuggled against his powerful chest.

She was totally, utterly, done with him.

Maybe.

PETE EYED THE women from the Seaside cottage

community, or the Seaside girls, as he'd come to refer to them, on his way across the street. They hadn't spotted him watching them as they ogled the young construction workers from the patio of the Bookstore Restaurant. Pete had done the community and pool maintenance for the cottages at Seaside for about six years. He was a boat restorer by trade, but when he'd begun working at Seaside, his career hadn't yet taken off. By the time word got around that he was an exceptional craftsman, he was too loyal of a man to stop doing the maintenance work. Besides, the girls were fun, and he'd become friends with the guys in the community: Tony Black, a professional surfer and motivational speaker, and Jamie Reed, who'd developed OneClick, a search engine second only to Google. And then there was Jenna Ward, the buxom brunette with the killer ass, a cackle of a laugh, and the most intense, alluring blue eyes he'd ever seen.

Fucking Jenna.

He watched her eyes shift to him as he neared the restaurant. Other than his craftsman skills, reading women was Pete's next best finely honed ability—or so he'd thought. He could tell when a woman was into him, or when she was toying with the idea of being into him, but Jenna Ward? Jenna confused the hell out of him. She was confident and funny, smart, and too fucking cute for her own good when she was around her friends. Just watching Jenna sent fire through his veins, but when it came to Pete, Jenna lost all that gumption, and she turned into a...Hell, he didn't know what happened to her. She grew quiet and tentative when she was near him. Pete liked confident women. *A lily to look at and a tigress in the bedroom.* His mouth quirked up at the thought. He wasn't a Neanderthal. He respected women, but he also knew what he liked. He wanted to devour and be devoured—and with Jenna, who swallowed her confidence around him, he feared his sexual appetite would scare her off. Besides, with his alcoholic father to care for, he didn't have time for a relationship.

Jenna turned away as he stepped behind her. Her hair was longer this summer, framing her face in rich chocolate waves that fell past her shoulders. Pete preferred long hair. There was nothing like the feeling of burying his hands in a woman's hair and giving it a gentle tug when she was just about to come apart beneath him.

He held Joey, the female golden retriever he'd rescued a few weeks earlier, in one arm, placed his other hand on the back of Jenna's chair, and inhaled deeply. Jenna smelled like no other woman he'd ever known, a tantalizing combination of sweet and spicy. Her scent, and the view of her cleavage from above, pushed all of his sexual buttons, despite her tentative nature around him. But he had no endgame with Jenna Ward. No matter how much he wanted to explore the white-hot attraction he felt toward her, he respected Jenna and treasured her friendship too much to take her for a test ride.

"Hello, ladies."

"Aww. Can I hold her?" Amy jumped to her feet and took the puppy from his hands. Joey covered her face with kisses.

"She's a little shy," Pete teased. He'd found the pup in a duffel bag by a dumpster behind Mac's Seafood, down at the Wellfleet Pier. The poor thing was hungry and scared, but other than that, she wasn't too bad off. The first night Pete had her, the pup had slept curled up against Pete's chest, and they'd been constant companions ever since.

"Yeah, real shy. How's she doing?" Leanna asked.

"She's great. She sticks to me like glue." He shrugged. "I was just coming over to get her a bowl of fresh water, maybe a hamburger."

"Hamburger?" Leanna wrinkled her thinly manicured brow. "How about puppy food?"

"Puppies love burgers." Chicks were so weird with their rules about proper foods. He glanced down at Jenna, whose eyes were locked on the table. She usually went ape shit over puppies, and he wondered what was up with her cool demeanor.

"Want to join us for a drink?" Bella slid a slanty-eyed look in Jenna's direction.

He felt Jenna bristle at the offer. He should probably walk away and give her some breathing room. She obviously wasn't herself today. He was just about to leave when Amy grabbed his arm and pulled him down to the chair beside Jenna. *Great.* Now Jenna had a death stare locked on Amy.

Pete was beginning to take her standoffishness personally.

"Sit for a while. I want to play with Joey anyway." When Amy met Jenna's heated stare, she rolled her eyes and kissed Joey's head.

"How's the boat coming along?" Leanna Bray was a quirky woman, too. Her cottage had always been a mess before she met her fiancé, Kurt Remington. Every time Pete had gone by to fix a broken cabinet or a faucet, she'd had laundry piles everywhere, and sticky goo from her jam making seemed to cover every surface, including herself. Almost all of her clothing had conspicuous stains in various shades of red, purple, and orange. Kurt was as neat and organized as Jenna. He'd taken over the laundry and didn't seem to mind picking up after Leanna. In any case, her place was much more organized these days.

"She's coming along." Pete had been refinishing a custom-built 1966 thirty-four-foot gaff-rigged wooden schooner for the past two summers. Working with his hands was not only his passion, but it was also cathartic. He'd spent the last two years pouring the guilt over his father's drinking into refitting the boat.

"What will you do with it when you're done?" Amy Maples looked like the girl next door, with her sandy blond hair and big green eyes, and acted like a mother hen, always worrying about her friends.

Pete shrugged. "Oh, I don't know. Maybe I'll sail someplace far, far away." He'd never leave his father, or the Cape, but there were days…

That brought Jenna's eyes to him. Jesus, she had the most gorgeous eyes. They weren't sea blue or sky blue or even midnight blue. They were more of a cerulean frost, and at the moment, pointedly icy. *What the hell did I do?* He racked his brain, going over the last two weeks, but he hadn't seen Jenna for more than a minute or two. He couldn't imagine what he'd done to warrant her attitude.

Jenna raised her eyebrows in Amy's direction. "Time for *me* to go away." She rose to her feet, bringing her red-string-bikini-clad body into full view. The tiny triangles barely covered her nipples and the bottom rode high on her hips, exposing every luscious curve.

Pete shot a look around the patio—every male eye was locked on Jenna. Jenna wasn't even five feet tall, but she had a better body than any long-legged model. *How the hell can a woman have a body like that and not be one hundred percent confident at all times?* He stifled the urge to stand between her and the ogling men.

"Where are you going?" Bella's eyes bounced between Pete and Jenna.

"I'm going to do what I came here to do. There's a con-struction guy with my name on him over there." Jenna lifted her chin toward the sky, and her pigeon-toed feet carried her fine ass off the patio, across the grass, and directly toward one of the young construction workers.

"What's she doing?" Pete narrowed his eyes as Jenna approached a ripped construction worker. He expected Jenna to put her hands behind her back and sway from side to side like she did when she spoke to him—reminiscent of an excited girl rather than a sensual woman—adorable and confusing as hell.

"Oh. My. God." Bella rose to her feet, her eyes wide.

"Nothing, Pete. She's…Oh God." Amy put Joey in Pete's lap. "Take her. I um…Darn it." Amy reached for Bella's hand as they gawked, mesmerized by Jenna's bold move.

Her shoulders were drawn back, her beautiful breasts on display—proudly on display! *What the hell?* She put one hand on her hip, and holy hell, Pete didn't need to see her face to feel the slow drag of her eyes down that bastard's body in a way similar to how she usually looked at *him* when she thought he wasn't looking. But then she'd go all nervous when he'd approach.

What the fuck?

"Holy shit. She's going for it." Bella sat back down, as Jenna put her finger in the waistband of the guy's jeans and shrugged. "She's something this summer, isn't she?"

Jealousy clutched Pete's gut.

"Yes, and this summer's rock fixation? What's up with pitch-black rocks? She's never collected them before." Amy's voice trailed off as she watched Jenna in action.

Pete made a mental note of the rocks Jenna was collecting this summer. He'd spent five years taking mental notes about Jenna. Every summer she collected different types of rocks—egg-shaped, all white, gray, and oval. There was never any rhyme or reason that Pete could see for her rock selection, but she knew what she liked, and the ones she liked ended up all over her cottage and deck.

Jenna's eyes were fixated on the guy. *That* was the Jenna Pete had hoped would talk to *him*, and now…Now he was getting pretty damn pissed off.

"Those aren't local guys; they're contractors," he warned. "They probably have women in every town around here. Want me to intervene?" Jenna wasn't his to protect. They'd never even gone out on a single date, but somewhere in his mind, despite his confusion, she *was* his. Summers to Pete meant six to eight weeks of seeing Jenna, and over the last two years, while his father buried his troubles in alcohol, seeing Jenna meant even more to him. But until this very second, he never realized how much he wanted her, or how much she meant to him. Joey turned her tongue on Pete's chin. Frustrated, Pete lifted his face out of reach.

Leanna shook her head. "God. Look at her go."

Look at her go? You think this is okay?

"Pete, have you heard something bad about them? Should we worry?" Amy's voice was laden with concern. "Bella, maybe we should…"

Pete watched Jenna take her phone from her pocket and type something. A second later the blond guy took his phone from his back pocket and nodded.

"She gave him her number. I can't believe it," Leanna said.

"She wasn't shitting us," Bella said. "Damn, our girl's getting her groove on." She settled back in her seat and petted Joey. "Oh, Pete…*tsk, tsk, tsk.*"

"What's that supposed to mean?" He clenched his teeth so tight he thought they might crack.

"Nothing." Leanna smacked Bella's arm.

Bella set her eyes on him. "A woman like Jenna only comes around once in a lifetime."

He was just beginning to realize how true those words were.

"Bella, don't," Amy warned.

Bella shrugged. "Just sayin'."

He didn't know what to make of the woman who was a wallflower around him and a sex kitten around a random dipshit in the street. Jenna sashayed back toward the table with a grin on her face. That was Pete's cue to get the hell out of there before he was stuck listening to Jenna going on and on about that dipshit. He rose to his feet with Joey in his arms.

"Wait. Don't leave," Amy pleaded. "You didn't get Joey her water."

"I've got to get going." With Joey in his arms, he headed off the patio. Jenna brushed past him without so much as a word, and it pissed him off even more. He couldn't escape fast enough.

"Guess who's going to the Beachcomber tonight? Oh my God. He's even hotter up close." Jenna's voice echoed in his mind as he crossed the street to get Joey a bowl of water from Mac's.

Holy Christ. Like I needed to hear that shit.

CHAPTER TWO

"JENNA, YOU CANNOT go out with a guy you met in the middle of the road." Bella stood in front of one of Jenna's bedroom closets later that evening as Jenna sifted through outfits.

Her one-bedroom cottage didn't have much space, but the space it did have was supremely organized. Jenna was so OCD that she organized her clothing by color, season, and length of the outfit. There were two small closets in the tight master bedroom, one on either side of the door. She'd hired Pete a few years earlier to lower the rods to accommodate her four-eleven stature and to build shelves above and below, leaving just enough room for shoes along the floor.

"What are you talking about? How do you want me to meet men? They don't exactly line up outside my front door with résumés in hand." Jenna held up a black sundress. "What do you think?"

"Too sexy. He'll think you want to get down and dirty," Amy said from her perch on the bed. "She does have a point, Bella."

"Yeah, I know, but I think this is just Jenna rebelling."

Bella pulled a white sundress with puffy sleeves from the closet.

"No. No way. Who am I, Little Miss Innocent? Hell no. Rebelling against what, anyway?" Jenna snagged the dress from Bella's hands and placed it back where it belonged— with the other short, white dresses.

"Rebelling against Pete not being interested." Bella shook her head at a red dress Jenna pointed to.

"That's not called rebelling. It's called moving forward. Why do you care if I look for someone other than Pete anyway? You got the man you wanted—and Caden's like a dream come true. A loyal police officer who worships the ground you walk on. Shouldn't you want the same for me?"

"I care because I love you, Jenna. And you, my friend, are still hooked on Pete." Bella cocked her head and held Jenna's stare.

"What is with you? I'm not hooked on him, and I'm not getting any younger. Leanna got her man, you got yours, and now it's mine and Amy's turn. Right, Ames?"

"Don't drag me into this, but Leanna said she thinks you're doing the right thing," Amy said. "She and Kurt went back to their beach house a little while ago, because she has a big jam order to fill and was going to work late tonight and early tomorrow, but she was all for Jenna's new approach to dating." Leanna owned Luscious Leanna's Sweet Treats, a jam-making business that she ran out of a cottage on Kurt's bay-side property. She sold jam, as well as baked goods she made, at the Wellfleet Flea Market and to restaurants and grocery stores around the area.

"And what do you think, Amy?" Jenna plucked a black miniskirt and white button-down, sleeveless top from a hanger and set them on the bed beside Amy.

"I don't know. I feel bad for Pete. He looked like he wanted to kill that construction guy." Amy smoothed Jenna's blouse.

"Charlie," Jenna corrected her. She'd told them his name four times already, and she was annoyed that her friends refused to use it.

"Charlie. Right," Amy said.

Jenna's cell phone vibrated, and Amy snagged it from the center of the bed. "It's a text from your mom, Jenna."

"Oh, God. *Please.*" The last thing she needed was to spend thirty minutes talking to her mother about anything. Gina Ward had been acting so ridiculous that her lifelong friends were tired of dealing with her. And while Jenna was with her friends, they were battling about Pete, whom she really didn't want to talk about. She'd gone to talk to Charlie only to escape the way Pete made her entire body hum. She knew that if she didn't hightail it away from him, she'd fixate on him all summer long. She wasn't even sure that Charlie was enough of a distraction to keep her feelings for Pete at bay, but she had to try.

"Jenna, she's having a hard time. Want me to read you the text?" Amy asked.

"Why not? It's not like she won't text me eight hundred times in the next hour anyway." She slipped on turquoise and leather sandals and surveyed them, then set them back in the closet.

"J, it's Mom." Amy smiled. "I love how she still does that, like you wouldn't see her name on the phone."

"She's still getting a grip on that kind of stuff," Jenna said.

"Hope you're having fun. I was thinking I'd come visit for a few days if you won't come see me. Okay?"

"*Ugh.* That's the last thing I need." She took the phone from Amy's hand and texted her mother back. *I'm really busy. Let's talk about it in a few days.* Jenna and her mother both lived in Rhode Island, though they lived almost an hour away from each other when Jenna wasn't at the Cape. The Cape was only about two hours from her mother's house, but she had no interest in leaving Seaside and going back to deal with her mom, when she could be drowning her Pete Lacroux woes in Charlie. Maybe.

"Let me show you what I'm dealing with." Jenna scrolled through her pictures and held the phone out toward her friends.

"Oh my God." Bella laughed.

Amy's eyes widened. "Oh, hon. Your poor mother is really having a hard time. She's dressed like Madonna, or Madonna's grandmother."

"Exactly. See what I'm talking about? Too tight, too

short, not to mention that these outfits went out of style ages ago, and she wants to go dancing." Jenna shoved her phone in her skirt pocket. "Dancing. My mother. The woman who spent her nights needlepointing in front of the television and her Sundays at church. Suddenly she's lost her mind."

"No, Jen." Amy reached for her hand. "She's lost the man she loved, and that's not an easy thing to go through after thirty-plus years of marriage. She probably feels like her whole life's been ripped out from under her."

"I know. I'm trying to be patient, but come on. It's been *two years*. Two years since their divorce. Shouldn't she be building a new life and not mudding things up for me when I'm trying to get my own life in order?"

Bella looked at her watch. "Oh gosh. I have to go soon. Caden and I are taking Evan up to P-town tonight to see a comedy show." Provincetown was an artistic community about thirty minutes from Wellfleet. Bella handed Jenna a tie-dyed aqua sarong. "It's supposed to be chilly tonight."

Jenna looked at the sarong and wrinkled her nose. "With a body like Charlie's, do you seriously think I'll be cold?" Jenna dressed in the skirt and top, leaving the top two buttons of her blouse open. She slipped on the sandals she'd chosen, a pair of dangling silver earrings, and a big red plastic ring that looked like a flower and covered the entire space between the knuckles of her index finger.

Bella planted her hands on her hips. "Jen, what are you doing? You're not the kind of girl who goes out looking for sex, and with your girls on display like that, any guy would think you're up for a good time."

Jenna rolled her eyes and brushed her hair away from her face. She'd always worn her hair in a bob cut just below her ears, but over the winter she'd grown it out, and she liked the way it felt brushing against her shoulders. She felt sexier, and this summer, she needed all the sexy she could muster.

"No, I don't look like that, and I'm not looking for sex. Although it has been so long since I've gotten any that I wonder if my body's revirginized itself. You guys heard Pete say he might sail away. What do you expect me to do? Hang around vying for his attention for another lonely summer? He's not interested. Period. Now let me get into the swing of summer dating again. I'm totally out of practice, and it's so much more fun than dating back home. Everything is better here, and not that I'd remember, but I bet the sex is better here, too."

Bella held up her finger. "I can attest to that. Come here." She grabbed Jenna's arm and pulled her into a hug. Jenna face-planted between Bella's breasts. "I don't expect you to wait around for Pete to make a move. But I swear to God, Jenna, if you turn into a scrump-and-dump whore, I'll kick your ass."

Jenna laughed. "I know you will, and I love you for it. I just want..." She pushed from Bella's arms and gazed out the window. "I want someone to adore me like Caden adores you. I want to experience that moment when our bodies come together for the first time and my stomach dips like I'm going downhill on a roller coaster. That first moment of bliss when everything I worried about—my breath, what I wore on the date, if sex would change things—disappears, and all that remains is total, unencumbered ecstasy. You know that moment when your mind falls to pieces, and it's all you can do to remember to breathe?"

Amy fell back on the bed with her hand over her heart. "I want that moment, too."

"I know that moment well." Bella sighed.

"We know," Amy and Jenna said in unison.

"So, then, what's your plan?" Amy sat up and asked.

"I don't have a plan. When I saw Pete this afternoon and he still wasn't looking at me like…Well, you know, like he *wanted* me, and he said he might sail away…*Ugh*! And you know what's even worse? I was jealous of his adorable little puppy. I wanted to take her from his arms so I could climb into them and snuggle up against his chest and have him hold me like he wanted to protect me." Jenna sighed dreamily. "That's stupid, I know, because I love puppies. I just had to get out of there and refocus my attention on moving forward. I've been stuck for too many years."

"I meant your plan for tonight, goofus," Amy said. "I know you think you're over Pete."

"Which you're totally not," Bella added.

"Yes, I am. Or at least I am trying to be." Jenna pulled Amy to her feet and they went into the living room. The interior of Jenna's cottage was painted white. Her furniture was Scandinavian in design with sharp edges and neutral flavors of beige with black-and-white accents throughout. The living room was only about twelve feet long and ten feet wide, with a kitchen that was really more of a nook tucked off to the side. The bathroom was built off the living room, and the master bedroom took up the back of the tiny cottage.

Jenna patted Amy's hip as she walked past and weaved around the coffee table. "Okay, I have to run. I'm meeting Charlie at the Beachcomber."

"That was smart. No need to be locked in to driving with him. You never know if he's a freak or not." Amy motioned for Jenna to spin around. "You look really cute, but, Jenna, are you sure you want to do this? You've wanted to be with Pete for so long that I can't help but feel sad that you're supposedly done with him. It should be him you're going out with tonight, not *Charlie*." She lowered her voice and said Charlie's name like a curse word.

"Yeah, well, he had his chance, and obviously I'm a nimrod around him. Can't you just put your pretty little ideas away and support me on this?" Jenna stuck out her lower lip in a feigned pout.

"Okay, okay, fine. You win."

Jenna bounced up and down on her toes and hugged Amy. "Thank you. I feel better now. Walk me to my car so I'm not so nervous. I haven't been on a date in forever." She took Amy's hand—borrowing a little of her strength and confidence to carry along with her on her date—and followed Bella outside.

"Do we need an emergency call for tonight?" Amy asked. An emergency call was when they called each other at designated times while they were out on dates, just in case the one on the date needed an excuse to leave. If Amy called and Jenna was having an awful time, she could tell Charlie she had to tend to an emergency—and *voilà*, the date would end.

"Yes, she does." Bella pulled her phone out and set an alarm. "It's seven thirty. I'll call you at eight fifteen."

"I'll call you at nine," Amy assured Jenna. "Why does this feel so nerve-racking? Bella didn't need an emergency call when she first went out with Caden."

Bella climbed into her car. "Maybe because Jenna picked up a construction worker."

"Oh, please. So what? You picked up a cop." Jenna settled into her car and reached for Amy's hand. "When are Tony and Jamie getting here?" Jamie's grandmother, Vera, owned the cottage on the far side of Leanna's, and Tony owned the cottage on the opposite side. Vera was in her eighties, and Jamie came up during the weekends to look after her.

"Jamie's started some new project, so he's not sure when, maybe in a week or two, but Tony is booked solid with speaking engagements. He texted last night and said that between his surfing competitions and the motivational speaking schedule, he's not sure he'll come at all this summer." Amy's eyes filled with sadness. She'd had a crush on Tony for years, and like Jenna with Pete, every summer she hoped for more.

"Oh no, Amy. I'm so sorry. I can stay home with you tonight," Jenna offered. Part of her hoped Amy would ask her to say.

"Go. Have fun. I'm fine. I have a juicy romance novel to read." Amy tucked her hair behind her ear and pushed Jenna toward her car.

"Aww, Ames. We both need to get a life, don't we? You can't hang on to the hope that Tony will finally come to his senses and realize you're the best woman on the planet any more than I can wait around for Pete to notice how magnificent I am." Jenna smiled and pointed to her head. "Men are thick. I'm telling you, thick."

Amy glanced at Tony's cottage, then brought her attention back to Jenna. "Yeah. I know. Let's see how your summer goes before I throw my hope into the wind."

Jenna blew her a kiss and then headed for the Beachcomber with her heart beating so hard she was sure she'd pop the few buttons she'd secured. What was she doing? She didn't pick up men on the street, not even fine-looking, hard-bodied men. She thought about what Amy had said about Pete and she wondered if he really had looked like he was going to kill Charlie. The thought made her smile, and then it made her angry. He had no right to get upset, especially since he never seemed to think she was worth asking out.

As she pulled into a parking spot at the Beachcomber, her cell phone rang. *Mom.* She might as well get it over with now, or her mother would call her a hundred more times before the night was over.

"Hi, Mom. I'm sorry, but I've only got a minute. I'm on my way to meet someone."

"Oh, *really?*" Her mother was using the new and improved, overly dramatic and far too interested tone that grated on Jenna's nerves.

"Don't get your hopes up. We're just having a drink, maybe going dancing." Jenna loved to dance, but she hadn't been since she and the girls went dancing two summers ago. She only wished she were meeting—and going dancing with—Pete instead of Charlie. *I'm definitely losing my mind.*

"Dancing, now, that sounds like fun. I was thinking, maybe since you aren't going to be coming home over the next few weeks, I'll just pop down to the Cape for a few days. I can sleep on your couch." The cottage had belonged to Jenna's parents before they stopped going to the Cape and gifted it to Jenna. Jenna had spent summers sleeping on her parents' pullout couch, but hearing her mother say she'd sleep on it grated on Jenna's nerves.

Jenna clenched her eyes shut. She loved her mother, but she also loved her summers at Seaside. They were *hers*, and she'd really like to keep it that way, but Jenna was also softhearted, and Amy was right; her mother was going through a hard time. Her father had decided to marry Cara, a woman just a few years older than Jenna, and Jenna was stuck in the middle of her father's happiness and her mother's crisis. She loved her father, but at the same time, she hated seeing her mother so upset. Even though her father hadn't left her mother for Cara—they'd divorced because they'd grown apart—it was definitely not a fun place to be, sandwiched between two people she loved.

It was too much to think about right now. She had a hunky man waiting for her inside the Beachcomber, and she was ready to be adored.

"Maybe, Mom. Let's talk about it in a few days, okay? Are you okay otherwise?" Her mother was always okay. That was, until the news of her father's impending wedding crushed her sense of self. She'd been so strong during the divorce that Jenna was confused at her reaction to the news of her father marrying Cara two years later.

"Oh, yes." She sighed. "I'm okay. Just miss you, I guess. Nights are long when I'm alone, but go ahead, honey. Enjoy your date. And who knows? Maybe when I come down we can go on a double date."

Oh God. Don't even go there. Jenna didn't grace her with a response to *that* unpleasant idea. "I'll talk to you tomorrow, Mom. Love you."

"Love you, too. Have fun, and be safe. Remember to

use—"

"Mom! Stop. We talked about boundaries, remember?" Ever since her mother's new endeavor to reverse time and become half her age, she wanted to talk about sex and all the things that went along with it. It was enough to turn Jenna's stomach, and right now, she wanted to be turned on by a hot construction worker, not turned off before she even entered the restaurant.

PETE WIPED HIS hands on his jeans, feeling the gritty particles of recently sanded wood against his palms. He had been working on the schooner all evening, in an effort to keep from dwelling on the fact that Jenna was out on a date with that damn construction worker. The scent of sawdust and damp earth filled his lungs inside the boat barn he and his father had built five years earlier. The barn was large enough to hold boats up to forty-eight feet, giving Pete room to work freely around the perimeter with ladders and other accoutrements. He stepped back and assessed the schooner. It rested on six jack stands and was an easy twelve feet tall and equally as wide. To a land lover, the schooner would feel massive. To Pete, it felt just right. Comfortable. But in truth, the schooner did more than fill his love of refitting boats. Schooners were his father's passion. If his father were his old self, he'd be by Pete's side, working late into the night, rejuvenated by the feel of his hard work vibrating through his chest as he scraped and sanded the wood until it was smooth as silk. He'd be with Pete when he finished refitting the damn thing and finally took it out on the water.

Pete was holding on to a shred of hope that one day his father would get the help he needed and regain control of the life he once enjoyed, thereby giving Pete back the freedom to live his life the way he used to.

Pete ran his hand through his hair, conjuring up the image of his father as a younger man, his two front teeth overlapping just a hair, adding to his youthful appearance. Neil Lacroux had eyes as dark as night and hair the color of wet sand—perpetually mussed as if he'd just toweled off. Even pushing sixty, Neil held the attention of women and half of the men wherever he went. Pete heard his father's playful taunts as if he were right there beside him. He'd lift his chin and pretend to see some nonexistent flaw on the boat that Pete had left behind. *Hey, jackass. What's with the ridge along the bow?*

Jackass. Pete laughed under his breath, but as always, it didn't mask the ache of missing the father that he'd spent his life looking up to. Neil had always been a drinker, but after Pete's mother died, Neil spiraled into the bottle. It had been a slow realization for Pete, as his father owned the local hardware store and he'd been able to mask his drinking during the day, but once the sun fell, Neil followed its downward path straight to the bottom of the bottle. Pete had no idea how his father managed to make it through each day, but then again, the Lacrouxes were experts at pushing emotions aside until they were forced to face them head-on. He supposed that coming home to the empty house his father once shared with his mother might do that to a man.

Pete swallowed the ache that swelled in his throat and filled his veins with a slow burn that never quite fully diminished. He patted his thigh to distract himself. Joey bounded to his side, tail wagging, nose in the air as she vied for attention. Pete knelt beside her and scratched behind her ears.

"Ready to go inside, girl?" He kissed the pup on the snout, then pulled the doors of the oversized barn closed behind them.

The wind chimes sang a gentle melody against the breeze sweeping up the rocky bluff surrounding Pete's bay-side cottage in Eastham. He inhaled the damp sea air. The fishy, salty smell brought back fond memories. Joey trotted beside him down the sandy path that snaked through the grass toward his cottage, and Pete smiled as he remembered the fun he and his siblings had growing up at the Cape. It seemed like just yesterday when he and his younger brothers, Hunter, Matt, and Grayson, were running around like wild banshees on the beaches, their baby sister, Sky, toddling along behind them. Their hair was always too long, their clothing sandy and wet around their bare, calloused feet. Looking back, he wondered if they drove their mother crazy, but Bea Lacroux would never admit to any such thing. She adored her children, and her husband, until she took her very last breath.

Pete pulled open the screen door and waited for Joey to go inside before shrugging out of his jacket and tossing it on the kitchen table. He washed his hands, then pulled a can of soup from the cabinet, pulled the tab, and emptied it into a bowl. He set it on the floor for Joey.

"Beef stew. Enjoy, girl." He opened another can and heated it in the microwave. He ate standing up, his hip leaning against the counter. Pete had learned to cook from his mother, and he was a damn good cook, but he rarely took the time to cook a real meal for himself, much less enjoy one. When his siblings visited, which hadn't been often over the past two years, he'd cook for them, but when it was just him, a can of soup was fine. He thought about Jenna at the Beachcomber with that asshole construction worker and pictured the guy eyeing her across a dimly lit table. *Asshole.* He tossed the can in the trash and threw the spoon in the empty sink.

Thinking of Jenna brought his mind back to his sister, which always brought his thoughts back to his father. He snagged the business card for Tatum Rehabilitation Center from beneath a magnet on the refrigerator and ran his thumb over it. He flipped it over and eyed the handwritten emergency number on the back and remembered asking the counselor if there was ever a time that getting someone into rehab *wasn't* an emergency. He placed the card back beneath the magnet on the refrigerator and pulled out his phone to call Sky.

Sky was twenty-four years old, and she'd been the closest to their mother. After their mother died, Sky fell apart. She was only twenty-two at the time and on the cusp of a promising career with an art museum in New York. Sky had stopped calling Pete and their brothers, and after not hearing from her for almost a week, Pete had put his life on hold and gone to New York.

"Hey, big brother. What's up?" Sky always answered the phone the same way, and it made Pete smile. When he'd gone to New York, she was so depressed that he'd had to drag her out of bed each day. He's stayed by her side as she cried, yelled, screamed, laughed, and worked through every emotion known to man—and finally, after ten days or so, she came out on the other side of the grief that had consumed her. She later quit the job at the museum. *Too confining.* Pete was still waiting for her to find a career she loved.

"Hi, sis. How's life?"

"Life's good. I've been drawing a lot, painting, and oh, I almost forgot to tell you, my band started playing these impromptu concerts at the park. Total fun."

Pete laughed. "Sounds like you're having a good time. How about work?"

Sky sighed. Pete pictured her tossing her long brown hair

over her shoulder and rolling her eyes. "Fine. I'm still working at the co-op."

The co-op. Not exactly the career he hoped she'd find. She was a bright and talented artist. "Enjoying it?"

"God, Pete, lighten up. Yes, I'm enjoying it. I know you want me to find my niche, and I will. Someday."

"I know you will. Do you need anything? Are you okay financially?"

"Yes, Pete. I'm fine. More importantly, how are you and Dad? I'm trying to clear my schedule so I can visit soon. I've tried to call Dad the last few nights, but he never answers his phone."

Pete grimaced. He'd spent two years protecting Sky from finding out about their father's drinking—convincing her to stay with him when she visited instead of with their father and intervening when she was planning a surprise visit.

"We're both fine, but Dad's pretty busy these days with the store. He's been going to bed early." He hated lying to her, but he worried that his father's drinking might send her spiraling back into the dark place she'd found after their mother died. "Maybe you should wait a few more weeks to come visit." The need to get his father help took a leap on his priority list.

Sky sighed. "Okay. I miss you."

"I miss you, too, Sky. If you need anything, call me."

"I always do." She called him when she was missing their mother, or when a guy she was dating pissed her off—and it was all Pete could do not to drive to New York and kick the shit out of the guy.

A few minutes after they ended the call, the clock chimed, drawing his attention to where it hung on the wall beside the refrigerator. He'd managed to avoid thinking of Jenna and Dipshit's date while he was talking to Sky. *Or at least to admit to myself that I was thinking of them.* Now, as the seconds ticked by with annoyingly loud precision and Joey rested her chin between her paws with a loud sigh, adrenaline flooded Pete's veins. How would Jenna protect herself if he tried something? What if he got her drunk and she was too out of it to defend herself? She had no idea what she was getting into with that guy. Hell, how could she? He was a stranger. Didn't she learn anything in kindergarten?

He dug his keys from the pocket of his jeans and stared down at Joey. "I'll just make sure she's okay, girl. That's it. I'll be back in less than an hour. Promise."

By the time he pulled into the parking lot of the Beach-comber, Pete had thought up all sorts of unsavory situations in his mind. No matter how they began, each ended with Jenna wrapping her arms around Pete's neck, gushing with appreciation.

The Beachcomber was built at the top of a dune over-looking the ocean. Pete listened to the music coming from the deck at the back of the restaurant, which he knew was lit up with colorful plastic lights. Bands played nightly during the summer, and tonight the music was loud and the tune was surprisingly less beachy and more reminiscent of the seventies, soulful and deep.

Pete drew his shoulders back as he headed around to the other side of the restaurant. A gusty, cool breeze swept across the dunes, rustling the dune grass. He heard Jenna's laugh before he caught sight of the wide smile that lit up her whole face. Jenna had a loud laugh that some might say sounded like a cackle. They'd be right. It did, and he could single it out anywhere—in a crowded bar, over a band, on a crowded beach—it was a laugh that always drew a smile from Pete, except tonight. His insides churned at the idea of her laughing with that dipshit construction worker instead of him. He ran his hand through his hair and looked away, realizing that he hadn't even bothered to clean up after working on the boat for hours.

"Hey, babe. You coming in? I'd love a dance." A stacked brunette ran her finger down his chest.

Summer chicks. Summer on the Cape brought loose women and horny men. Although even in the desolate winter months, there was never a shortage of women interested in Pete. He raked his eyes down the brunette's body. He should have gotten hard just thinking about that body against his, but the only body he wanted against him was Jenna's. Jenna's laugh pulled his attention across the deck.

"No, sorry. I'll have to pass." He circled the deck, moving toward the sound of Jenna's voice.

"Asshole," the woman mumbled as he walked away.

He lost track of Jenna as he rounded the dance floor, where half-naked twentysomethings clad in short shorts and bikini tops, or tank tops and board shorts, twerked and grinded against one another. He looked down at his black T-shirt, speckled with sawdust, and his dirty jeans, streaked with varnish and caulk. It was dark out, and the tiki lights weren't that bright. He hoped no one would notice. He moved in closer just as Jenna pushed through the crowd, her hand trailing behind her, attached to Dipshit.

Pete's hands fisted and his eyes narrowed. Jenna turned and placed one hand on Dipshit's chest, the other still holding on to his hand. It took all of Pete's focus to refrain from storming onto the dance floor, swooping her fine little body into his arms, and whisking her away. *Fuck this. I'm only here to make sure she's okay, and she's fine. She's fucking fine.*

Jenna turned, and their eyes caught. Her smile faded, and that befuddled look he knew too well fell into place like a mask—eyes wide, mouth agape. Her hand dropped from Dipshit's chest and she fidgeted with the edge of her skirt—and hell if Pete didn't find her reaction adorable.

Too fucking adorable.

CHAPTER THREE

THE NEXT MORNING Jenna crouched beside the basket of flip-flops on the front deck of her cottage. Crows cawed from their perches atop pitch pine trees surrounding the small community. The damn things had been cawing since dawn, grating on Jenna's nerves, which were already fried. She'd been up all night organizing and reorganizing in an effort to figure out what the hell Pete was doing at the Beachcomber last night. She turned at the sound of tires on her crushed-shell driveway.

Leanna jumped out of her 1968 Volkswagen Bus, or as she called it, her *happy mobile,* because of the hand-painted beach scene that ran from front to back and the gigantic blue dragonfly covering the driver's door. Her father had restored the van as a college graduation gift. Never one for subtlety, Leanna adored the bikini-clad women that covered the center of the van and the half-moon with a face painted on the rear panel.

"Did I miss coffee?" Leanna set a plate of scones on the table.

Jenna shaded her eyes from the morning sun and smiled

up at her friend. Leanna's tank top was already streaked with jam. Her cutoffs had red finger marks along the hip.

"No. In fact, we need to get Bella and Amy because I'm going to burst if I don't get out of my own head." Jenna set the flip-flops that she was stacking in neat color-coordinated piles into the basket by the door. "Come on." She pulled Leanna by the hand, and as they rounded Jenna's cottage, they ran into Bella and Amy, coffee mugs in hand.

"We were just coming over." Bella was still in her nightie, which barely covered her ass, while Amy had on flannel pajama pants and a T-shirt that read, *Purrdy,* above a picture of an animated kitten wearing lingerie and lying in a provocative pose.

"Sorry we took so long. I wanted to bring you these, but it took me forever to find them." Amy reached into her pocket and handed Jenna a pair of thick, black sunglasses.

"What are these for?" Jenna put on the glasses on the way back to her deck, where her tepid coffee cup awaited. They settled in around the table.

"It's Tuesday." Amy nodded toward the pool. "I figured if you're really trying not to focus on you know who, better to make it hard for you to see him."

"Shit. It's Tuesday?" Pete cleaned the pool Tuesday mornings. Jenna ran to the edge of the deck and looked down by the pool, where Vera was already sitting beneath an umbrella reading. Luckily, Pete's truck was nowhere in sight. She looked down at her clothes before joining the others. At least she'd already showered and changed into her bikini and cutoffs. *Wait. Why do I still care what he thinks?*

"Don't worry. You look hot." Bella held up a scone like she was toasting champagne.

"I don't care if I look hot." *Bullshit.* "I'm pissed at him anyway." Jenna snagged a scone and shoved it in her mouth. Raspberries melted in her mouth alongside a buttery shortbread flavor that caressed her taste buds into a frenzy of delight.

"Jesus, Leanna. How do you make these so good?"

"I use the right amount of ingredients, and I don't mix up the salt and the sugar," Leanna answered. Jenna couldn't cook if her life depended on it. For a woman who needed everything in order, when it came to ingredients and directions, she had yet not to ruin whatever she was making. Needless to say, Jenna ate a lot of toast, salad, and frozen dinners.

"Ha-ha. I did that once," Jenna said with a smile.

"Twice," Amy said.

"Thirteen times," Bella added.

"Whatever. I think if you queried men, they'd choose a woman being good in the bedroom over the kitchen." Jenna popped another piece of scone into her mouth. "I happen to be amazing in the bedroom."

"Hey! I happen to be good in both, thank you very much. More importantly, why are you pissed at Pete?" Leanna cocked her head in question.

Jenna leaned forward and lowered her voice. "He showed up at the Beachcomber last night and totally screwed up my perfect date!"

"Whoa. Hold on." Bella set down her coffee and held her hands up, palms out to silence everyone's gasps. "Pete showed up? Coincidentally, or showed up like"—she deepened her voice—"*I'm gonna check out my competition?*"

"I don't know. I was up all night trying to figure it out, but whatever it was, he was there. And, of course, when I saw him, I froze." Jenna threw her head back with an exasperated groan.

"Oh, hon, I'm sorry." Amy patted her forearm. "But can we rewind just a tad? *Perfect* date? So body boy had more going on than pecs and privates?"

Jenna laughed. "Pecs and privates. Love that, and especially love that it came out of our prim-and-proper sister's mouth. Yes. He was interested *and* interesting. It turns out he's a big-time reader, and you know me and books. We talked about all sorts of things."

"And?" Bella ran her hand through her thick blond hair.

"And nothing. The minute my eyes connected with Mr. I'm Not Interested, I lost it. I was like a mute bimbo. I couldn't even dance. And the jerk took off right after he saw me." She pointed at Bella and narrowed her eyes. "I think Pete was spying on me."

Bella, Leanna, and Amy exchanged knowing looks and coy smiles.

"Mm-hm." Amy smirked. "So, our friend Pete might be more jealous than we thought. I told you he had that look in his eyes when you and body boy were talking."

"Charlie. Okay? His name is Charlie."

The sound of tires on gravel sent their eyes to the road. Pete pulled up in his old blue truck, one arm casually hanging out the window, tanned biceps on display.

"Shit," Jenna whispered.

"Hey, ladies." He waved and flashed a killer smile that made Jenna's entire body tingle.

She turned away, embarrassed that while she was supposed to be pissed at him, her body betrayed her.

"Hey, Pete." Amy waved. "Want a scone?"

Jenna slapped her leg under the table.

"Oh! Sorry. I forgot." Amy covered her mouth and flashed a smile at Bella.

"My ass, you forgot," Jenna grumbled.

"No, thanks. I'm just on my way to clean the pool but wanted to check on the landscaping by the fire pit. Theresa said animals were digging in the plants. See you around." He parked at the laundry building, catty-corner to Jenna's cottage. Theresa Ottoline lived in the big house on the other side of the laundry building. The big house was the original house on the Seaside property, before the land was subdivided and the cottages were built. Theresa was a stickler for rules and spent time at the cottages during the winters when most of the Seaside owners couldn't be there. As such, she was the elected property manager for the third year in a row.

As soon as Pete was beyond hearing distance, Jenna smacked Amy again. "What was that?"

"I'm sorry. I'm used to being nice to him, and I still don't believe you're over him." Amy picked at her scone.

"You're supposed to be my friend, not his. Jeez, Amy, and you—" Jenna pointed at Bella, who was smiling with a glint of mischief in her eyes. "What was that look between the two of you?"

"I saw it, too," Leanna said. "They're up to something."

"No shit. I smell two blond rats." Jenna got up and moved to the chair beside Leanna. "At least I have one loyal friend."

"Oh, bullshit. You have all of us. We're loyal as hell and you know it." Bella shrugged. "We just know you, Jenna. You're as OCD with Pete as you are with everything else in your life. Once you set your mind on something, it sticks like glue. And your mind has been on Peter Lacroux forever. There's no way in hell *Charlie* measures up to Pete. I don't care how good of a body he has. What's Pete, chopped liver? That man's sizzling hot."

No shit, Sherlock. "That was the *old* Jenna. The new and improved Jenna realizes when she's taken on a losing proposition. The new Jenna liked being out on a real date with a man who was interested in more than what I say, but in me as a woman—as opposed to Pete, who can't see this body for what it's worth."

They all turned at the sound of Bella's cottage door closing. Caden and Evan, Caden's fifteen-year-old son, came around the side of the cottage a minute later.

Caden smiled when he saw Bella. "There's my beautiful wife-to-be."

"Hi, babe. Hey, Ev, ready for work?" Bella rose and hugged Caden.

Caden looked handsome in his police officer uniform, and even though he and Bella had been together for a year, he still looked at her like he was as hot for her as the first night they'd met. Jenna longed for *that*. She'd had boyfriends and she'd dated one or two guys for more than a year, but she'd never been with a man who adored her the way Caden adored Bella or Kurt adored Leanna. And now that she'd witnessed what true love could be, there was no way in hell she was settling for anything less.

"Ready to roll," Evan said. Last summer, unbeknownst to Evan, he'd been hanging out with a few kids that were breaking into cottages and cars. They'd broken into Vera's cottage and scared her half to death. Evan had stopped hanging out with them as soon as he found out what they were up to, and once school started, thankfully, he'd met a nice group of kids with similar interests. Evan had worked hard to regain the trust of the Seaside residents, and Bella was proud of him.

"I'm taking him over to TGG before my shift." Caden put an arm around Bella's shoulder. TGG, The Geeky Guys, was one of the companies taking part in the work-study program Bella had developed for the high school. Although Evan's job with them wasn't part of the program, Bella had connected Evan with them last summer when she learned of Evan's love of computers and programming. Evan had spent time with Jamie last summer, learning to program, and had been working part-time with TGG ever since. "Did you ask everyone about the movie tonight?"

"Not yet." Bella turned her attention back to the girls. "They're putting on a documentary film behind Town Hall tonight about shark migration on the Cape. It's being put on by the Brave Foundation. Want to go?"

"It's gonna be so cool," Evan added. "The guy who runs the foundation is going to be there, so we can ask him anything. Dad said I could ask him if I can go out on one of their shark-tagging missions."

"That's Dane Braden," Leanna said. "His sister, Savannah, is married to Kurt's brother Jack. We're going to see it, but I didn't think you guys would be interested."

"No way. Really?" Evan pushed his shaggy brown hair from his eyes. He'd grown three inches over the winter and stood almost eye to eye with Caden. He was beginning to fill out and wasn't quite as lanky as he'd been last summer.

"Yeah. I bet Kurt can get you on the boat if there's space available." Leanna dug her phone from her pocket and typed in a text. "I'm texting him. I'll let you know."

"I'm in," Amy said. "Jenna? Want to go with me?"

"Sure. Charlie and I didn't make plans, so why not?" The truth was, Charlie had asked her out for tonight, but when she'd seen Pete, her mind had begun playing tricks on her, and she'd begun comparing the two men. And no matter how much she tried to deny it, there was no comparison. Pete already owned too big of a piece of her heart to open it to anyone else.

"Great. So we'll all go. It's at eight." Caden kissed Bella again. "See ya, babe. Ready, Ev? I want to talk to Pete before we take off."

Bella stared after them. "God, I love them."

"We know," Leanna, Amy, and Jenna said in unison.

They sat on Jenna's deck and talked about Leanna's business and Bella's new life on the Cape. Jenna could barely concentrate when Pete drove by on his way to the pool.

"Jenna, you look like you're worried about being chosen for the Hunger Games. What's up?" Amy tucked her legs beneath her on the deck chair.

"I'm just...You guys, you don't really think Pete was checking up on me, do you? I mean, he's never seemed very interested. Why would he be interested now?"

"You've never given him any competition before. It's always been all about Pete. Every summer, *Pete, Pete, Pete.*" Bella waved her hand. "Now, with Charlie, you've shaken Pete up like a snow globe and upended all that stuff in his head."

Leanna's phone vibrated and she read a text. "I hate to

change the subject, but that was Kurt. He said he'll do what he can for Evan and that Dane loves to take people out on the boat, so it looks good."

"Thanks, Leanna," Bella said. "Please thank Kurt for me, too. Evan will be so happy. After last summer's fiasco, and how hard he's worked to rectify things with everyone, I'm glad this might come through for him."

"I'm excited for you guys to meet Dane and his girlfriend, Lacy. She's just like us. I'll call and see if she wants to hang out tonight since Dane will be running the show. Would you mind?"

"Of course not. Bring her along." Bella smiled and waved to Caden and Evan as they drove by on their way out of the community.

"Can we circle back to my issue for a minute, please?" Jenna waved her hand. "I'm in serious agony here. I've reorganized everything in my entire house, and I'm about ready to start on each of yours." Jenna tugged at her bikini top, which was headed for a wardrobe malfunction.

"Yes. Focus. I just got my cabinets back to the way I like them after the last time she got ahold of them." Leanna brushed her dark hair from her eyes.

"Kurt loves when I organize your cottage." Kurt was as organized as Leanna was disorganized. When Jenna had organized the cabinets in their cottage after Leanna had spent the weekend there while Kurt attended a writer's conference, he'd praised Jenna for a week.

"Yes, that he does. Thank God he didn't rescue *you* from the water." Kurt and Leanna met on a stormy night when Kurt rescued Leanna's dog, Pepper, after he'd been swept out to the deep water.

"Oh, please. We'd totally knock heads. He likes quiet, and I'm anything but quiet." *And he's not Pete.* Jenna pressed her palms on the table. "Okay, so here's the deal. I have a confession."

"You love Pete; we already know," Amy said as she nibbled on a piece of scone.

"No. Maybe. I don't know. The truth is, Charlie asked me out for tonight, and I really liked him, but Pete showing up got me all confused, so I told Charlie I had plans."

"Face it, girlie. You're hooked on Petey," Amy said in a singsong voice.

Jenna groaned and buried her face in her hands. "No, I kind of regret telling Charlie no. And if I am still hooked on Pete, then I'm an idiot."

"No. He's the idiot for waiting so long to really take notice," Bella said.

"Yeah, but who hangs on to a crush for this many years? I think I have to go out with Charlie again, don't you? I mean, to be fair, he really was pretty great." Jenna ran her finger along the edge of the table, remembering what it felt like to be with Charlie. "He was attentive and not at all like I expected. I thought he'd be rough around the edges, which I know is a gross generalization because he's a construction worker, but he wasn't at all. He was easy to talk to and fun and…" *Not. Pete.*

"So, what's the issue?" Amy leaned her elbow on the table, her chin in her palm. "Did you kiss him?"

Jenna smiled.

"She did," Bella said. "And?"

"And he kissed me good night despite my being a mute bimbo…It was nice. He's a good kisser."

"Therein lies the problem," Bella said. "Nice? Really? Nice?"

"It was. He was sweet and kind, and—"

"Come on. Your first kiss should never be *nice*. It should be wild, passionate, intense." Bella slid her eyes to Leanna. "Right, Lea?"

"Absolutely." Leanna glanced at her cottage. "Your first kiss should basically suck the air from your lungs and leave you mindless."

"Spineless," Amy added.

"You're such romantics. It should leave you wanting to rip his clothes off and take him right there and then." Bella raised her brows in quick succession. "Listen, Jenna. Your first kiss should leave you hot and flustered. Anything short of that? Or *nice*?" She wrinkled her brow. "No one wants to take *nice* to bed."

Jenna rested her forehead in her hands. *Maybe Pete thinks of me as nice.*

"I would take *nice* to bed," Amy said.

Jenna turned her head, looking up at Amy from her bent-over position. "That doesn't make me feel any better."

"Well, I would. I like nice. I like hot and sexy, but nice is...nice." Amy glanced at Tony's cottage.

"Jesus, Ames." Bella rolled her eyes. "There's no way Tony is *nice* in bed. With a body like that, my money's on animalistic. Pure passion. Take-me-to-the-moon-and-back passion."

Jenna shot to her feet. "Okay, well. I think I need to give Charlie a second chance. I'll bring him with me tonight. Is that all right, Amy?"

"Sure. Blow me off for a *nice* kisser." Amy shrugged one shoulder.

"You could set him up with Amy, and then you could ask Pete out," Leanna suggested.

"No sloppy seconds for me." Amy pushed to her feet. "I need to go take a shower."

"And I need to bonk my head against the wall about a hundred times before going to the library. Anyone want to join me?" Jenna arched a brow in Amy's direction. Amy never turned down a trip to the library.

"I'm in for the library, but you can head bonk by yourself."

The roar of a motorcycle drew their attention back to the road.

"Holy cow. Who is that?" Amy's eyes widened as a muscular, tanned man parked by the laundry room and stepped from the motorcycle.

He pulled off his helmet and Jenna gasped. "Charlie? Still think he's *nice* in bed?"

Bella grabbed Jenna's hand. "Nice just got a whole lot hotter."

FRUSTRATED, EDGY, AND still confused over the way his body and mind were reacting to Jenna, Pete put the cleaning supplies in the pool house and forced a smile for Vera. She often sat down at the pool in the morning, before the sun got too hot. She'd tried to spark up a conversation with Pete when he came down, but he was in no mood to chat, and he was in no better frame of mind now.

Today marked one of the very few times that Jenna had been home when he was cleaning out the pool, and she didn't peek at him from her deck or *happen to* walk by with Amy, Leanna, or Bella. Not only did she completely ignore the fact that he was there, but she'd fricking turned away from him when he stopped by in his truck. She might be shy around him, but she'd never before intentionally turned away. *She did at the Bookstore Restaurant.*

He'd taken it as a good sign that she'd come home last night. At least that indicated that she probably hadn't slept with Dipshit.

Who was he kidding? It indicated exactly nothing.

Shit. Stop thinking about her.

Yeah, that's not happening anytime soon.

He waved to Vera. "Have a nice morning, Vera."

She smiled and nodded as he climbed into his truck. A motorcycle roared into the complex as Pete started up his engine. Seeing Jenna with that guy last night should have been enough to quell his attraction to her. Instead it fueled his passion for her and made him realize how close to losing her he really was. Caden had invited Pete to a documentary at Town Hall tonight, and he thought he might use that as a chance to get closer to Jenna. Until now Jenna had been sexy as hell, confusing as rain on a sunny day, and safely nestled in the friend zone. Pete was about to kick the damn friend zone into oblivion.

He was going to drive by Jenna's cottage one last time. If she ignored him again, he'd forget her altogether. He wasn't a glutton for punishment after all. That's exactly what he'd do. Forget that she was ever interested in him. He'd drive out of Seaside, and the next time he returned, his mind would be solely focused on his duties as related to the cottages and pool maintenance.

Jenna crossed the road in front of his truck wearing her red bikini top and a pair of cutoff shorts that bared the curve of her ass. Pete's eyes lingered on her ass.

Her eyes were locked on the guy climbing off the motorcycle.

The construction guy drives a Harley? Pete white-knuckled

the steering wheel. *Son of a bitch.* He shifted his attention back to the road as he rolled past, just as Dipshit bent down and took Jenna in a hot and heavy kiss.

Look at the road. Look at the goddamn road.

His eyes did not get the message. They shifted right and caught on Jenna, her arms wrapped around Dipshit's neck, her sweet hips pressed against his, and that was no little kiss. He was devouring her.

Pete hit the gas.

There was no way he was going to let that asshole take Jenna from him. So what if she confused the hell out of him, or lost that blazing confidence around him? So what if his nights were interrupted by phone calls from his drunken father? One way or another, he'd make damn sure that he was on the other end of Jenna's next kiss, and he'd damn well make her forget the Harley-driving construction worker ever existed.

CHAPTER FOUR

"THAT WAS QUITE the PDA." Amy looped her arm around Jenna's as they walked down Main Street toward the Wellfleet Library.

"Tell me about it. That man knows how to kiss." Jenna had been floored when Charlie showed up earlier that morning, even more so when he took her in a deep, passionate kiss. She'd been trying to convince herself all day that she'd enjoyed it. "But it just felt *nice*."

"Oh, Jenna. I want a nice kiss like that." Amy leaned her head on Jenna's shoulder and sighed as they passed Town Hall.

"Want me to set you up with Charlie?"

"What? He's your date tonight, not mine." Amy laughed. "I'd never take another woman's man."

"Yeah, he is my date, but…"

"Oh Lordy. What is it?"

"Charlie's a great guy, but I still didn't feel sparks. It was a good kiss. A great kiss, even, but it wasn't a mind-numbing kiss."

"Oh no. No, no, no. Jenna."

"I hoped it was going to be. Believe me, I tried. I even deepened the kiss with the hopes of feeling that tingling sensation that would bring me up on my toes." Jenna shook her head. "Nothing. Zilch. He had his hands in all the right places. His body...oh my God. It felt so good against mine, but the kiss? Eh." She held her hand level with the ground and wiggled it from side to side.

"Why? It looked amazing. Even Pete was gawking at you two."

"I've been trying not to think about Pete, thank you very much." But he was all she *could* think about as they walked into the library. "I made a point of not looking at him when I crossed in front of his truck. I thought he'd just drive by, you know? But I heard his truck slow down, and then when Charlie kissed me, I was so focused on trying to feel something that I lost track of Pete altogether."

"Hi, ladies." Candy Taylor waved from behind the desk. Candy was in her late twenties and she'd worked at the library during the summers since her junior year of high school. Now she was married, with a little towheaded boy named Jason. Jenna thought she'd probably still work behind the front desk thirty summers from now.

"Hey, Candy. How's Jason?" Jenna leaned over the desk and picked up the framed picture of Jason that Candy changed every few weeks.

"He's on a lobster kick. I gave him a taste of mine one night, and now he thinks he should have it every night."

Candy set down the book she was reading and tucked her blond hair behind her ear. "I swear, I've never heard of a four-year-old even liking lobster."

"It could be worse. He could want all of your chocolate." Jenna wiggled her eyebrows. "This is adorable. Was it taken on the pier?"

"Yeah. He loves to go fishing there. Hey, I don't suppose either of you wants to volunteer to help at the annual book sale this year? We're shorthanded, and, Jenna, I know how you are about organizing. We could really use you."

The annual book sale was a big event in Wellfleet. People planned their weekends and vacations around it. The sale was held in the front yard of the church and overflowed into the alley between the church and Abiyoyo, a novelty store on Main Street. Jenna and her friends enjoyed going to the sale, and Jenna had volunteered a few times. Working hadn't been on her agenda for this summer, but it might be a good distraction from her mother and Pete.

"What kind of help do you need?" Jenna asked.

"We need people to handle the sales, organize the books, and you remember how it was when you volunteered. People drop off books all day long, so we also need people to coordinate the incoming books. If you want to help and have the time, we could also use some help in here getting ready before the sale."

Amy and Jenna exchanged a glance. Jenna had no interest in giving up her time in the sun, but she wouldn't mind helping later in the day, and she could tell that Amy was thinking the same thing.

"Can we help in the late afternoon or early evenings?" Jenna asked.

"That would be awesome. Whatever you can do. A day, a few days. Whatever works for you two. We appreciate any help we can get." Candy wrote down her phone number. "Just let me know."

Amy and Jenna spent the next two hours working their way through the romance and suspense titles, and after they'd each chosen a handful of books, they went around the corner to the Juice Café and shared a veggie pizza. Then they went back to Seaside and lay out in the sun, enjoying their newly borrowed books.

Vera was gathering her things when they arrived.

"Oh, I'm sorry I missed you girls, but I've had enough sun for one afternoon," she said with a smile. Vera wore her hair in a pixie style, similar to Jamie Lee Curtis's hairstyle. She wore a beach cover-up over her bathing suit and a big floppy hat.

"Want me to walk you up?" Jenna asked.

"Goodness, no. I'm fine. You girls enjoy your time, but the next time you go to the harbor, I'd love to join you. I fear Jamie's not going to be up for a while." Duck Harbor was one of Vera's favorite beaches, as well as Jenna's.

"You've got it, Vera." Jenna waved and watched her walk back up to her cottage.

Just being at the pool made Jenna think of Pete. It had taken all of her willpower to look away from him this morning, and—Lord help her—when Charlie kissed her, she'd wished it was Pete kissing her like she was all he ever wanted and holding her like she was all he ever needed.

They stayed by the pool until the sun began to set and they saw Bella walking around the quad. They carried their blankets and books and joined Bella on her deck.

"Hamburgers?" Jenna asked.

"Yeah. I don't have any tomato, though. Do you?" Bella pointed to a plate of lettuce. "I need mayo, too. I probably should have gone to the grocery store today."

"I'll get some. Can you throw one on for me?" Jenna called over her shoulder as she crossed the quad—the grassy area between the cottages. She noticed Amy and Bella whispering to each other. She was sure they were talking about her and Charlie's kiss. *Ugh. The kiss.* The kiss that should have set her world on fire but instead set her mind spinning in circles. She'd invited Charlie to join them tonight with the hopes of stirring some sort of feelings inside her stupid body, but it was like her private parts were on vacation. She didn't even get a fluttery belly when they'd kissed, and she hadn't been able to stop wondering what it would be like to kiss Pete ever since.

She brought a plate of tomato and mayo back to Bella's and found her and Amy whispering again.

"Why do I feel like I'm missing out on something?"

Jenna asked as she walked into Bella's cottage.

"You're not," Bella called through the screen door. "Margaritas are in the bucket in the freezer. Bring 'em out?"

Amy went inside to help Jenna. "I'll get the glasses."

Jenna carried the bucket of margaritas out to the porch with Amy on her heels.

"When is Charlie getting here? Should I cook him a burger?" Bella asked.

"He's meeting me there. He had to go home and shower after work, and he had to run a few errands. Where's Evan?"

"He's at Bobby's. They're meeting us there, and Leanna said she and Kurt are meeting us there, too. She had to fill a rush order this afternoon, and she said Lacy is going to hang out with us. Should be fun." Bella loaded the burgers onto a plate, and as they sat down to eat, Caden pulled up. "There's my handsome hubby-to-be."

"God, you guys need to come up with new pet names. You make me feel very single." Jenna took a bite of her burger.

"Hey, babe." Caden leaned down and kissed Bella, then patted Jenna on the shoulder. "Heard you had a magnificent kiss today."

Jenna covered her mouth, which was full of burger, and glared at Bella.

"What? It looked pretty magnificent to me." Bella laughed.

Jenna rolled her eyes.

"Uh-oh. You mean a kiss that looks that good to one woman might not actually be that good to another? I don't think I want to know this." Caden went inside the cottage.

"She didn't feel a zing," Amy whispered.

"No zing?" Bella's eyes filled with worry; then they widened. "See? You aren't over Pete. I mean, unless this guy has a forked tongue or something, what else could it be? He had the whole possessive hold thing going on, and, girlfriend, your body was plastered to his, so I'm sure he was doing all the right things."

Jenna pushed her plate away. She wasn't hungry after all. "When you first kissed Caden, you *knew*, right?"

Bella glanced inside the cottage and leaned closer to Jenna. "Don't you remember? He turned me inside out. Still does."

"Charlie didn't even fold down my edges, much less turn me inside out." Jenna sighed. "I'm gonna go shower and get this date over with."

"Why did you even invite him to come with us if there wasn't a spark?" Amy asked what Jenna had been asking herself all day.

"Because it must be me. If Charlie had kissed either of you, you'd have felt a goddamn zing. I want a zing! It isn't fair. I want a zing so badly I'm ready to fake it."

Jenna let out a frustrated breath. "I keep hoping something will kick in. He's hot and sweet, and…" She stepped off the deck.

Bella shifted her eyes to Amy, and as Jenna walked across the lawn to her cottage, she was sure they thought she was just as nuts as she did. She went inside and stared into her closet. She had no idea what she wanted to wear. Did it even matter? She was with a hot guy and felt nothing. Maybe her body really was broken. It had been a long time since she'd had a real date. Could a person's body just turn off like that?

No. She completely lost all semblance of intelligence around Pete, and her body went all tingly. She was still alive in some way, even if it was a mindless way.

Mindless. She mulled the word over, then went to the window and gazed out at the pool. She'd missed peeking at Pete when he was cleaning the pool that morning, and now that he'd seen her not only practically throw herself at Charlie, but then kiss him in what apparently looked like a *magnificent* kiss, he probably wouldn't want anything to do with her. Thinking about Pete made her stomach quiver. Was that out of longing for what she'd never have, or was it something more?

Jenna wanted it to be so much more. She wanted a kiss that made her mindless. *I want Pete to make me mindless.*

Being mindless would be so much better than being mindful while kissing. So mindful that she couldn't put her finger on what was missing. *A great kiss should steal my ability to think.* She sighed loudly, and then she went into the bathroom and turned on the shower. She'd give this one more shot. *Dress sexy, act sexy, and damn it, no more evaluat-*

ing. And she was going to kiss sexy! When had kissing become such a pain?

She stepped into the shower and relaxed her head back—until the water turned ice-cold. Jenna screamed and scrambled from the shower. She wrapped a towel around herself and pushed the lever all the way to hot. She stuck her finger under the stream of water and still it was ice-cold. She turned it off, stomped out of the bedroom, yanked a picture off the wall, and flipped open the fuse box. No fuses were tripped. *Great. Now what?* She threw open the door and ran over to Bella's cottage.

"Bella? I need Caden," she said as she breezed through the cottage door.

Bella ran her eyes down Jenna. "He's not here. What's wrong, and why are you in a towel?"

"My hot water isn't working. If Caden's not here, and Tony and Jamie aren't here, what the heck am I going to do?"

Bella grabbed her keys and dragged Jenna outside. "You have to call Pete. He'll come fix it. But I have to leave. I'm meeting Caden. Now. I'm meeting him now."

"Can I use your shower?"

Bella's eyes widened. "Um. Of course, but you need hot water. You should call Pete."

"But—"

"Call him. He'll come fix it, and you never know. If the hot water doesn't work, the toilet could be next." Bella climbed into her car.

"The toilet? Why?" No toilet? Overnight? *This cannot be happening.*

"Plumbing," Bella said out her car window as she backed out of the driveway. "Call Pete before he goes out for the night."

"Ugh!" She waved to Bella and turned to go to Amy's, but she was backing out of her driveway, too. Damn it. Jenna wanted to cry. She glanced at Vera's cottage, but what could an eighty-year-old woman do to help? Maybe she should just shower at Bella's, then not worry about the damn hot water.

Or the toilet.

Oh God.

She dragged her ass back to her house and called Pete. She hadn't exactly been nice to him lately, and she wouldn't blame him if he ignored her call. She hadn't tried to be a jerk. She was afraid that if she fell into their normal friendly pattern, her crush would seize her and she'd never get over him. She'd spend every summer in the future longing to rip his clothes off and acting like she didn't know how. She knew how. Damn, did she know how! She was no stranger to being the aggressor in a relationship, but with Pete, her stomach got all fluttery, and she spent more time staring at him than anything else. It was ridiculous, really, and it kind of pissed her off. She was a grown woman, not a teenager. She should be able to walk right up to him and say, *Pete, let's go out for a drink.* Then make a move during the evening. But they were friends, and they'd gone for drinks plenty of times with the rest of their friends, and she'd never once made that move. Neither had he. *Maybe he doesn't feel the same.*

Her call went to voicemail. She tapped her foot as she waited for the beep. "Pete, this is Jenna, over at Seaside." *Duh.* Like he doesn't know that? Jeez, even on the phone she was a nimrod around him. "My hot water isn't working. Would you mind coming over to fix it? I'm sorry. I know it's late, but Bella said the toilet could go next, and—" The voicemail recording cut her off. She stared at the phone. *Stupid phone. Stupid shower. Stupid Peter Lacroux.*

This summer was supposed to be about Jenna finally taking charge of her life and finding her own happily ever after—with someone other than Pete. She'd found a really great guy. A damn hot one, too, but she had a sneaking suspicion that it was Pete that was messing with her ability to detect zings in their kisses. She'd spent too many years ogling him, hoping and praying to make something happen, and all the while, turning into a shrinking violet around the one man who did more than make her body zing.

She hurried back over to Bella's house and showered, only realizing after she stepped from the shower that she'd forgotten to grab her clothes to change into. This was totally not her night. Wrapped in her towel, she hurried back outside and across the quad to her house, stopping cold at the sight of Pete's truck in her driveway.

Oh God.

She'd had so many fantasies about Pete in her house when she was naked, but absolutely zero of them had anything to do with him repairing anything. Maybe breaking a bedspring or two, or crashing into a wall with her in his arms—*Oh God.* She needed another shower. A cold one.

Jenna fanned her face as she took one hesitant step after another across the deck to her screened door, where she peered inside. Pete was nowhere in sight. *Thank God.* He must have run down to the pool or over to Theresa's. She could run in and dress quickly. She pulled open the door and ran through the living room, looking over her shoulder in case he showed up—and she slammed into a wall.

"Ack!" Jenna screeched. Her hands flew up to push her cheek from the wall—*a wall with legs. Shit. Double shit*—as her towel fell to the ground. She clenched her eyes shut and ran her hands over the wall of muscles she'd smacked into, then fisted her hands in the soft cotton shirt that covered them.

Nonononono.

Please be a stranger.

Please, please, be a stranger.

"Hi, Jenna."

Zing! Pow! Bam! Pete's deep, sexy voice slid through her ears straight to her toes, leaving a trail of fire on everything in between. She clenched her eyes shut tighter. "If I can't see you, you can't see me. Right? Please lie to me." His chest felt amazing. Spectacular. *Lickable.*

She felt him lean forward a little, as if he were looking over her shoulder *at her bare ass.* He laughed, a low, sexy, zing-inspiring laugh that shot right to her naughty parts and woke them up with such force that her nipples stood at attention. *Against his chest.* Jenna heard a whimper slip through her lips.

"You're sadly mistaken, Jenna. I can see a whole hell of a lot of you right now." He whistled. It was the type of whistle construction workers sounded off as women walked by.

Jerk.

Sexy jerk.

Sexy jerk who smells like heaven wrapped in a soft cotton T-shirt.

"I guess you want your towel?"

She thudded her fist against his chest, unable to force another word from her throat. He'd seen her big ass. Her big *white* ass. She should have put on tanning lotion and…*Oh my God! What am I thinking? I'm buck naked in Pete's arms!*

"Don't freak out or anything when I bend down to get this towel." His voice was calm, like he was in total control, which was totally unfair.

"Mm-hm," she managed.

His big, strong hand slid down her side and stopped at her waist. How had she missed his hand gripping her arm in the first place? She felt her body begin to tremble, and she knew he could feel it, too. It was as obvious as a beach umbrella struggling to remain erect during a typhoon. She clenched her fists tighter in his shirt.

His grip tightened on her hip, and holy mother of grace did it feel good.

"If you keep hold of me like that, I'll never be able to pick up your towel."

Jenna's fingers flew open.

He laughed again and—thankfully—bent a little, as if he were going to retrieve her towel. His other hand, still holding her waist, slid seductively lower. She clenched her thighs to quell the desirous ache between her legs. He made a sound in his throat. Something between a grunt and an appreciative *Hm!* Then he crouched down a little lower, his cheek grazing her nipple, sending sizzling pinpricks through her entire body. She couldn't help it. She gripped his shirt again. She needed support before she fell right over. She'd never stood buck naked before a man who was fully dressed before. Beneath a man in the bedroom, sure. Above a man in the bedroom? Sure, sometimes, though not as often. But full frontal nude in front of Pete Lacroux?

Shoot me now. Please, please, let me drop dead.

She felt him rise to his full height again, his hand slid back up to her waist, where it felt like it had settled in for the night. His thumb pressed just below her ribs, his fingers gripped her back possessively, and when she remembered to breathe again, she inhaled lungs full of Pete. *Masculine.*

Sinfully sexy. Earthy.

She was going straight to hell for what she did next. She gripped his shirt tighter and inhaled again, hoping that smell would permeate her skin, her hair, her eyelids, for Christ's sake. She must have died and gone to heaven in the three minutes that this episode took place. That was the only explanation that made any sense, because suddenly she could breathe, she could hear noises from the cars on the main road, and holy smokes, she could feel a breeze coming in from the front door, which was wide open. Holy shit. Her door was wide open. Anyone could see her big white ass. She had it all wrong.

She was in hell.

She felt the towel wrap around her from behind.

"Better?" Pete took a step back, her claws still attached to his shirt as he handed her the ends of the towel.

She nodded, eyes still closed.

"Don't worry. I didn't look."

She opened one eye and looked up at him. That was so much worse. His chin was peppered with stubble, and his chest rose and fell with each breath. Now that she knew what those pecs felt like, each breath felt like it reverberated against her palms again. When she met his eyes, oh God, those glorious pools of brown sucked her right in. Jenna bit her lower lip to keep from grabbing his chest again.

"I fixed your hot water." Pete held her gaze, and he didn't look embarrassed or rattled, which only made Jenna more nervous.

"Th-thank you." Jenna couldn't move. She needed to walk past him to get into the bedroom and get dressed, and her legs were stuck. Glued to the floor.

"Are you going to the movie at Town Hall tonight?"

Oh shit. She was supposed to be there already. She managed a nod.

His mouth quirked up. "I'll see you there, then."

He walked toward the door, and it was all Jenna could do to remain standing. She closed her eyes, relieved and frustrated at once. She didn't hear the screen door open, and she sensed him standing behind her in the small living room. Was he looking at her? What was he thinking? Why wasn't he leaving?

All sorts of crazy thoughts went through her head, like turning around and launching herself into his arms and kissing him silly. Her heartbeat quickened at the thought.

"Jenna?"

"Mm-hm?" She couldn't move.

He was silent for a long time. Maybe two full days; Jenna wasn't sure. Or maybe two minutes.

"Call me if you need anything else."

When the screen door closed behind him, Jenna let out the breath she'd been holding. Her insides were trembling. She closed her eyes and took a deep breath, and when she opened her eyes, a smile lifted her lips.

My zinger isn't broken after all.

CHAPTER FIVE

THE LAWN BEHIND Wellfleet Town Hall was crowded with couples and families sitting on blankets and in beach chairs, gazing up at the Brave Foundation's documentary, playing on the back of the tall, white building. An old-fashioned popcorn machine sat atop the concession stand that was set up on the path leading from Main Street to the back of the building. Pete was trying like hell to concentrate on the documentary, as shark migration had become a major problem in New England, but he couldn't help watching Jenna and Dipshit instead. *Charlie.* He was actually a nice guy, and Pete felt a little guilty for thinking of him as Dipshit. A little, but not enough to stop the thought, especially after having Jenna's naked body pressed against him. It had taken all of his focus and determination not to kiss her until thoughts of anything other than them disappeared.

He watched her now, sitting beside Dipshit, fidgeting with the edge of her cutoffs. Her wide-necked long-sleeved shirt was falling off her shoulder, and her lean, tanned skin begged to be kissed. If he were sitting with her, he'd lean her back against his chest and wrap his arms around that tiny little waist of hers; then he'd lower his lips to her shoulder and kiss every inch of skin between her shoulder and her beautiful neck. After the way she trembled beneath his touch when he couldn't keep from placing a hand on her as he retrieved her towel, he knew that those kisses would raise goose bumps all over her incredible body. Hell, he was hard just thinking about touching her.

He shifted in his chair and forced himself to turn away. Pete wrung his hands together, catching bits and pieces of the documentary. *Following food...More dangerous to drive a car...Seals...*He was still trying to figure out what had actually happened at Jenna's. Her hot water had been turned off, which meant she had probably turned it off. That had been the first thing he'd checked when he'd arrived at her cottage, and it excited him. He'd thought she'd feigned the need for a repair just to see him, but then she'd acted like she always had—nervous and unable to talk around him. Granted, she had lost her towel. He grinned at the thought. If anything, it would have been the perfect time for her to give him an indication that she wanted him, and when she didn't, it had totally thrown him off. He was still off-kilter.

"I'm going to get popcorn. Anyone want to go?" Jenna rose to her feet and tugged at the frayed edges of her shorts.

Hell yes.

He tried to act cool, lowering his chin and sliding his eyes to the others as they passed on the invitation. He watched Jenna walk away, her ass swaying seductively as she disappeared into the darkness beside the building. Pete couldn't believe Dipshit was stupid enough to let a woman like Jenna go for popcorn alone. He was the man. He should have gotten it for her or escorted her. If Jenna were Pete's, he'd make damn sure she was taken care of properly. He waited a minute before getting up and heading in the same direction.

The concession area was lit only by candles on either end of the table. Jenna stood before the popcorn stand with her fingertips on the table and a smile on her lips as she watched the popcorn pop. Her hair ran down her shoulders, and as Pete approached, he thought about the curve of her naked hip beneath his hand. The air shifted and heated as he moved behind her and glanced back at the others, sitting far enough away that they couldn't see them. He couldn't resist placing his hand on her hip again. Jenna went rigid beneath his touch and sucked in a breath. Pete leaned down, his cheek beside hers, her intoxicating scent wrapping its tentacles around Pete and drawing him a step closer. His thighs grazed her ass as he whispered, "Hungry?"

Hungry? What the hell? It had been a long time since Pete had had to court a woman. They usually came to him, and he was out of practice.

Jenna nodded. Another mousy response. Not at all what he'd hoped for. He took out his wallet and paid for her popcorn, and when the elderly gentleman handed her the bucket of popcorn, he had no business keeping his hand on her waist and guiding her from the table onto the dark path, but he didn't care. Every silent step brought them closer to the others. Pete's pulse quickened at the thought of sitting away from her again, watching that guy put a hand on her thigh. He hooked his finger into the belt loop of her shorts and tugged Jenna around so she was facing him—and clutching the damn popcorn. He stared into her troubled eyes. The sounds of the movie faded into the night. Jenna's lips parted; she barely came up to Pete's solar plexus. One tug brought her hips against his. Her breasts brushed against his abs, and damn, did they feel good.

He leaned down so they were eye to eye, her lips a whisper away.

"Why won't you talk to me?" It wasn't what he'd intended to say. In fact, he hadn't intended to say a goddamn word, but he had to know. Why could she talk to a guy like Dipshit when she fell apart around Pete?

"I…" She swallowed hard and tightened her grip around the popcorn.

"I don't bite, Jenna." He reached up and brushed her hair from her shoulder. His fingers lingered in her soft waves and skimmed over her neck. Her skin was warm, and he was tempted to slide his hand beneath her hair, wrap his fingers around the back of her neck, and pull her in to a kiss—but he knew he wouldn't want to stop there. Not with the memory of her bare body still so fresh. He lowered his hand to his side and waited.

Her brows drew together, then eased, then drew together again. She closed her mouth, then opened it again. She was struggling, and he wanted to take her in his arms and hold her until she felt safe enough to say whatever was so difficult for her. This was new and unfamiliar territory for Pete, both his patience and the eagerness for a woman who was so different from the way he was with the women he usually dated. Hell, he didn't need a woman right now at all. Then again, need had nothing to do with the desires coursing through him.

Want was sailing this boat.

Seeing her with Dipshit had amped up his desire. Seeing her naked turned his curiosity to an intense craving. His body demanded Jenna. *Only Jenna.* He searched her eyes again, hoping for some indication that he was on the right track. Beneath her worry was pure, unadulterated lust. *Holy hell.* It was right there in her eyes. Had it been there the whole time? Had he just overlooked it? Lust he understood. Lust was familiar territory, but on Jenna it was laced with something deeper. A connection that snaked into his core and rooted there, momentarily severing his ability to think past what they both felt. He heard clapping in the background and knew their time was coming to an end.

"It's okay, Jenna. I can see this is hard for you. Take your time." He lowered his lips until they brushed her ear and whispered, "One day it'll be my name coming off your lips as you fall apart, and I promise you, after that, when you forget how to talk, it'll be worth every erotic, sensual second."

JENNA SUCKED IN another breath. *Oh God. Erotic. Sensual.* His voice, his words, his confidence, spiraled around her, taunting, teasing, practically stroking her. She shuddered with his promise.

"And when you remember to breathe again, you'll beg for more," he whispered.

The bucket of popcorn slid down against her belly as her arms went limp. Pete slid one strong hand beneath the bucket. He rose to his full height, the popcorn bucket tucked against his side, and he turned Jenna toward the grass where the others were sitting. She sucked in a jagged breath as he took her elbow in his hand and guided her back to her seat. *Beg for more?* Oh God, yes. She wanted to beg for so much more. She'd waited years to hear something like this from Pete, and now she was struck mute? *Say something! Oh God, I can't even talk.* She couldn't even wish she could drop dead, because she didn't want to, no matter how upset she was over her inability to respond. Finally. *Finally*, Pete wanted her.

When they were just a few feet from their friends, he leaned down again and whispered, "Breathe, Jenna. Your date is waiting." Then he walked back to his chair as if he hadn't just made a promise that she'd hear in her mind until the day she died.

Jenna moved as if she were on autopilot, lowering herself to the blanket beside Charlie and settling the popcorn in his hands. Charlie said something, but his words were lost in the fog of Pete's promise. Jenna tried to smile and felt it fall short. The movie had ended, and Dane Braden, the founder of the Brave Foundation, stood before the crowd, but his words were also caught in the web of Peter Lacroux. Jenna squinted, trying to at least pretend she was listening, but her eyes kept shifting to Pete. He looked so damn handsome sitting beside Caden, knees up, feet flat on the ground, his muscular arms leaning casually on his knees. He cocked his head and caught her staring. Jenna dropped her eyes, sure everyone near them could hear her heart thundering in her chest and certain the desire bubbling inside her would come bursting out if she tried to speak.

Dane talked for half an hour, during which Jenna's eyes darted to Pete a hundred times—and each time he managed to catch her. His face was somber at first, but now, as she chanced one more glance, the right side of his mouth kicked up and he arched a brow; then he lowered his chin even more and sent her a seductive stare that pinned her in place. The world silenced around her, and then slowly she became aware of a flurry of movement.

"Jenna, are you going to sit there all night?" Amy yanked her up by the hand. "Jeez, woman."

Charlie reached for her. "That was fascinating, wasn't it?"

"Fascinating." *Thrilling. Terrifying* also came to mind.

"Are you guys up for a drink?" Lacy Snow, Dane's girl-friend, was a tall blonde with thick spiral curls that hung past her shoulders and a smile that eased even Jenna's crazy nerves. "I know Dane would love to hang out with everyone." She glanced at Dane, talking with a group of people by the building. Jenna recognized the dreamy look in her eyes—it was exactly how she used to look at Pete.

Used to. When she looked at Pete now she no longer saw the quiet man who moved like a shadow, doing exactly what he was supposed to do at all times—the man she was initially attracted to. Now he appeared to be so much more. Now she saw a man with an edge, in control, mysterious. A man who was ten times as alpha as any man she'd ever met but confident enough to keep it to himself. The type of man she'd always dreamed of being with—and it scared the shit out of her and intrigued her in equal measure.

She didn't need a drink to make it through this night. She needed an entire bottle.

THE BAND AT the Beachcomber played a mix of top forty and country music. The deck was dimly lit, the music was loud, and the dance floor was packed. They claimed the only empty table, a table for four on the corner of the deck, and thanks to a helpful waiter, they were able to secure extra chairs from around the room. The ten of them squeezed in around the small table. Jenna sat beside Charlie, directly across from Pete, who was sitting beside Amy. Dane and Lacy were at one end of the table, and Bella and Caden sat at the other, with Kurt and Leanna squeezed in at the corner.

"That was a fascinating documentary, Dane," Caden said. "So you're a shark tagger and a marine biologist, and you combined the two when you founded the Brave Foundation?"

"Brave's mission is to use education and innovative advocacy programs in an effort to enlighten those that are fearful of sharks, and work toward their protection, and in a broader sense, protecting the oceans as well. Tagging is part of the process." Dane pulled Lacy closer to him and kissed her temple. "But enough about work. Kurt said Evan wanted to come out on the boat. Why don't we make a day of it and all go out for an afternoon? Lacy could use some girl time. We've been on a research mission in Bermuda for the past three weeks, and she's probably pretty sick of me."

Lacy wrapped her arm around Dane's middle and pressed her body to his. She narrowed her baby blues and looked into his dark eyes. "Never, but I would love to hang out with Leanna and the girls on the boat." Lacy smiled at Leanna. "We can sun ourselves while the boys play fishermen."

"Sounds great to me. Kurt's ahead of his deadline, so he can take an afternoon, right?" Leanna reached for Kurt's hand.

"I wouldn't miss it for the world." Kurt brought her hand to his lips.

Jenna felt something against her foot and glanced beneath the table. Pete's giant boot was pressed against her sandal. She bit her lower lip, unsure if he'd meant to do it, or if she should move her foot away. She glanced up at him and he pressed it harder.

She swallowed.

"Let me know when you're thinking of going and I'll try to get the time off," Caden said.

Charlie placed a hand on Jenna's thigh, and Jenna felt her cheeks heat up. She knew he was probably waiting for her to invite him on the boat trip. She chanced another glance in Pete's direction and he arched a brow. He was amused by Charlie's hand on her thigh? What the hell did that mean? Pete shifted his eyes to a blonde on the dance floor. Despite her decision not to be wrapped up in Pete this summer—a battle she was slowly losing grip on—jealousy wrapped its claws around her chest and squeezed tight.

"Charlie, can you get away for an afternoon to go with us?" Jenna kept her eyes focused on Charlie. She felt guilty for using him to get back at Pete, but Pete had left her high and dry for too many years for her to simply fall into his lap, even if there was nothing else on earth she'd rather do. Of course, if she fell, she'd probably turn into a blundering idiot and he'd boot her away faster than she could blink an eye. *Stop it. Stop thinking about him!*

She couldn't help it. She thought of her body pressed against his in the cottage and his hot breath caressing her skin. *Every erotic, sensual second.* She dropped her eyes with the thought. She shouldn't have invited Charlie. It wasn't fair to him since her stupid mind was still hung up on Pete.

Charlie accepted her offer and draped an arm around her. His smile pounded the *guilty* stake into her heart a little deeper.

"Great. Amy? Can you make it?" Lacy asked.

"I can always make it. I never have any plans." Amy ran her finger around the rim of her glass.

Pete draped an arm over Amy's shoulder. "I could hook you up with a nice guy."

Jenna's stomach clenched.

Amy tucked her hair behind her ear. "That's okay. I could have a date if I wanted one. I just…" She shrugged.

"She's waiting for a particular pro surfer to come knocking at her cottage door." Bella raised her eyebrows.

Amy rolled her eyes.

"If he's not careful, he'll have missed the boat." It took all of Jenna's willpower to keep her eyes trained on her glass and not lift them to look at Pete's face. She wanted to read his eyes and see if her words hit home. Instead, she downed her drink in one gulp and hoped to hell they did.

"Oh, I don't know," Pete said. "Amy's gorgeous and sweet. She's funny, and she's loyal to each of you. I think she's probably worth waiting for."

"Aw, thanks, Pete." Amy patted his leg.

Worth waiting for?

"Maybe you need to be more forward with Tony and let him know what you want," Pete suggested.

Jenna didn't have to look to know he'd shifted his gaze to her. Heat blazed across the table.

"Oh, I think he has a pretty good picture," Bella said.

"Lacy waited more than a year for our schedules to work out so we could finally be together." Dane smiled at Lacy. "Some things can't be rushed."

Jenna snuck a peek at Pete and he shifted his eyes away.

He took a long pull of his drink. "Exactly." He eyed the blonde on the dance floor again.

Jenna's stomach clenched tight with jealousy.

Lacy kissed Dane's cheek. "Well, you're the most romantic man I know, so you were definitely worth waiting for."

"Romance is so hard to come by," Amy said. "To me, the most romantic thing a guy could do is to take care of you when you're sick, or something simple, like carry your bags when he sees you're struggling."

"Or ride your pink bicycle just to see you?" Leanna touched Kurt's cheek, and he leaned in for a kiss.

"Those are all romantic, and Kurt looked adorably sexy on that pink bike." Jenna smiled at Kurt, who rolled his eyes.

"I wasn't kidding, Kurt. To me, sexiness and romance aren't about doing what people expect; they're about caring enough to do the things that aren't expected, or loving a person enough to see things in them that others didn't. Like making her coffee just the way she likes it, or like Caden installing new locks on Bella's doors and windows, or, I don't know, singing just to see your girlfriend smile, even if your voice cracks."

"Singing? Got that, Charlie?" Amy laughed.

"Don't look at me. I can't carry a tune across the street." Charlie took a sip of his beer.

Pete shifted his eyes to Jenna, and for that brief second, she knew exactly what romance was. Romance was the look in Pete's eyes, the connection that they were both fighting tooth and nail. He looked back at the blonde on the dance floor.

Or maybe not.

When the blonde headed for the ladies' room, Pete followed. "Excuse me."

Oh no you don't. Jenna was not about to be teased with promises of erotic, sensual experiences and then thrown away for some blond bimbo. She pulled her shoulders back, inhaled deeply, and rose to her feet. "Excuse me a sec. I think I see someone from the library." She stalked into the restaurant, then circled around to the back entrance to the hall that led to the restrooms. She didn't even know what an erotic experience was, although bondage and other things came to mind.

She froze at the thought. No, she had to be wrong. Pete wasn't like that. Sweet, docile Pete? *Ha!* The only thing docile about Pete was—oh hell. She couldn't even pretend there was anything docile about him anymore. She forced her feet to carry her around the corner to the entrance of the restrooms. As if to prove her thoughts, Pete stood with his arms crossed over his chest, his biceps twitching, powerful legs planted like tree trunks, and his eyes locked on the blonde from the dance floor. He shifted his gaze and caught sight of Jenna. A coy grin slid north to his eyes. He touched the blonde's arm, said something, nodded, then closed the gap between him and Jenna.

Jenna stumbled backward until her back hit the wall. Pete leaned a palm on the wall beside her head. He leaned down so they were eye to eye. Before he could say a word, Jenna's thoughts burst from her lips.

"What are you doing?" She was breathing so hard her boobs rose like they were riding the swell of an ocean liner.

"You're speaking to me?"

She narrowed her eyes. "Jesus. You're…" *Making me hot and bothered, and confused. Wickedly confused.*

He arched a brow, and she wanted to smack that amused look off his face, then plaster her lips to his.

"Jenna, if you have something you want, just tell me."

Kiss him. Just press your lips to his and—"Ugh!" She pushed past him and stormed into the ladies' room.

"Something I want. Something I want?" She paced the floor, ignoring the looks from the blonde he'd been talking to and the two brunettes washing their hands at the sink. She grabbed a paper towel and wiped a bead of sweat from her brow.

"He has that effect on women."

Jenna spun around and faced the blonde.

"Pete. I assume that's who you're talking about. The guy I was talking to who had a bead on you the minute he saw you?" She raked her eyes down Jenna's body. "He's a big tease, choosy as hell." She moved in closer, like she was Jenna's best friend, and lowered her voice. "Only, I hear that when he's not teasing, which apparently doesn't happen as often as we might think, he'll blow your mind." She licked her lips. "And he'll leave you begging for more."

Holy crap. "Ha—have you...been with him?" *I don't want to know. Don't tell me. Please don't tell me.*

"Pfft. Me?" Blondie laughed. "Don't I wish. I'm not even close to being in his league."

Jenna quickly assessed her: chesty, lean, pretty, but not overly made-up. Her hair fell to the middle of her back in lustrous waves, and she had legs that went on forever. If *Blondie* wasn't in his league, Jenna wondered if she was even good enough to sit on the bleachers.

CHAPTER SIX

JENNA BANGED ON Amy's bedroom window. She had two bottles of Middle Sister wine in one arm and a roll of premade chocolate chip cookie dough in the front pocket of her hoodie. It was pitch-black in the development, as there were no streetlights, and Amy's bedroom was on the side of her cottage. Jenna wasn't tall enough to see in her window. She hung on Amy's windowsill and called to her in a loud whisper.

"Ames! I need you!"

She heard Amy groan.

"Amy! Ames! Hurry! It's cold out here."

Amy's face appeared in the window. Her blond hair was a tangled mess. They'd come back from the Beachcomber an hour and a half ago, and Jenna had tried to sleep, but every time she closed her eyes, she heard Pete's promise.

"What's wrong?"

"I can't sleep." Jenna bounced on her toes and held up a roll of cookie dough. "I brought goodies!"

Amy's eyes widened. "Cookie dough? I'll be right out, but I'm bringing my blanket."

"Bring me one, too!"

Amy came outside in her flannel pajama pants and a hoodie with two blankets in her arms.

"Wanna get the girls?" Amy yawned.

"Yeah. Do you think it's okay with Kurt and Caden?"

Amy shrugged. "When have they ever stopped us?" She grabbed Jenna's arm and dragged her to Leanna's window. "Give me a hand," Amy whispered.

Jenna put the bottles and cookie dough on the ground and clasped her hands together so Amy could step in them and peek in the window. Amy tottered to the side.

"Whoa!"

"Shh," Jenna chided. "Hang on to the windowsill."

Pepper, Leanna's dog, barked.

"Oh, shit!" Jenna jumped back, sending Amy flat on her ass.

"Ow!" Amy rolled on top of Jenna and laughed.

"Pepper." Kurt silenced the pup with one word. "Leanna, I think the girls need you."

"Shit, shit, shit." Jenna covered her mouth. "We woke Kurt up!"

Kurt looked out the screen. "It's okay. She'll be out in a minute."

Bella's front door opened, and she came out in her nightie. "Jenna? Amy?" she whispered over her deck.

"Over here." Amy waved.

"You're going to wake Theresa!" Bella ran over in her

bare feet, her arms crossed over her chest. She helped them up. Leanna joined them a minute later, wearing one of Kurt's sweatshirts—and it looked like nothing else.

"What are you doing? It's two in the morning," Leanna said.

"Jenna couldn't sleep," Amy explained.

Jenna held up the cookie dough in one hand and the wine in the other. "I have goodies. Please, please, please don't be mad."

Leanna rolled her eyes. "Mad? Never. Where to?"

Jenna bit her lower lip, opened her eyes wide, and bobbed her head in the direction of the pool.

"Chunky-dunking? No, I'm too tired," Bella said. Chunky-dunking was what they called skinny-dipping.

"Piggies only?" Jenna stuck out her toes and wiggled them.

Bella reached for a bottle of wine and cranked it open. "Okay, piggies only."

At the pool, Jenna unlocked the gate as quietly as she was able, with Bella shushing her every three seconds.

"If Theresa hears you, we're all in trouble," Amy reminded her. The pool closed at eight o'clock, and swimming after dark was prohibited. They weren't sure what would happen if Theresa really caught them, but they didn't want to find out.

They tiptoed onto the pool deck and sat around the edge of the pool.

"It's cold!" Amy said, pulling a blanket around her shoulders.

"Oh, it is not." Bella's legs dangled in the water. "Pass the cookie dough."

Jenna tore open the cookie dough, ripped off a chunk, then passed the tube to Bella.

"Why couldn't you sleep?" Bella asked. "Maybe because the sexual tension between you and Pete was so thick I was afraid it would swallow you whole, and poor Charlie didn't seem to have a clue." Bella stuffed cookie dough in her mouth and handed the tube to Leanna. "Besides, you haven't given us one shred of detail about what's going on, and if you don't give it up soon, I'm going to let Leanna loose in your kitchen."

Leanna batted her lashes. When Leanna cooked, she left no counter, floor, or table untouched. Sometimes even the ceiling was peppered with jam or flour or other ingredients that had no business being on a ceiling.

Jenna took a swig of wine, then an even longer one at the thought of Leanna being set loose in her clean kitchen. She passed the bottle down the line, as the cookie dough made its way back toward her. "My life has turned into a really bad comedy of craziness."

"Oh, Jen, I'm sorry you feel that way." Amy leaned forward and looked at her around the others. "You have a great life."

Bella smiled. "I take it your hot water got fixed. I saw

that you used my shower. You lined up everything in my shower by height."

"Sorry." Jenna broke off another hunk of cookie dough. "Pete fixed it. You're not going to believe what I'm about to say, and I can't even believe I've waited this long to spill it, but with Charlie being sweet and sexy all night and Pete stalking me like prey…"

"See? Five bucks." Bella held her hand out to Leanna.

"I thought Pete was just being sweet." Leanna took a long drink of wine and handed it to Amy. "I hate that you guys all know and see things about men that I don't pick up on, like when Jenna was talking about orgasms all last summer and thinking about Pete, and I was clueless."

"If she's thinking about orgasms, she's thinking about Pete. That's a given," Bella said.

Jenna pushed to her feet. Goose bumps covered her legs. She hurried behind the girls and plopped down beside Amy, hoping to steal their warmth. "See? It's all your fault this is even an issue. If you'd stop bringing up Pete and me in the same sentence like I can't live without him, then maybe I could feel a zing when I'm with Charlie."

The others shared an eye roll that felt like it shook the earth.

"Ugh!" Jenna clenched her eyes shut and spoke as fast as she could. "I ran into him in the living room and my towel fell off; then I clutched his chest for dear life while he stood there thinking God knows what. Then he promised me erotic sex and told me to tell him what I wanted." Eyes still clenched shut, she fisted her hands and crossed her arms over her chest.

"Holy crap," Amy said.

"Naked clutching? Erotic sex?" Bella said. Jenna heard movement in the water, then sensed Bella's presence behind her.

"Tell him what you want?" Leanna sounded breathless.

"Open your goddamn eyes!" Bella shook Jenna by the shoulders.

Jenna's eyes flew open and was met with Bella's wide, toothy grin. Jenna couldn't help but smile, but at the same time, she wanted to cry.

"Oh no. No, no, no." Bella sat down behind her. "Jenna Jane, what on earth is wrong with you? Please don't cry. You know I'm not good with tears."

"She's overwhelmed. She's loved him forever." Amy patted Jenna's back.

Leanna handed Jenna the bottle of wine. "It's a lot to take in." She crinkled her nose. "Are you sure we're talking about Pete? Our Pete? Quiet guy, tall? I can't even imagine him saying the word *erotic*. *Sexy* maybe, but *erotic*?"

Jenna downed the wine, closing her eyes as the tangy liquid slid down her throat, quelling the panic inside her.

"Not only did he say it, but the man said it like he was good at it, and then...Oh my God, I can't believe I didn't tell you. When I went to the ladies' room, he had this blond bimbo cornered, and she said *she* was out of his league, and that he was a like a wild animal in the bedroom." Jenna shook her head. "*Blow your mind*, that's what she said. If she's out of his league, what the hell is he doing saying that stuff to me?"

"You're a hundred times hotter than any woman at that bar," Amy said.

"This is what you always wanted, Jenna. *He's* what you've always wanted," Bella reminded her.

Jenna covered her face and groaned. Then she peeked out over her fingertips. "I'm not sure I even know what erotic sex really means. Bondage? Anal? Threesome?"

"Jenna!" Amy covered her mouth.

"I think our sweet Pete has a dark side, and it scares me a little," Jenna admitted.

Bella swatted the air. "Look at Caden. He's Mr. Polite on the streets, but hotter than hell in the bedroom."

"He's freaking hot on the streets, too, Bella, and you know it." Jenna looked away.

"Yes, but so is Kurt, and Pete, of course," Leanna said. "Kurt's an animal in the bedroom. My docile, quiet wordsmith turns my world upside down." Kurt was about as even-tempered as they came, and as a writer, he often lived in his own head.

"We know," Amy and Jenna said in unison. Leanna and Kurt often forgot to close their windows when they were fooling around, and they weren't exactly quiet lovers.

Jenna lay back and looked up at the stars. "But what does it *mean* when a guy says *erotic* and *sensual?*"

Amy folded her hands in her lap. "Don't ask me. I'm vanilla or chocolate. You're talking about funky flavors I've never tasted."

Jenna bolted upright. "Ha! God, I love you, Ames." Jenna set serious eyes on Bella. "Well?"

"Why do you look at me?" Bella laughed. "Who knows? But I don't think it's any of the stuff you're worried about."

"Oh." Jenna heard the disappointment in her own voice and it surprised her. "I mean, oh, good."

"Yeah, whatever. What's the big deal? It's not like you're sexually repressed." Bella tore off a chunk of cookie dough and handed it to Jenna. "I mean, threesome, that would be a deal breaker for me, but you know what I mean. He's a guy. He probably meant really good, hot sex. Passion and power, a lethal combination."

"Finish the wine. I'm getting cold." Leanna reached for one of Amy's blankets.

"That's because all you're wearing is Kurt's sweatshirt," Amy said.

Leanna arched a brow. "If you slept with my fiancé, would *you* wear clothes?"

Amy took a swig of wine. "If I slept with your fiancé, you'd beat my ass, so it wouldn't matter what I wore. I'd be dead."

Jenna sighed. "Can we focus? I have one more confession."

All eyes locked on her.

"When I was clutching him for dear life, buck naked…"
She drew in a deep breath. "I didn't feel a zing."

Bella was putting a chunk of cookie dough in her mouth,
and she stopped with her hand in the air. "What?"

"It was more of a *ZING, POW, BAM!*"

Amy squealed and hugged Jenna. Bella wrapped her arms
around Jenna from behind. Leanna jumped to her feet, and
then all four of them were jumping in a circle, hugging and
laughing in a celebratory dance.

Bella tripped and reached for Amy on her way down,
pulling both of them into the pool. Jenna doubled over in
laughter and fell forward, headfirst into the water. The three
of them broke the surface in fits of laughter, clinging to one
another as they swam for the side of the pool.

"Shh!" Leanna reached for their hands. "Shh. Theresa's
going to catch us!" As they climbed from the pool, Leanna
wrapped blankets around them. "Theresa's light is on. We're
so dead."

"Hurry." Jenna ran to the gate and held it open.

"The bottles!" Amy ran back, gathered the bottles, and
joined Bella under her blanket. "So, why did you invite
Charlie on the boat, anyway?"

Jenna's teeth were chattering as she tried to lock the gate.
She dropped the lock. "Darn it." She fumbled in the
darkness for it. "Shit. Oh my God. Oh, here it is." She lifted

it with a smile and worked at hooking it to the chain again. "I did it to make Pete jealous." Jenna felt silly saying it out loud, but it had seemed like a good idea at the time. She locked the gate as the beam of a flashlight lit up the center of the road.

"Cripes!" Amy grabbed Bella's hand. "Run!"

They ran in a huddle behind the cottages on the other side of the road, laughing and shushing one another, then peered around the corner at Theresa as she unlocked the pool gate and walked onto the deck.

"My vote is to show up at Pete's house wearing nothing but a raincoat tied at the waist," Bella whispered. "Throw the man on the floor and devour every inch of him. Give him a taste of his own medicine. Leave him begging for more."

"Bella!" Amy whispered. "She gets flustered around him. How is she gonna...you know?"

"Oh shit. She found the cookie dough wrapper." Jenna pointed to Theresa, who stood on the pool deck with one hand on her hip, the other holding the wrapper.

"Quick, into Amy's!" Jenna took Amy's hand and pulled her toward her cottage.

"I think Pete's either trying to pull Jenna out of her stupor when she's around him, or he's, you know, laying it all on the table so Jenna can either decide to put down roots or go seed some other lawn." Bella followed them into Amy's cottage. They closed the curtains and kept the lights off, while Amy hustled into the bathroom and grabbed towels for all of them except Leanna.

"I'm not seeding anyone's lawn," Jenna hissed. "But I have to admit that I'm not over Pete. The man practically gave me the big O with nothing more than a whisper and a hand on my *naked* hip."

"You are a naughty, naughty girl, Jenna. I'm kinda jealous." Amy handed Bella and Jenna towels.

Bella peered out the front curtains. "Shh. She's standing in front of Amy's cottage."

"What now?" Amy whispered.

Bella closed the curtains and waved them all into the room at the back of the cottage. "Now Jenna has to decide if she's planting roots in Mount St. Peter or playing in the sand with Charlie." Bella patted Jenna's shoulder. "Just remember one thing. You're a woman, and women can be just as fierce as men. You've never been afraid of a man in your life, so whatever's running around in that cute little organized head of yours probably has nothing to do with being afraid of *him*. Maybe you act afraid of Pete because of what letting Pete see the real you means in your own head. What it means to *you*."

"I don't get it," Leanna said. "Do you mean like how I was worried that I'd be out of sync with Kurt and how you kept your love of frilly things from Caden? Well, and the rest of the world, but you know what I mean."

"Maybe," Bella whispered. "I'm not sure. But Pete's the only guy Jenna has ever really liked, and he's the only guy she isn't able to talk to. It has to mean something."

Amy yawned. "Jenna, I think you shouldn't worry about erotic anything, because in my experience, guys are all talk with not nearly enough follow-through. It's like how they all think six inches is really eight."

"Right," Leanna agreed. "You know, guys are so dumb like that. We don't walk around saying we're double D's when we're C's."

"Um…" Jenna looked down at the two bowling balls strapped to her chest.

"You put us all to shame." Bella glanced down at her own perfect C's. "But Caden likes mine, so I'm happy."

"Hey, can we not talk about things we don't *all* have?" Amy pointed to her chest. "I think B cup is pushing it over here."

"I'd give you some of mine if I could," Jenna offered.

"I know you would. I think you should just follow your heart, Jenna." Amy patted her own heart. "If it turns out Petey is a perv, you can stop seeing him."

"We're not even seeing each other, and he makes my heart go ten types of crazy." *Good crazy. Exciting crazy.*

"That's not a bad thing, hon." Amy yawned again. "I have to go to sleep or I'll be whipped tomorrow."

Jenna scrunched her shoulders and clenched her eyes shut. "Don't hate me, but I told Charlie I'd go out with him this weekend."

"Why on earth are you leading him on?" Bella ran her fingers through her hair, which was a tangled mass of wet blond waves.

Jenna shrugged. "Guys lead girls on all the time, and he's really nice and hot. Who knows? Maybe a zing will appear."

"Miss Zing Pow Bam, I doubt you're gonna zing for anyone but Pete. I've got to get home." Bella tiptoed to the front window again and peered out. "Caden has an early shift tomorrow, and I always get up with him."

"You're so sweet, Bella. I lie in bed for twenty minutes after Kurt gets up and listen to him typing on his laptop. It's comforting."

"I want comforting," Amy said with another sigh.

"Oh shit." Bella closed the curtains and covered her mouth.

"What?" Jenna pulled the curtains back. She spotted the cookie dough wrappers on the porch and slammed the curtains shut. "Shit, shit, shit. She knows it was us."

"Great." Amy sank onto her couch. "Now she thinks I'm the bad one."

"Oh, hush," Bella said. "No one ever thinks you're the bad one. We'll see what happens tomorrow."

"Well, girls, are we on for the beach tomorrow?" Leanna asked.

"Yeah," they all agreed.

On the way back to her cottage, Jenna thought about what Bella said about being afraid of something other than Pete. She thought of her parents' divorce and her mother floundering to navigate a future that she hadn't planned for or wanted. She pulled the screen door open and pushed the uncomfortable thoughts away. Maybe Bella was right, and what she was afraid of was staring her in the face every time her mother called. Maybe there really was no happily ever after.

CHAPTER SEVEN

PETE STOPPED BY the hardware store early Wednesday morning and found his father in the back office, punching figures into a calculator. He unhooked Joey's leash. She burst forward and climbed into his father's lap. He needed a distraction this morning, after Jenna's reaction—or lack thereof—last night. He focused on his father as he slowly spun his old rolling desk chair toward Pete. His eyes lit up as he petted Joey. He loved that dog as much as Pete did. He greeted Pete with a wide smile.

"Peter, how's it going, son?" His hair stood on end, and his jaw and neck were peppered with two days' worth of stubble, an indicator of at least one hard night.

Damn.

Not for the first time, Pete felt guilt and anger clawing at him. Guilt, because he knew his father needed help and he loved him too much to force him into rehab, and on its heels, anger, for being too weak to do what his father so obviously needed him to.

"Hey, Pop. I just came by to see how you're doing."

His father set Joey down, and the pup barked and sniffed

his shoes. "Working the books. It's a pain in the ass," he grumbled. "I have no idea how your mother did it for all those years, bless her heart." He stood and embraced Pete.

Out of habit, Pete inhaled, smelling for hints of alcohol. Thankfully, there were none, but Pete wasn't fooling himself. He knew alcoholics could mask their dirty little secret too many ways to count. Still, Pete breathed a sigh of relief. He didn't think he'd ever tire of the warmth of his father's embrace. Softer around the middle now from age and alcohol, Neil still had strong arms that carried the memories of the attentive father he'd always been, and memories of their close-knit family, which had become frayed by rattled emotions with their father's drinking.

"I told you I would find a bookkeeper to do it for you."

Neil swatted the air as he headed into the store with Joey trotting alongside. "*Pfft*. Family business doesn't mean hiring someone off the street, you know." It was a bone of contention among his father and all of his children. Pete's younger siblings had found careers off the Cape. Like Pete, they didn't have any interest in working in a hardware store, and although it made Pete sad to think about, he knew that when his father retired, they'd likely sell the store, and Lacroux Hardware would become a thing of the past.

He followed his father to the register. "So, you're doing okay, then?" The store hadn't changed in years. It was a typical hardware store with stocked metal shelves, linoleum floors, and no decorations other than the OPEN sign hanging from the door. His father had never been one for frivolities.

"Fine, fine." His father picked up an inventory clipboard and proceeded to the paint aisle.

Pete ran his eyes over his father's polo shirt and jeans, both clean and unwrinkled. A thread of hope weaved its way through Pete's heart. It was a pattern he'd tried to break, hoping a new day would bring a wake-up call for his father before a heart attack did. As much as it pained him to know that there would likely be no alarm going off in his father's head, when Pete had first realized he had a drinking problem, he'd approached him about getting help, and his father had been knee-deep in denial. Weeks later, his brothers had staged a full-on intervention, much to Pete's dismay. Their efforts had caused a fissure in their relationship with their father for a few hard months—with the exception of Sky, who had been oblivious to their attempts. While his brothers could escape their father's wrath of denial by going back to their respective lives, Pete remained. Eventually, Pete relented the fight, unwilling to lose the father he loved in that manner. Guilt-ridden was now a perpetual state for Pete, as he knew that if he didn't intervene, every day he saw his father might be his last.

"Okay, Pop. Then I'm gonna head out. Do you want to come by tonight and help with the boat? I could use a hand with the caulking." *Come on, Pop. Just one night.* Pete may have given up pushing his father to get help, but he never gave up hope that if he could convince his father to get back into the hobby he used to live for—refitting boats, as he'd taught Pete to do—that he might think twice about diving headfirst into the bottle the next time the urge took hold.

His father mumbled under his breath, something about *too much work*.

Pete leashed Joey and hesitated for a second, his mind and heart battling over trying again to convince his father to get help. He replayed the last conversation they'd had about it in his mind. *Hey, Pop, drinking isn't going to bring Mom back. Why don't we check out an AA meeting? I'll go with you.* His father's eyes had narrowed, a rare scowl settling on his lips before he turned his back to Pete in a dismissive manner and grumbled, *AA. I don't need AA. Go on, son. I've lived my life. Go live yours.*

He only wished he could.

AFTER SPENDING THE day at the beach, Jenna and Amy threw on sundresses over their bathing suits and went to the library to help prepare and organize for the annual book sale.

"Want to grab dinner at Mac's after this?" Amy asked.

"Uh-huh." Jenna stood before a box of books, withdrawing one after another, flipping through them, then writing the price for each on the inside cover before placing them neatly in the appropriately labeled boxes, alphabetized by author, of course.

"Can you believe Theresa didn't say anything this morning about the cookie dough wrapper when she saw us?" Amy asked. "It's like she wants us to know that she knows we're the ones who broke the rules, but she doesn't want to confront us."

"It doesn't have anything to do with us. I think she wants Bella to know that she knows, without giving Bella the gratification of seeing her get upset." Jenna eyed Amy. "But that's Bella's thing. You know she loves to prank Theresa, and she'll keep doing things that she's not supposed to until she gets a rise out of her—all done with love, of course."

"Of course. We all love Theresa."

"Ames, I've been thinking about Pete." She watched Amy, who kept her eyes trained on her books, but smiled with Jenna's admission.

"Yeah?"

"Yeah." She priced three more books in silence.

"Are we playing mental telepathy? You know I suck at that game."

Jenna laughed. "I just don't know what I think, but I'm thinking about him. You know, we're friends, and I love that, but I want so much more, and at the same time, I don't want to risk our friendship."

"True." Amy continued penciling in prices.

"And I've never really *told* him I was interested, and now that he's shown an interest, he makes my heart go even wilder, making it even scarier to try to let him know how I really feel."

"Yes."

Amy was doing what Amy did best, drawing out Jenna's thoughts by refusing to give her answers. She was patient to a fault, and when it came to Pete, Jenna knew she needed to be handled in that fashion. Telling Jenna she loved Pete brought out her defenses. This summer was supposed to be about finding happiness regardless of Peter Lacroux. *Liar, liar.* She'd been locked in her own mind for too long, running circles around Charlie and always circling back to Pete.

"I also think Bella was right, that he's never had competition for my attention before." She set down the book she was holding and faced Amy. "So, now that Pete has made it clear that he wants to take our friendship to the next level I should probably figure out how to talk to him so I can give him the same chance I gave Charlie."

Amy lifted her gaze to Jenna. "But?"

"But..." Jenna joined Amy and took the book from her hands and set it down. She leaned her butt against the table, and Amy did the same. "Suppose when the competition is gone, he's no longer so hot to trot for me?"

Amy pressed her lips together for a second. "I wish I had an answer, but honestly, that could happen."

"Yeah, I know. Sometimes I wish you could lie."

"I can lie, just not very well. Who knows? Maybe it won't happen." Amy turned back to the books. "What then?"

"Mad, erotic threesomes with anal sex?" Jenna sashayed back to her table.

"Eww. You're a pig." Amy laughed.

"Ha!" She threw her head back with the laugh and turned back toward Amy. "I don't know what then, but the next time he corners me, I'm not going to let my stupid body steal my ability to act like I would with anyone else. I'm going to climb his body like scaffolding"—she moved her hands and feet up and down as if she were scaling him— "wrap my legs around his waist, and kiss those amazing lips until he realizes that there is no woman on earth as incredibly smart and sexy as me!"

Amy's eyes widened.

"Okay, as me, you, Leanna, and Bella, of course, but you know what I mean."

Jenna closed her eyes and spun around. "That's exactly what I'll do." She opened her eyes and found Charlie standing with his hands on his hips, straight off the construction site, his tank top drenched in sweat and black gunk, and a smart-ass grin on his face.

Oh shit.

"Now, that's what I'm talking about." He closed in on Jenna, lifted her up, and sealed his lips over hers, stroking her tongue with deep, intense motions that should have sent her legs around his waist, only she was too wrapped up in thoughts of Pete.

Jenna opened her eyes wide, midkiss, then slammed them closed again. Kissing Charlie made her feel a little queasy—far from anything resembling a *zing*—and maybe relieved that he thought she was talking about him. She couldn't even begin to imagine how to handle the explanation if he found out she was talking about someone else.

She heard the back door to the stockroom open, and Jenna's eyes sprang open. She was still in Charlie's arms, eye to eye with his hungry stare—and in clear view of Pete, standing just inside the door with daggers shooting from his eyes and steam practically streaming from his ears.

"Pete." Jenna didn't know if she'd actually said his name or not. She pushed from Charlie's arms and landed with a thud on the floor as Amy spun around—and Pete stormed out of the building.

"Bummer," Charlie said. "He must have been in a hurry."

Yeah, a hurry to get away from me. Jenna's heart sank at the look on Pete's face.

"I just wanted to let you know that we're out of town on another site for the next few days, but I'll call you," Charlie said. "I'm looking forward to the boat ride with you on Saturday."

Jenna was still staring at the door, too shocked to move. She heard Amy join them, saw movement in her peripheral vision.

"You kissed her silly, Charlie." Amy bumped Jenna with

her elbow.

Jenna shook off her stupor and forced a smile for Charlie. *The boat trip.* "Great," she lied.

"I've got to run." He kissed Jenna's cheek and whispered, "Maybe after the boat ride I'll let you climb me like scaffolding."

Shitshitshit.

PETE DROVE DOWN to the pier, cursing a blue streak. What the fuck was he thinking? He couldn't get the image of Jenna lip-locked with that guy, her body pressed against him, out of his mind. He'd heard her and Amy talking about working at the library today, and he'd convinced himself that the only way to get past this mess was to lay his feelings on the line with Jenna. Let her know how much she meant to him, regardless of the obstacles in his life, and that he was interested in much more than just a sexual relationship. But she was most definitely *with* Dipshit, and he was obviously wasting his time. He threw his truck into park and stared out over the water.

Joey pushed her chin onto Pete's lap and huffed out a sigh.

Pete stroked his head. "What am I gonna do, girl? Stake my claim or walk away?" Damn if he wasn't incapable of walking away from Jenna. He took Joey for a walk along the beach, trying to work through his emotions. They sat on the beach and watched the sun set.

Pete's cell phone rang, startling Joey. *Pop.* He marked sunsets by his father's drinking, and hell if it wasn't that time again. He closed his eyes before answering the call and facing his father's drunken ramblings.

"Hey, Pop."

"Pete...Peter, Peter, listen, Pete."

Pete pushed to his feet and headed back to the truck. "I'm here, Pop."

"I can't find her, Pete. She's gone."

His chest constricted. Alcohol brought his father's longing for his mother to the forefront in the most painful of ways. "I know, Pop. I'm on my way." He turned the truck around and headed toward his father's house.

Like a child afraid of the boogeyman, Pete had come to fear the sight of his father's dark house. He longed for days gone by, when his parents' home was lit up with life, and visiting meant an evening of a home-cooked meal and laughter.

He mounted the stairs of his childhood Cape-style home. Joey's nails tapped out a beat beside him on the porch decking. Pete had refinished the porch last summer in an effort to get his father to focus on something other than the loss of his wife. When he was just a boy, his father had taught him how to channel the ache and ire of his emotions into physical labor, but somehow his father had lost sense of that ability after his wife passed away.

He closed the door behind him, and the silence of the old house pressed in on him. There was no need for him to call out to his father or to wander the house looking for him. He knew he'd find him in the same upholstered chair, an empty bottle beside him, a glass on the end table, and a single reading light casting an eerie yellow glow over his mother's sewing table.

The worn wood floors creaked beneath his heavy boots. Pete glanced into the dark living and dining rooms as he passed. They were, as always, neat and orderly with no hints of the nightmare that consumed his father after dark. He passed his parents' bedroom and went through the kitchen, picking up an empty bottle from the counter and tossing it in the trash without allowing himself to think about what it meant. Dwelling on his father's problem only made it harder to deal with.

His mother's sewing room looked just as it had two years earlier, when she'd died of an aneurysm while sewing a button on one of his father's shirts. Pete had tried to get his father to sell the house, but Neil was a stubborn man, and he insisted on remaining in the house, forming yet another layer of guilt for Pete to wear. He'd secretly been relieved that his father didn't want to sell the house. Every room held fond memories for him, too. Memories not just of a mother who'd doted on her children but had also scolded them with a stern look, followed up by a pat on the head and a hug.

Oh, Peter. You know I love you, but you can't do those things.
Those things covered everything he'd ever done, from racing
down the middle of the road on his bike to skipping school.
He smiled at the memories. His mother had tried hard to
raise them well, and she'd done a damn good job, only Pete
got all of his father's stubbornness and all of his mother's
softness, rendering him unprepared and, he worried, unable
to fix his father's troubles.

He crouched by his father's side. Neil's jaw was agape,
and his arms hung limply off the sides of the chair. Pete
loved him so much he ached, and it killed him to know that
his father's love for his mother was what led him down this
awful path. He lifted the black-and-white framed photo of
his parents' wedding day from his father's lap and ran his
fingers over their images. His mother had worn her hair
short later in life, but in the photo, at twenty-four, the age
his sister, Sky, was now, she'd worn her dark hair almost to
her waist. In the picture, her hair was pulled over one
shoulder, her wedding veil perched on the crown of her
head. Her head was tilted back, a smile gracing her full lips
and radiating in her big, round eyes. His father was looking
at her with love in his eyes that danced off the photograph
and tugged at Pete's heart. His father looked young and virile
in his dark suit, with his hair slicked back.

Pete set the picture on the end table and assessed his
father. Alcohol was stealing all signs of the man he'd been.
His father looked broken. Done.

"Pop. Come on, Pop." Pete nudged his arm.

Joey licked his father's fingers.

Neil grumbled and shrugged away from Joey.

Over the months, Pete had tried to pinpoint the most difficult thing about his father's drinking. The first few times he'd found him, he'd thought the hardest part was getting him into the bedroom and settling him in for the night. Other times he'd thought it was living the lie, knowing that the people who knew his father had no idea the hell he endured after dark. But recently, he'd come to believe that the worst part of his father's disease—and he had to remind himself often that his father did in fact have a disease—was his own inability to right his father's course.

That thought was what coated him in guilt. He wasn't sure if his thoughts were selfish or not. Now wasn't the time to ponder it as he hoisted his father's body from the chair, wrapped his arm over his shoulder, and secured his strong arm around his body, taking his full weight as he brought Neil through the kitchen, down the hall, and into the bedroom.

His father's head lolled back. "Good boy. Bea? Where's Bea?"

Pete laid his father on the bed, then removed his father's shoes and placed them by the closet.

"Bea?"

"She's not here, Pop." He moved his father toward the center of the bed and placed two body pillows against his father's sides. He'd purchased the pillows last year, when he finally realized that the reason his father was falling out of bed was that he was reaching for his mother. The pillows did the trick. They seemed to fool him into feeling like she was nearby. Neil hated blankets, but Pete always felt better if he had them just in case he got chilly. He pulled the blankets up to his father's waist and then lowered himself into the rocking chair in the corner of the room.

He leaned back and closed his eyes, listening to the steady rhythm of his father's breathing. This is what his life had become—a cycle of work, fearing his father's calls, and fearing the day the calls stopped and his father's breathing silenced forever.

Joey stretched on the hardwood floor by his feet and yawned. Pete reached down and ran his fingers over Joey's head. He'd never thought of himself as lonely until he'd taken Joey into his life. Caring for her made Pete realize how much time he spent alone. He enjoyed taking care of Joey. Who wouldn't enjoy unconditional love from an adorable puppy? Pete knew that, to some extent, Joey filled a gap in his life that his father had left behind. He and his father had been close before his mother died. His father had taught him how to restore boats, how to sail, and how to play football. He'd taught each of Pete's siblings different things. He catered to their likes and dislikes. Matty, two years younger than Pete, was into academics, and his father would bring home nonfiction books that kept Matt enthralled for days.

Hunter and Grayson, now twenty-eight and twenty-six, were into hunting, fishing, and of all things, steel and metalwork. His father had taken them to Plymouth to learn from a steelworker there. Sky loved anything music and arts related. He smiled at the memory of his father cursing as he built a small art studio in the backyard. The eight-by-ten structure that Sky was forever disappearing into, and that he and each of his brothers had snuck girls into throughout their teenage years, still stood in the backyard.

Pete had always been protective of his siblings, which was something his father was proud of. He'd learned from the best. Neil had always been their family's fierce protector. Not that there was much to shield them from in the small town of Brewster, Massachusetts, but as Pete grew older, he realized that his father had protected them from the silent troubles of life. Years when the store wasn't doing well and they barely had enough money for groceries and when his mother had surgery when they were young and he'd told them that she was going away to take a class for a few days. He hadn't ever wanted his children to worry about things they couldn't control, which was probably why Pete protected Sky from their father's drinking.

If only their father felt compelled to protect them now, from his own demise. If only that need could be strong enough to make him change.

If only.

His phone vibrated, pulling him from his troubled

thoughts. He withdrew it from his pocket and saw his brother Matt's name flash on the screen.

"Hey, Matty," he said quietly.

"Pete, how's it going? How's Pop?" Matt lived in New Jersey, and out of all of his brothers, Matt was the most reasonable and open to talking about their father.

"Funny you should ask. I'm here with him now." Pete went into the living room so as not to wake Neil. Joey walked sleepily beside him, then plopped onto the living room floor.

"Can you talk, or should I call back?" Matt knew the score with their father, as each of their siblings did, with the exception of Sky. They were all willing to help pay for rehab, and they'd gone to bat to try to convince their father to get help, to no avail. Pete knew they felt guilty that he was the only one who lived close enough to care for his father, and Matt called often, as if it might help. Only Grayson seemed to have a chip on his shoulder over his father's alcoholism, and at times, his frustrations shot like spears directly at Pete, but Pete could handle it. He even understood it. There were times he'd like to shake some sense into his father. If Pete were the type of person to lash out, he'd probably do so at one of his brothers, too, just as Grayson lashed out at him. Because in the Lacroux family, unconditional love was a given, even when it hurt.

"He's flat-out. I can talk." He paced the small living room. The walls held a trail of family pictures, depicting the fun they'd had over the years. The couch and rocking chair were the same ones that had been there when Pete was young. No frivolities here, either, other than the curtains on the two front windows, handmade by his mother a few years before she died. The house wasn't fancy, but it was home.

"How are you holding up?" Matt's voice was deep and empathetic. He was the most careful of Pete's siblings, always weighing risk to benefit of whatever he did. Pete pictured him sitting behind the desk in his study, wearing a pair of trousers and a dress shirt open at the collar. He had the same wet-sand-color hair as their father and deep-set eyes with lashes so long and thick they looked fake.

"Pretty good. Can't complain."

"Dude, I'm not Grayson. I'm not going to give you shit about not getting him into rehab. It sucks having to be there and pick up after Pop. You don't have to minimize it. The man needs help, and you're a saint for sticking around."

Pete exhaled loudly. "I'm anything but a saint, and Grayson should give me shit. Pop does need help."

"True, but cut yourself some slack. He's a stubborn old goat. One day he's going to wake up and realize what he's doing, and we all know that we owe you, Pete."

Matt spoke as if Pete were doing a miraculous thing by caring for their father. But Pete didn't feel like he was doing even half the job he should. He made a mental note to push his father once again the next time he saw him. He couldn't make progress if he didn't try.

"You don't owe me anything. If you were here, you'd do the same thing. What's going on with you, Matt?"

"Not much. Mom's birthday is next weekend, and I know how hard that is for Dad. Are you ready for that? Do you want me to fly into town for the weekend?"

"No, the less disruption the better. If last year is any indication, he'll drink himself into a stupor and sleep, pretty much like every night."

Matt sighed. "Well, if you change your mind, let me know. By the way, Sky was talking about coming out next summer to stay with Pop. You okay with that?"

Their younger sister was always making plans, but the summer to Sky could mean eight weeks or three days. Sky was eight years younger than Pete. When he'd left for college, she was just a kid, and after graduation, when he'd gotten his own place to live, Sky had been only twelve years old. It had been forever since they'd lived in the same house, but Pete had kept a close eye on her throughout the years. He'd protected Sky from his father's drinking for two years, and if he had his way, he'd protect her from it until it was no longer an issue—if that time ever came.

"She's all over the map. I'll just be damn sure to get Pop straightened out before then. It's a year away, so who knows how many times she'll change her mind between now and then."

Matt laughed. "Yeah, she said she's thinking of making a go of things in Provincetown. God only knows what that means. Tattoo artist, art, music, animals. P-town has everything she loves." Matt sighed. "God, it would be nice to be twenty-four again."

"No shit. I'd love to see her, so whatever she decides is fine, but she'll stay with me, not Pop. She'll go ape shit over Joey."

"Yeah, you might want to rethink letting her come out. She might never leave. How's the boat coming along?"

Talking with Matt was a nice distraction from both his father and Jenna. "It's coming along. I don't have much time to work on it, though."

"I know. Sorry Pop falls on your shoulders, Pete. We can try another intervention to get him into rehab. I don't know why you fight that so hard."

"Sometimes I don't, either." But he did—the fallout after their last intervention had nearly irreparably severed their relationships with their father. Pete couldn't begin to fathom the shape his father would be in if he were left to his own devices without someone to get him into a safe place at night. Pete's biggest worry was that his father might just continue drinking until he killed himself.

He pushed the thoughts away and finished explaining. "When he's sober, he fights the idea of rehab tooth and nail, and when he's not, there's no talking. Another intervention will make him feel like it's all of us against him again."

"*With* him, Pete. *With him.*"

"Yeah, I get it. If you guys want to do that, be my guest,

but don't leave me with the mess. Someone has to commit to staying in town so when he flips out and doesn't end up in rehab, one of you can be here to deal with it. Short of that, I'm going to keep talking to him when it feels right to do it and hope he comes around."

"I hear ya. I've got to run, but, Pete, remember, you've got to have a life, too, and taking care of Pop is no life."

Pete rubbed his temples. "I've got him covered, Matty. Thanks. Good to talk to you."

For a long time after his call with Matt, Pete sat in the living room thinking about his father and his siblings, and finally, himself. It didn't take him long to realize the answer to his earlier question about staking claim to Jenna. Pete would never turn his back on his father, and Jenna deserved a better life than being tied to an alcoholic's son. He had no choice but to remain in the friend zone.

He wasn't sure that was even an option anymore.

CHAPTER EIGHT

BY SATURDAY MORNING Jenna was fit to be tied. She hadn't seen Pete since he'd stormed out of the library, and she'd spent Thursday and Friday vacillating between calling him to explain and feeling like what she did was none of his business. She'd pouted and bitched and tried burying her feelings in sweets, but nothing calmed her nerves. Even talking it out with Bella, Amy, and Leanna hadn't helped her figure out what she should do, or if she should do anything at all. Her phone vibrated and Charlie's name appeared on the screen.

"*Ugh.*" Something was seriously wrong with her. Charlie was strong and sexy, interesting, and, probably by any other woman's standards, a really good kisser. Most women would swoon over his looks and fall in love with his attentive nature—any woman except Jenna, that is. He'd called her several times while he was out of town, and Jenna had tried to remain focused on those calls, but her mind had drifted to Pete. She knew that was a horrible sign, and she should have uninvited him on the boat trip, but she wasn't good at breaking up, and doing it over the phone seemed rude.

She answered his call, hoping he might cancel their plans.

"Hi, Charlie."

"Hey. I just wanted to let you know that I might be five minutes late to the marina, but I'll be there. Don't worry."

Did he have to be so damn considerate? "Okay, no problem. If you can't make it, just let me know so I can tell Dane."

"I wouldn't let you down like that. I'll be there."

Of course you will.

After their call, she plopped onto the couch and closed her eyes. *Why can't I just feel something for him? Then this would be easier.*

Damn Bella for being right. Pete was the man she loved, and probably the only man she ever would.

"Knock-knock," Bella said as she walked through the door wearing a blue sundress over her bathing suit. She narrowed her eyes and pointed at Jenna. "Let's see…You've got on your least-favorite bikini, your favorite cutoffs, and your favorite earrings. But your face tells me that the yellow bikini was worn for a reason and the other stuff was an afterthought. Does that mean you didn't break up with Charlie?"

Jenna met her gaze but didn't say a word. She knew she didn't have to.

"Jenna! You promised you were going to do it last night." Bella sat beside her on the couch. "What are you thinking?"

"I was thinking that it would suck to be broken up with over the phone."

"The man thinks you want to scale him like a mountain," Bella reminded her.

"Climb him like scaffolding," Jenna corrected her.

"Whatever. What happens after the boat trip when he's ready to do you and you're ready to dump him?" Bella exhaled loudly. "And what happens when you're stuck on the boat with both Pete and Charlie?"

Jenna shot upright. "What?"

"Leanna told me this morning that Pete's going. I didn't remember him saying he was that night at the Beachcomber, but apparently, he and Dane swapped numbers to talk about boats and…" She shrugged.

"Bella, this is terrible. I can't go. How can I even face Pete? It's *him* I want to climb like scaffolding, and he stomped away when he saw me sucking face with Charlie." Jenna paced. "This is bad. Very, very bad."

"You could call Charlie and cancel. Tell him you're sick or something."

"I can't do that. He just called and confirmed. Jesus, Bella. I'm not cut out for this. I shouldn't have approached Charlie in the first place. I should have come down here this summer and just ogled Pete for a few weeks, too chickenshit to let him know how I really feel, and let it go at that."

"You guys ready?" Amy peeked through the screen.

"No," Jenna snapped.

"She didn't break up with Charlie," Bella said.

"Cripes! Jenna." Amy joined them inside the cottage. "You know Pete's coming, right?"

"How come you both knew about him coming and I didn't know?" Jenna asked.

"Leanna told me just now, but I don't know how Bella knew." Amy shrugged. "It doesn't matter. How are we going to deal with this?"

"I'm not going." Jenna plopped back onto the couch.

"You're going," Amy and Bella said in unison.

"Maybe this is all a coincidence," Bella said with a softer tone. "Maybe Pete stormed out of the library because he forgot something."

"Oh, that makes me feel better. So he's not interested. I just imagined the whole, erotic, sensual whisper in my ear that made me practically orgasm right on the spot. That must be it. I'm delirious." Jenna covered her face with her hands and groaned.

"Okay, okay. This is fixable. First, change out of the yellow," Bella directed. "If Pete's on the boat, you want him to want you, and everyone knows the yellow one is not your fave suit. Even Pete. So wear something that says, *I'm psyched to be here!*"

"You're insane," Jenna snapped.

"You know I'm right. What do you think every time Amy wears her hair in one of those awful headbands pulled back like a twelve-year-old?" Bella arched a brow.

"Hey…" Amy wrinkled her brow.

"A very sexy, cute, beautiful twelve-year-old," Jenna said to Amy. "Who doesn't want to do whatever we're doing that day."

Amy rolled her eyes.

"Exactly. Now go change." Bella pushed her to her feet.

"What about poor Charlie?" Amy asked.

"That's the part I'm not sure about. If Jenna won't break up with him beforehand, then I don't think there's any way around this. She'll have to just pretend everything is normal." Bella paced.

"Oh, Pete will love that!" Jenna called from the bedroom.

"She's right. Holding a guy's hand isn't exactly a turn-on to another guy. Besides, it's mean to use Charlie like that." Amy crossed her arms and tapped her cheek with her index finger. "I've got it. You should tell Pete. Call him and say something like, *Hey, just wanted you to know that Charlie's definitely coming today, but I wish he wasn't.*"

"Then Pete won't show up. She just needs to be herself and let whatever happens, happen. We'll be there to save her from anything too traumatic." Bella gasped as Jenna came out of the bedroom in her jade bikini. "Holy shit. *I'd* do you in that bathing suit."

Jenna pulled her shoulders back, put her hands on her hips, and turned sideways. "Good, right?"

"Barbie-doll good," Amy said. "You make me look like an ironing board."

"I think you have a great figure, Amy. These babies are not all that fun." Jenna lifted her boobs. "There's always a question in the back of my mind if a guy likes me for me or for my tatas."

Bella rolled her eyes. "Both, of course. They *are* men. Come on. We have to leave or we'll all miss the boat."

DANE BRADEN'S FISHING boat moved swiftly through the ocean. They'd been on the water for more than an hour, and Pete regretted being there for most of that time. The first few minutes were cool, when Dane explained to Evan that the chair secured to the deck of the boat was called a fighting chair, used when reeling in a big fish or a shark. He explained how he strapped himself into it when they had a shark on the line, giving them better control and more power. Constructed of wood and metal, with a foot plate that allowed for more stability, the chair rotated with the movement of the fish. Since they weren't going to fish for sharks today, Evan was perched in the chair, soaking up the sun in a pair of dark sunglasses and listening to his iPod.

Pete shifted his eyes around the boat. Lacy, Leanna, Bella, Amy, and Jenna were sunning themselves on the front deck of the boat in their bikinis. Jenna's hair whipped around her face. She looked beautiful with the sun beaming down on her flawless skin. Their laughter carried in the wind, and Pete got lost in the sound of Jenna's joy. He debated joining them just to be near her, but thoughts of last night with his father held him back. When Charlie joined them and sat down beside Jenna, Pete turned his attention to Kurt, Caden, and Dane, hanging out by the helm. He glanced back at Jenna a minute later, trying to convince himself that he was lucky for their friendship and he should leave it at that. She had Charlie, and he had his father to contend with.

Aw hell. He still wanted much, much more.

"Who's ready to chum the water?" Dane called to the women and Evan.

"I'll do it!" Evan climbed down from the chair.

"Lace?" Dane waved her over. He was Pete's height, with a body sculpted by years of deep-sea diving. Lacy smiled as she came to his side and caressed his shoulder. Dane's powerful physique dwarfed her feminine frame.

The others joined them, and when Charlie draped an arm over Jenna's shoulder, Pete felt a spear of jealousy. Ever since his conversation with Matt, he'd been dwelling on what he'd said. *You've got to have a life, too, and taking care of Pop is no life.* He was so damn torn over the whole situation. He wanted Jenna—in every way, not just as a friend, and even though the thought brought enough guilt to drown him, he was pissed over his father's drinking and how it was standing in his way.

Dane whispered something in Lacy's ear, and she reached for his hand.

"I'm okay," she said quietly before turning to the others and explaining. "I get a little quivery around sharks, but I can always go belowdecks if I get nervous."

Dane squeezed her hand.

Bella went to Caden's side. "I was asking Caden this morning what I should do if I get nervous. Now I know."

"Evan, come on over and let me go over a few things with you. First and foremost, when you see a shark, never try to touch it, lean too far over, or do anything risky, got it? They're not dogs. You can't hand-feed them." Dane spoke with a serious tone.

"Yes, of course. I don't want to go near them. I just want to see one," Evan explained. "I promise, I won't do anything stupid."

Dane pointed into the barrel of chum while he explained to Evan how to chum the water. Pete's attention was drawn to Jenna. She was listening intently, with her brows pushed tighter, her arms crossed over her narrow rib cage. Pete wanted to stand behind her and feel her back against him, warm from the sun. He wanted to whisper in her ear— something, anything, that would make her smile or blush. He wanted to be closer to her.

He wanted to love her. Publicly. Not just in his mind and in his heart. Every day brought the depth of his love to the surface, and he was doing all he could to keep from thrusting it upon her, and because of his father, he knew he shouldn't.

An hour later, the others were gathered around the edge of the boat, watching the chum slick for sharks and listening to Dane tell stories about his shark-tagging adventures. Pete couldn't take it anymore. He couldn't spend one more second watching Jenna and Charlie. He went belowdecks to get a cold drink. He grabbed a soda from the fridge, flipped the tab, and took a long, icy swig.

"Would you mind handing me one?" Jenna's voice was different. Stronger.

Pete turned, and Jenna closed the distance between them, her eyes locked on him. Heat rolled off of her and ignited with each step. She didn't dart her eyes away. Her voice was confident and seductive, so different from the Jenna he usually encountered. He liked her. A lot.

"Actually," she said, moving in front of him. "I can get it."

She bent to retrieve the drink, giving Pete a clear view of her incredible ass. *She's better off without me.* The thought came quickly but didn't take hold as she opened the soda and took a sip, then dragged her tongue slowly across her lips. He set his soda on the counter, wanting to do so much more than lick her sensuous lips. He knew he shouldn't, but he took a step closer, all of his senses on high alert. His heart thundered in his chest, and an instant rise trapped against the zipper of his jeans. She smelled of suntan lotion, and desire wrapped around them like powerful arms, drawing him nearer as she gazed up at him. He took the soda from her hands, his eyes never leaving hers as he set it aside.

"Shouldn't you be with your boyfriend?" He shouldn't ask. He shouldn't care. But every fiber of his being wanted to kiss her.

"He's not my boyfriend." She narrowed her eyes.

Pete wasn't a game player, and if this was a game to her, he had to know. He'd had enough summer flings; he didn't need to ruin their friendship for one. The lust in her eyes told him this was no game to Jenna.

Voices rang out from the deck and he shot a glance at the stairs, unwilling to move away. He stepped closer, brushing her thighs with his.

"Do you play tonsil hockey with all the guys who aren't your boyfriend? If so, I must have missed the invitation." He rested his palm on the wall behind her and leaned in close, testing the waters, his vow to remain in the friend zone forgotten.

"N-no." She blinked several times. Her chest rose and fell as her breathing hastened. Her eyebrows drew together; then she set her shoulders back, just a fraction of an inch, but Pete noticed. Hell, he noticed everything in those quick seconds—the scent of her breath, the way her thighs tensed against his, the shape of her eyes.

She sucked in air. "You don't need an invitation."

Desire surged forward, chasing worry, friendship, and hesitation until they bound together and scrambled away, and he lowered his face to hers, their lips a second apart. His hand slid down the wall, and he clutched the back of her neck. His other hand found her lower back and pressed her body to his. They were both breathing hard. Jenna's body trembled against him, and *holy fuck* did she feel good. He slid his lips to the corner of hers, grazing the edge of her mouth and then further still. His cheek rubbed against her silken skin, and she sucked in air again. He was savoring the moment, because once their lips met, there was no turning back. He pressed kisses along her jaw, and her head lolled back, her lips slightly parted, her eyes closed. She grabbed the waistband of his jeans, holding him against her as he trailed openmouthed kisses down her neck. Her skin was hot from the sun, salty, and so damn sweet, he didn't want to stop there. He could only imagine how blessed sweet the rest of her tasted. He ran his hand up her ribs, brushing the swell of her breast with his thumb.

"Jesus…" she said in one long breath.

He tightened his hold and nipped at her earlobe. "When you're with me…" He kissed the back of her neck. "How about if mine is the only name coming off your lips?" Her breathing quickened again; her taut nipples pressed against his chest. He pressed both hands to her cheeks, hard, his thumbs against her jaw—a last chance for her to beg off. He wanted to be gentle, but gentle left the boat the minute she said he didn't need an invitation. Indecent thoughts he'd tried to stop himself from pairing with Jenna raced through his mind. If he was going to be with Jenna, really be with her, he needed to know she could handle—and wanted— him *before* he tasted that sweet mouth of hers.

But when he looked into her beautiful eyes and felt her eager body, it struck him like a ton of bricks.

She was there with Charlie. She wasn't his to claim. No matter how much she felt like she was, no matter how hard he was or that he was practically salivating at the thought of kissing her, she wasn't his to enjoy. Pete did not want to share Jenna.

He forced himself to bring his mouth to her ear again.

"When you're done with your boy, Jenna, and you want me. *Just me.* You let me know." His voice sounded rough and gravelly, laden with frustration.

Releasing her was the hardest thing he'd ever done, until he took a step back and unfurled her fingers from his jeans, breaking their connection altogether. Jenna let out a loud breath, panting, her eyes slowly refocusing on him.

"Wha—? Why?"

It was a fair question, and the anger in her beautiful eyes was fair, too. He wanted to take her in his arms and devour her, but he wouldn't. Once their lips touched, she was his. And he was hers. All Pete had to offer her was the truth.

"I don't share well. Not you, Jenna. I can't share you."

He felt her hot stare follow him as he stepped away; then

her hand clutched the back of his jeans and she yanked him back. Pete was a formidable presence against her petite frame. He turned with her efforts and Jenna threw her arms up, coming up short of his neck, which almost made him laugh because she was so fucking cute, all hot, bothered, and ready to devour him. But laughter wasn't on his mind as he gripped her waist and lifted her easily so she could do what she pleased. He was powerless to resist the love he felt for her. Jenna's arms circled his neck as he backed her against the wall and sealed his lips over hers in a hard, deep crash of a kiss. She met stroke after insistent stroke of his hunger. She buried her hands in his hair, her nails digging into his scalp as they deepened the kiss. Her legs wrapped around his waist, holding her up, freeing his hands to grope and—good Lord, her body was supple, her breasts, sheer perfection. She could damn well handle him, and now he knew she wanted him, too. Just him.

With one powerful arm around her waist, the other feeling her up—yes, feeling her up, because there was no other way to describe the way he took what he'd been wanting, what he'd tried to ignore for too long—he turned with her in his arms and lowered them both to the padded bench behind them. Holy hell, it was all he could do not to take her right there. She rocked her hips against his groin, and he grabbed a handful of her sweet ass, pressing her harder against him, until he could barely think.

"I'll see where she went." Bella's voice sailed around

them as they made out like horny teenagers.

Footsteps descended the stairs, and Pete knew he should pull away, but Jenna was intoxicating, grabbing his hair, kissing him like he was the very oxygen she needed to survive. He wanted to stay right there, kissing her, loving her.

"What?" Bella's voice again, coming closer.

Fuuuck.

He tore himself from Jenna, leaving her gasping for air, sprawled across the bench. He lifted her to a sitting position and then plopped down beside her, hoping his erection would somehow disappear and knowing there wasn't a chance in hell it would.

Bella was looking behind her, up toward the deck. She turned, her eyes darted between them, and worry shifted across her features. "Oh. Shit."

There was no way for them to hide the urgency of their need. He was sure it dripped from their pores. Jenna's hair was a tangled mess, her cheeks were flushed, and if that wasn't enough to give them away, between his raging erection and her erect nipples...*Aw hell.* Pete ran his hand through his hair and turned his attention to Jenna. He wasn't about to try and explain to Bella. She knew exactly what was going on, but he didn't want Jenna to be embarrassed, and the last thing she needed was for Charlie to find out. *Charlie.* Pete bit back his distaste that Jenna had come with Charlie and that now he'd have to relinquish her to him again. He ran his fingers through her hair until she looked more kempt, then cupped her cheeks and stared deeply into her eyes.

"Jenna," he whispered, and rested his forehead against hers.

"Holy moly." Bella took a step toward the stairs, then turned back.

Pete waited for Jenna to say something, and when she didn't, he kissed her cheek and took her hand in his. "Go out with me tomorrow?"

She nodded, a slight smile on her lips, and in her eyes was pure, unadulterated desire that snuck inside him and softened his rough edges. Only then did he realize what he'd been too thick to see for all these years. Jenna didn't need words. She didn't need to be aggressive like the women he was used to, telling him that she wanted him, staking claim to him in a way that left no doubt. There was more want in her eyes, more real emotion, than any woman had ever verbalized. How could he have been so blind for so long? Jenna was the perfect combination of confidence and sweetness, and dear Lord, tomorrow could not come soon enough.

JENNA FELT LIKE she'd sprouted wings and jumped from the top of a tower. She was soaring, weightless, among the clouds. Pete placed her hand on her thigh and covered it with his own, and then he smiled. Oh, how she loved his smile. His lips. The man could kiss—and hold, and touch, and, *Oh God. I like you. I like you so damn much.*

"Are you okay?" His voice was tender and caring.

She nodded, or at least she thought she did.

"I don't want you to have trouble with Charlie, so I'm going to go up to the deck, but, Jenna, I need you to know that leaving you is the last thing I want to do."

"Maybe so, but go. Please go," Bella urged as she shot another look up the stairs. "Jesus, you two look like…Forget it. You know what you look like."

Pete's eyes never left Jenna. She felt protected and cherished in a way no man had ever made her feel with nothing more than a kiss, a touch, and a thoughtful tone.

"Okay?"

She forced herself to nod. When he rose to his feet, he took her next breath with him and she longed for him to return.

Pete stopped beside Bella. "You know I don't want to leave her."

Bella pushed him toward the stairs, her eyes frenzied. "Yes. I know. Now get the hell up there before she gets in trouble."

He turned back, his eyes locking on Jenna again. Her breath caught in her throat. "I didn't want to do this when you were here with another guy. I'm sorry, Jenna. It wasn't my intent to make you uncomfortable."

"Oh dear Lord." Bella rolled her eyes. "She knows. It was passion. You guys couldn't help it. Whatever." She gave him a hard shove toward the stairs, and his lips curved into a smile.

"It was so much more." He shifted his gaze to Bella. "But you can minimize it if it makes you feel better."

He disappeared up the stairs, and Jenna let out a loud breath. Bella rushed to her side and grabbed her hand.

"Oh my God. What happened?" She snapped her fingers in front of Jenna's face. "Hello? Jenna?" Each word was a harsh whisper, a reminder that Jenna had become unhinged and she needed to fix herself. Now.

Jenna breathed deeply. She trapped her lower lip in her teeth and clenched her eyes shut, wanting to remember every second of being in Pete's arms: the brush of his stubble against her cheeks, the way he held her tightly, like she was his, the way he kissed—goodness, the way he kissed. She felt as though she might burst. When she opened her eyes, she met Bella's concerned gaze.

"You know what you said a first kiss should be?" Jenna asked.

"Yes."

"This was a million times better."

CHAPTER NINE

THE TRAIL LEADING to Duck Harbor Beach was a long one that snaked over the dunes with no trees to shade and cool the sand. The first time Jenna had come to Duck Harbor with Pete, they'd come in the afternoon with their friends from Seaside. By noon the path was scorching hot, and by three o'clock, even walking in flip-flops was painful, because sand seeped over the edges, sizzling from roasting for hours in the hot sun. Jenna had complained on the way over the steamy dunes, and Pete had knelt before her and given her a piggyback ride to the beach while the others made fun of them. They'd come to Duck Harbor with bottles of wine and a basket of snacks, to watch the sunset. It was years ago, but Jenna recalled it as if it were yesterday. The sun had left layers of purple and orange in its wake, and she and Pete had sat beside each other. When she shivered with the cool night air, he'd wrapped his zip-up sweatshirt around her shoulders with the easiest smile.

She sighed, thinking of how she'd felt warmed by his jacket, his scent soaking into her senses. She'd relived their kiss so many times since yesterday that she'd memorized every breath. He was so different from the man she thought he'd be that he'd taken her by surprise. Heck, she'd taken herself by surprise when she'd pulled him back for a kiss, but she wasn't taking any more chances. She wanted him to know how she felt about him.

I think he got the hint.

Jenna set down her romance novel and flipped onto her back with a sigh. She'd talked to her mother for an hour this morning, and she made a point of omitting any mention of Pete. Her mother went on and on about the new outfits she'd bought, outfits that sounded too young for Jenna, much less her mother. Jenna had tried to be patient with her, and when her mother brought up coming down to the Cape again, Jenna agreed to the idea, but put off choosing a date until she knew where she and Pete were headed. She'd come to Duck Harbor to try to ease her nerves about their impending date, but it wasn't working. She was sure she'd somehow swallowed a nest of bees.

She sighed again.

Amy set her book down and turned onto her back. "You're doing it again."

"Hm?" She and Amy had been lying in the sun since nine o'clock that morning. Vera had joined them and was sitting contentedly beneath a large umbrella, wearing a straw sunhat and a sheer cover-up over her bathing suit, a thick book in her hands. Like Jenna and Amy, Vera was an avid reader, which made them perfect companions for a lazy beach day.

"You have that *just been done* look," Amy whispered. "I'm a little jealous."

"I know about that look," Vera said with a twinkle in her eyes. She patted her hair and smiled.

"Vera!" Amy laughed.

"I do *not* have that look. My eyes are closed." Jenna scrunched her nose, then wiggled her lips, but she didn't feel as though her face had been portraying anything telling.

"Jenna dear," Vera began. "Women don't need to see other women's eyes to know when we're thinking about men. Our skin resonates desire. Why, you could no better hide that than the bay could refrain from washing away at low tide."

"I'm that transparent? Wow. Vera, I wish I would have known that yesterday morning. That's probably why when I finally got the guts to break up with Charlie, he wasn't surprised."

"Oh yes. I'm sure that's why." Vera sighed. "Men know these things, too, but some take longer to recognize it than others."

"You can say that again," Amy agreed. "I just can't believe I missed the whole thing with you and Pete. I didn't even realize you were gone. Everyone was taking pictures of the shark, and Lacy and I were so focused on not being nervous that we were talking about high school just to keep our minds busy. It wasn't until Charlie called your name and

Bella went to find you that I realized you were gone. And, of course, a minute later I noticed Pete was gone, but by then I knew I had to keep Charlie out of there, so…that was fun."

Jenna turned to face her. Amy's blond hair was gathered over her left shoulder. She was shading her eyes and watching a man walk down the beach. Amy had a subtle tan, and there wasn't an inch of extra meat on her, but she wasn't like some pin-thin women who looked like broomsticks with bras. Amy's slim hips and small breasts had curves, even if lean, and her caring personality made her even more attractive. Jenna had no idea how Tony Black didn't want to wrap her up, take her home, and keep her all to himself. She was as good and honest as they came. Jenna knew that Amy playing middleman with Charlie must have been very uncomfortable for her, especially since Amy wasn't a good liar. She could omit information, but asked a direct question, she was more likely to spit out the truth and *then* slap her hand over her mouth, wide-eyed and apologetic.

Jenna reached for her hand.

"I'm so glad we're friends, Ames. Thank you for having my back."

"You'd do the same for me."

"Yeah. I would. And I'm so sorry that Tony isn't here this summer."

Amy smiled, but it didn't reach her eyes. "It's okay. He called me this morning to say he wished he were here with us."

Us. Jenna wished Tony would have said *here with you* to Amy. Amy needed a distraction, and Jenna knew just the thing. She pushed to her feet and bounced on her toes. "Rock hunting time!"

"You're such a goofball. Fine, but I'm not carrying heavy rocks back to the car, so you can forget that idea right now." Amy pushed to her feet and slipped on a bright red, floppy sun hat.

"Vera, would you like to join us?" Jenna asked.

"Yes, I think I would enjoy a short walk." Amy reached for her hand, and Jenna attached herself to Vera's other arm.

Jenna loved Vera like a grandmother, and each year she was surprised to see how well Vera was holding up, especially after last year's scare. They walked along the shore with their feet in the cold water. The bay beaches were rockier than the ocean side. The perfect rock-spotting venue for a rock collector like Jenna.

"Remember, we're looking for—"

"Pitch-black rocks. I remember. Why pitch-black?" Amy bent to retrieve a rock and held it in her palm for Jenna to inspect.

"That's dark gray, but close." Jenna splashed water with her toes. "I thought this was going to be the summer I gave up on Pete," Jenna explained. "I never thought we'd cross from friendship to anything more, no matter how much I wished for it. And with all the stuff going on with my mom, black seemed a fitting way to mark the summer."

"One day you girls will realize that you have very little control over matters of the heart." Vera nudged Jenna's arm and pointed to a dark rock.

Jenna picked up the perfect black rock, thinking about what Vera said. "How can that be, Vera? People scheme all the time to connect with the person they're attracted to." Jenna held up the rock. "This is perfect. Thank you." She tucked it into her bikini top, below her breast, as she'd done so many times before. With no pockets in bathing suits, Jenna had to be creative. She resituated her bikini top, then took Vera's arm again.

"Oh yes. Women and men alike. They all scheme and plot, but rarely do those plots end the way they think they will. In my experience, forever loves, the ones that are meant to last through thick and thin, happen all on their own." Vera smiled down at Jenna.

"See, Jenna?" Amy raised her brows. "I don't have to look for a man. The right one will find me."

"I guess that could be true, but, Vera, if that's the way love works, then why is it taking Pete so long to realize I'm his…?"

"A little assumptive, are we? Just a day ago you couldn't even talk to him." Amy arched a brow.

"Okay, so maybe I'm not his…"

"His…" Vera repeated. "You'll search your whole life to figure out what word encompasses all that your true love represents. I still can't think of one word to describe my late husband. Comforting, yes. Loving, warm, angry sometimes." She sighed. "Passionate. Frustrating. Safe. Warren was everything to me, and even that seems too simple of a statement. You're on the cusp of your best years, girls, and every day you'll grow a little wiser."

"My twenties were pretty darn good," Jenna said as she retrieved another rock, inspected it, and tossed it into the water.

They stopped and waded up to their ankles in the water.

Vera patted Jenna's hand. "You'll find something wonderful about every decade, but when you're in your twenties, you're just learning about yourself, your body, your desires, your pet peeves. Some couples can adapt to the changes that happen while you're becoming women and men are coming into their own. But most couples these days don't have the patience to love and grow together. They're only interested in instant gratification, and when things fall short, they shrug and move on to the next person. My generation wasn't better at too many things, but we seemed less self-involved. Less interested in proving we were valuable in a relationship. Things were slower. Families were units that did everything together. Oh, girls, we had such fun." Vera reached for their hands. "We ate meals together without distractions. We could go hours without background noise, and we only knew what our friends were doing when they called or sent handwritten letters. Or, of course, when we loaded up the car and drove to see them."

"But things change, Vera. People are busier. Everything's more expensive, so we need to work harder. And there's Facebook to keep in touch." Amy looked at Jenna for validation.

"True," Jenna agreed.

Vera's eyes warmed even more, then filled with empathy. "It takes very little to make a happy life, girls. That's the piece that everyone seems to forget. All those things people think they need—bigger houses, better cars, titles behind their names, gold-engraved invitations—they can never replace the warmth of trust and love, or the feeling of hugging a good friend, and I don't mean a virtual, computerized hug."

Vera blew out a breath and began walking down the beach again, still holding their hands. "The right relationship will leave you wanting for nothing. It will fill the spaces that others plug up with material things. And for those people, it's when those material things are no longer enough that people turn outward, when really, they should turn their attention to their relationship and remember why they fell in love in the first place."

"Vera, you make love sound so easy," Amy said.

Vera laughed as they turned back the way they'd come. "Relationships are the most difficult thing you'll ever do in your life. Childbirth? A breeze compared to living with a man. But again, the right partner will help you blossom. The wrong one will watch you wilt."

Jenna thought about her summers on the Cape and how different they were from the other nine months out of the year, when she was strapped to her cell phone and calendar, and every minute was spent darting from one commitment to the next. There was no comparison to working versus being on vacation, but she let her mind wander, and she imagined what her life might be like if she put away her cell phone and turned off her computer in the evenings the other nine and a half months out of the year. She could read a million more books. She might even have time to paint for fun, rather than only working on projects for her art students. She wondered what Pete did in the evenings. Did he chat online? Hang out at bars during the winter? Was he a reader? She imagined him working on his boat throughout the year, maybe spending time with his dad, having dinners once a week, like she and her mother did, and the thought made her smile. She wanted to find out, and she wanted to do all those things with him.

They gathered their beach supplies and headed back to the car. Vera was so well versed in Cape beaches, having vacationed there her whole life, that she wore socks and solid walking shoes to avoid the hot sand on the path back to the car. She looked hilarious, but Jenna didn't care. Her socks and shoes were simply part of who she was, like Jenna's OCD tendencies and Amy's sweet nature.

As she drove back toward Seaside, Jenna's stomach began doing flips again. She was beyond nervous about her date with Pete that evening. If their kiss was any indication, she wasn't sure she'd make it two minutes alone with him without climbing across the console of his truck and kissing that glorious mouth of his. She bit her lower lip as heat rushed to her cheeks. She shot a look at Vera, sitting in the passenger seat, watching her, with a smile on her thin lips.

Vera smiled. "It'll be fine, Jenna. Remember, this is bigger than you. Just let yourself go and follow your heart."

That's what she was afraid of. Her heart had been soaking in thoughts of Pete for so many years that she thought she might drown.

CHAPTER TEN

PETE DIDN'T USUALLY think a lot about first dates, because he rarely let them lead to much else, but there was no denying that he was nervous about his date with Jenna. He was full of *should I's*: *Should I kiss her right away? Should I bring her flowers? Should I hold her in my arms when I want to?* Fuck it. He was definitely going to kiss her. He was *not* going to bring her something as frivolous as flowers, and he was going to hold her every chance he got. He wondered if Jenna was as nervous as he was. He imagined her suffering over what she'd wear, pulling out nearly every outfit in her organized closet, and he laughed under his breath.

Normally, Pete would take a woman on a first date to a restaurant. A little conversation, a drink or two to ease the nerves, and he'd figure out the rest from there. But after their kiss—that amazing, rock-his-world-off-kilter kiss—he couldn't imagine sitting still in a restaurant, and taking her to his place for dinner was completely out of the question. He'd want to carry her to the bedroom the second they went inside.

His thoughts returned to their kiss. He'd felt guilty kissing Jenna when she'd gone on the boat with another guy, but when she tugged him back after he tried to do the right thing, he was powerless to stop the pull between them. When she looked at him with her big blue eyes full of want, need, and the slightest hint of disbelief, she caused a crack right down the center of his good intentions, and she stepped inside and stuck like glue.

Pete grabbed his keys from the counter and opened the door. Joey wagged her tail beside him. Joey loved going for rides in the truck, and she went nearly everywhere with Pete, but he couldn't very well show up on their first date with Joey in tow. Joey's tongue hung from her mouth as she sat patiently waiting to go on their next adventure. Pete crouched and loved her up, scratching her head behind her ears.

"Sorry, girl, but tonight you have to wait here."

Joey barked, tugging at Pete's heart. He couldn't believe he felt guilty leaving a dog behind on a date.

"I'll see you later, girl. Be good, and maybe I'll bring you on the next date." And he'd make damn sure there was a next date.

When Pete parked in Jenna's driveway, he wasn't surprised to see Bella and Amy scurrying out of her cottage like teenagers. He waved from his truck. He'd never dated a woman who didn't try to impress him and act a certain way. Jenna and her friends had never pretended to be anything but their zany selves, and until now he hadn't given that too much thought. He stepped from the truck and realized that it was one of the things he really liked about them all—and loved about Jenna.

He surveyed Jenna's deck on his way to her door. He'd been on her deck hundreds of times over the years, but tonight he saw it all differently. The rocks that lined the railing had always been simply rocks. Now it struck him that these were rocks *Jenna* had chosen. Rocks that she'd seen something special in and refused to leave behind. He'd seen the picture of the ocean nailed to the balusters on the far side of her deck so many times he'd forgotten it was there. Now he saw the beauty of it and imagined Jenna taking great care as she chose the driftwood as her canvas and spent afternoons painting the peaceful scene. His eyes swept across the deck to the basket of neatly organized flip-flops. Everyone at Seaside knew of Jenna's OCD tendencies, and as it had with the rocks, tonight his mind processed the information differently. He pictured her organizing the flip-flops with her brows drawn together, focusing on each color, lining them up, setting them neatly in the basket, then bouncing to her feet with the same wide smile he saw on her face now, as he approached the screen door and found her standing inside, watching him, with her palms pressed against the screen.

She sizzled in a white halter dress with flecks of blue and green that accentuated her small waist and revealed the swell of her breasts. She was so damn beautiful that Pete was momentarily struck mute. His gaze didn't remain on her enticing figure. It traveled north, drawn to the anticipation in her eyes. It felt natural to press his palms to hers and hold her gaze. She dropped her eyes to their hands, and her cheeks pinked up in a way he'd come to expect—and love.

JENNA HAD ANTICIPATED this moment for so long that she hadn't been able to sit still as she waited for Pete to reach the door. He looked soulful as he assessed her deck with serious eyes. She wondered what he thought of her crazy rock collection, and she suddenly realized that he knew all of her quirks. He'd hung the shelves in her closets and teased her about the way she color-coded her clothing and organized her shoes by heel height and color. *And you still asked me out.* He must be a glutton for punishment.

His hands were twice the size of hers. His palms were warm, pressed against hers through the screen. She couldn't stop herself from raising her eyes to his chest and staring at the space between the open buttons of his white button-down shirt. She'd seen his chest a million times, but somehow seeing just that patch of skin made her go all tingly inside. He was smokin' hot in a pair of snug-fitting jeans, faded at the thighs, with his untucked shirt and rolled sleeves. Casually sexy, like he'd strolled out of a Hugo Boss commercial.

"Hey there." Gone was the demanding need that his

voice held on the boat. His tone was soft once again, warm and inviting—and she was ready to walk right in.

"Hi."

"You look amazing." He held her gaze.

Jenna had worried over her outfit for almost two hours, trying on nearly everything she owned. Amy and Bella had made the final decision. *Sexy, flirty, fun,* was how they described her above-the-knee dress that showed too much cleavage. Even so, Pete didn't stare at her boobs, and that made her feel more comfortable. The way he was looking at her, like he wanted to climb through the screen and…hold her hand, made her feel even more confident. She worried that he'd be all about sex after their earth-shattering kiss and his whispered promises of erotic, sensual sex and begging for more. God knew she couldn't stop wondering what it would be like to be beneath him without the barrier of their clothing, but if she'd seen that look in his eyes, she would have worried that he wasn't into her, but rather into sex with her. She wanted both.

"Thank you," she finally managed.

"Can we open the door?" He arched a brow.

"Oh my gosh. I'm sorry." She dropped her hands from the screen, and as he opened the door and stepped inside, heat rushed in. Who knew a screen door could provide such protection? Pete reached for her hand and kissed her cheek. Holy moly, he smelled like he'd bathed in all things male and sensual. There were no words to describe the way his scent made her legs wobble. How would she ever make it through the date? He'd have to carry her if he was going to smell like that all night.

He reached into his pocket. "I brought you something."

You brought me something? Jenna was like a kid when it came to gifts. She didn't just love them; she adored them, and it didn't matter what they were. A pair of cheap flip-flops would make her bounce with excitement as much as a set of diamond earrings. Well, she assumed they would, as she'd never actually received a set of diamond earrings.

Pete opened his palm and displayed a jet-black rock. She glanced up at him, and her breath caught in her throat.

"Peter."

"When we were at the Bookstore Restaurant, I heard Amy say you were collecting black rocks this year."

"You…heard her say it? And you remembered?" Her heart melted a little more. The rock was warm from being in his pocket and was perfectly smooth, save for a tiny ridge across the center. She held it in her palm for him to touch.

"You have to feel this. It's so soothing."

"I just did."

"No, you gave it to me. Now concentrate. Close your eyes and feel the soothing qualities."

"Soothing?" He closed his eyes as he brushed his fingers over the rock. His brow furrowed, then relaxed. When he opened his eyes again, he smiled. "I can see how that would feel soothing."

She didn't expect him to have the same connection as she did with rocks, but the fact that he'd brought her a rock and he wasn't mocking her meant the world to her.

"I wasn't sure how you chose your rocks," he explained. "So if you don't like it, don't feel pressured to keep it. I know you're particular about the ones you keep."

Swoon! "It's perfect." It could have been purple for all she cared. It was from Pete, and that made it the most precious rock she'd ever owned. She hooked her finger in his jeans for leverage and went up on her toes to kiss him. Pete met her halfway, and the moment their lips touched, her legs turned to jelly and she fell back on her heels. Pete caught her with one strong arm around her waist and deepened the kiss.

She was floating again. Time stood still. She must be in heaven. *Bliss. Delicious.*

When their lips parted and their eyes connected, his darkened, intensifying the passion in them. Jenna's pulse quickened as he lowered his lips to hers again in a tender, slow joining that reached deep inside, drawing heat straight through her core and claiming a piece of her. It was such a powerful feeling, as if they'd each had half of a soul embedded deep inside them that finally found its match.

He slid his lips to her cheek and kissed her again. "Baby, I'm going to keep a collection of rocks on hand at all times."

Her laugh came out as a mew. She held the rock in her fist as he rose to his full height again, and she tried to focus on where to set the rock he'd given her.

"Where should I put it?" *Kiss me again. Kiss me. Kiss me now.*

She watched as he eyed the coffee table, with a bowl full of rocks she'd found in Chatham three summers earlier and the ostrich-egg-shaped rocks on the floor by the edge of her couch.

"How do you choose?" he asked.

"I have to feel drawn to the place where I put the rock."

He looked around the room, his eyes lingering on a painting she'd made a few years earlier. It was one of the most difficult ones she'd ever done, a scene of rocks in a puddle. Getting the movement of the water just right had taken her weeks.

"Why don't you ever paint anymore?" he asked.

"Too busy collecting rocks, I guess." She was shocked that he even remembered when she used to paint.

He nodded, then glanced at the rock in her hand.

"Oh." She remembered that she was telling him how she chose where to put the rocks. "I usually hold the rock for a while, and if it doesn't hit me, then I put it in this basket." She went to the kitchen, opened a cabinet beneath the sink, and pulled out a step stool. She held on to the counter and stepped up, then reached over the refrigerator to the cabinet and used her fingertips to fling it open. Pete put a hand around her waist.

"Why don't I get it for you?" He reached up and grabbed the basket that she would have had to climb onto the counter to reach.

"Thank you."

He set the basket on the counter, then took the rock from her hand and set it inside. Jenna standing on the stool brought them much closer to the same height. She didn't think Pete could look any sexier, but being almost eye level with him brought a whole new perspective. His chin was more chiseled, his lips fuller, and his strong, stubbled jaw begged to be touched. She could barely think past the bees swarming in her stomach as his eyes searched hers, but she wasn't befuddled or at a loss for her voice any longer. Last night's kiss had set her free. Pete was the man she'd wanted for as long as she could remember, and she wasn't taking any chances of him not knowing it. She brought her hands to his cheeks and met his gaze as he settled his big hands on her slim waist.

"I'm going to have to kiss you again," he said in a husky voice.

Jenna's heart was beating so hard she thought she might explode with anticipation. "If you must…"

He laughed as he brought his lips to hers and pressed a soft kiss to them, lingering just long enough to leave her wanting more. She leaned forward, and he held her up with one arm, kissing her in the middle of her tiny kitchen. She loved kissing him in the kitchen! In *her* kitchen! She'd imagined this very scene a million times in her head, and reality was so much better than fantasy.

"We might never go on a date at this rate," he said against her lips.

She smiled and gave him another quick peck, before arching back so she could look at his face. Vera was *so* right. There were so many adjectives flying through her mind about Pete—sexy, safe, possessive, sensual, caring, amazing, sweet, powerful, smooth, delicious—that she could never pick just one.

"We'd better go, or you'll be the talk of Seaside." Jenna felt him lowering her to her feet and she clung to his biceps. *Mm.* He had great biceps.

"Baby, I have a feeling we'll be the talk of Seaside for a very long time to come."

THEY PARKED AT Pete's house and walked down the beach to the crowded weekly beach jam, where local bands came together and played for the evening. The town of Eastham only allowed charcoal fires on bay beaches, and the group that ran the weekly beach jam had enormous hibachis custom-made by Pete's brother Hunter a few summers earlier. Hunter worked with steel. His passion was making sculptures from raw materials, but he made functional items from steel and stone for a living, and his uniquely sized and shaped hibachis were well known on the Cape. Pete liked having that family connection associated with his first date with Jenna.

He and Jenna held hands, and it all seemed so natural, being there with Jenna, surrounded by crowds of people smiling and dancing, that he was no longer nervous. Jenna gripped his hand so tightly that he wondered if she was.

"I'm glad you agreed to go out with me tonight," Pete said as they stood among the crowd.

Jenna turned in to him and brought her hands to his hips. "Me too."

"I probably should have taken you to dinner, or the drive-in."

"No, you shouldn't have. This is perfect. I'm not a wine and dine girl. I'm more of a…"

"Rock girl?" He tucked her hair behind her ear.

She flushed at the intimate gesture. "Yes, and a marshmallow girl."

Pete noticed an elderly couple struggling to carry their chairs. "I'm sorry, babe. But I'll be right back. I just want to help them." He nodded in the couple's direction.

Jenna pressed her palm to his abs. "Go. I'm fine."

Pete helped the couple carry their chairs down to the water and turned back, watching Jenna load a stick with marshmallows as she talked to a group of people around the bonfire. Pete's heart swelled, knowing that as badly as he'd wanted to be closer to her this summer, he finally could—even if it would be hindered by his father. He wondered again how he could have overlooked their connection for so long.

Pete had spent last night thinking of all the things he'd learned about Jenna over the years. Jenna was spontaneous, and despite her shyness around him before their kiss, she was one of the funniest women he knew. She wasn't high maintenance, craving glamour and glitz. Jenna wore colorful plastic rings and bracelets like they were diamonds, and she pulled them off like no one else ever could. She loved to laugh, and she seemed to like any type of music that she could dance to. And, of course, she loved the beach. He'd noticed that she also enjoyed being around people. As much as he wanted to keep Jenna all to himself tonight, there would be plenty of time for that. It was more important that she feel comfortable on their first date, and by the looks of her, smiling and chatting away, her hips swaying side to side to the beat of the music, it appeared she was very comfortable.

"Petey!" Jenna wiggled her insanely sexy hips from side to side in a little dance that he was sure was meant to look more cute than sexy by the way she was beckoning him over with her hand, but it captured the attention of every man who had come to the beach jam tonight.

Petey? He hadn't been called that since he was a kid. Hearing the nickname brought back happy memories of his mother, which brought his mind to his father's recent issues. Pete drew in a deep breath and forced those thoughts aside. This was his night with Jenna, and hopefully it would remain that way.

Pete had walked away for only a minute, maybe two, and Jenna had already corralled an entire group of couples around her.

"Pete, this is Chuck and Kerri, Wendy, Bob, Butch, and Lisa. This is Pete." She wrapped a hand around his forearm.

Pete loved her possessive move. He and the others exchanged hellos, and as the other couples began settling their marshmallows over the fire, Jenna thrust an empty stick toward him.

"Roast marshmallows with me?"

The band played another calypso song, and Jenna swayed to the music again. Pete forced himself to focus on her question rather than the urge to pull her hot little body against him.

"I don't eat them, but I'll cook them for you." There weren't many sweets Pete enjoyed besides chocolate. *And Jenna.*

Jenna grabbed his shirt and pulled him down so they were eye to eye. "Are you sick? Should we go to the doctor?"

He laughed with a shrug. "I'm not a big sweets guy."

She released his shirt. "Marshmallows aren't really sweets. They're…"

He arched a brow.

"Marshmallows." She wiggled her butt again. When he reached for the stick with the marshmallows on it, she pulled it out of reach. "You can't cook mine."

"Why not?"

"Because I'm really picky, and you'll take me home and never ask me out again." She looked up through her thick lashes with serious eyes.

"Aw, come on. You can't be that picky." He reached for the stick again, and she let him take it.

"Okay, but I warned you."

He knelt by the fire's edge and reached for her hand, bringing her down beside him. "How do you like it?"

She looked so damn cute, elbows on knees as she crouched on her heels, eyeing the marshmallows. "Golden brown. Not golden. Not brown. Golden brown."

Pete thought of her rock collection, her spotless cottage, and the way her closet was organized—by color, style, and length of the outfits.

Oh shit.

Golden brown.

The marshmallow caught fire and he blew it out before it charred. "Good?"

Jenna shook her head and stuck out a pouty lip. "Too dark. Here, let me show you." She reached for the stick and he held tight.

"Golden brown. I've got it." He tossed the marshmallow into the fire and loaded up the stick again.

"Not golden, not brown. Golden brown," she reminded him.

He held the stick over the fire, turning it slowly until the edges were brown and slightly bubbled, and then he offered it to Jenna. "Golden brown."

She inspected the marshmallow and shook her head. "See the white on the ends?"

"No one gets the ends, it's all about the middle." His competitive nature was kicking in. *The ends?* How the hell was he supposed to roast the ends and not burn the rest?

She smiled and settled a hand on his thigh. "You sure you don't want me to do it?"

If he could practically build a boat from scratch, he could damn well roast a fucking marshmallow. He'd get this right if it killed him.

"Yeah, I'm sure." He leaned in and stole a kiss.

When their lips parted, her eyes remained closed. "Mm. If only you could cook marshmallows like you kiss."

She opened her eyes, and he teasingly narrowed his and glared at her.

"I warned you that it wasn't easy to cook a marshmallow for me. Golden brown is not as easy as it sounds." She traced the seam of his jeans along his thigh.

"I have a feeling nothing with you is easy." He smiled to let her know he was only kidding. *Sort of.*

He cooked three more not-good-enough marshmallows as Jenna danced around him, calling out instructions: *Turn it before you burn it! Yes, perfect! Turn it again! Oh no, too dark.* Each time her smile faded anew; then her excitement would reappear as he loaded the next marshmallow on the stick.

The other couples had long since finished roasting marshmallows and were standing among the crowd by the band.

Jenna planted her chin in her palms. "It's okay, Petey. Some people are made for kissing instead of cooking marshmallows."

"I'm made for both," he practically growled. He set to work on another marshmallow.

Jenna crouched beside him again and began spouting off instructions. He silenced her with another glare, cooked the damn marshmallow, then turned the stick toward her for inspection.

"Princess, your marshmallow has arrived. Not golden. Not brown. Golden-brown perfection." After so many imperfect marshmallows, his nerves were strung so tight they twitched. He tried not to let on and forced a smile as Jenna set her mouth in a serious line and craned her neck, inspecting every ripple of the damn marshmallow.

Her eyes widened and her lips curved into a smile as she pulled the marshmallow from the stick with two fingers. "You did it! You can roast marshmallows as good as you can kiss."

She popped the warm, sticky marshmallow into her mouth. Her excitement was worth every ounce of Pete's agitation, which was dissipating quickly as he watched her luscious lips moving. Her eyes closed, and she moaned, as if the marshmallow was orgasmic. He couldn't wait a second longer. He pulled her onto his lap and sealed his mouth over hers. The sticky sweetness slid over their tongues, dissolving with the heat of their kiss.

"I told you I'm picky." She was still sitting on his lap, and he was already hard, and in no hurry for her to move.

"And I told you I could cook the damn thing." He brushed her hair from her shoulder and cupped her cheek. "You, my sweet marshmallow princess, are picky as hell."

She lowered her eyes and wrinkled her brow. "Does that mean you won't cook marshmallows for me anymore?"

He lifted her chin. "No. It means I've memorized exactly what it takes to satisfy you. Sixty-seven seconds on each side, held about five inches from the fire, then twenty seconds with the tip of the marshmallow aimed directly at the flames, but a few inches away so it doesn't burn."

"That's the sexiest thing I've ever heard anyone say."

She leaned in for another kiss, and Pete deepened it as she opened to his efforts. There on the crowded beach, with music filling the night and the smell of the bay mingling with the smoky fire, Pete felt his world shift into place.

WHEN THEIR LIPS parted, Jenna had to remind herself to breathe. Pete's kisses made her body hum with anticipation. She was still sitting on his lap, his strong arms wrapped around her, making her feel feminine and safe against his powerful breadth. She felt his desire hard beneath her bottom, and a thrill shuddered through her.

"Do you want to dance?" His voice was deep and carried an undercurrent of desire.

No. I want you to kiss me again. "You'll dance with me?"

"Babe, I'd do anything with you."

Zing!

Groups of people gathered around the band, dancing and swaying to the music. Pete pulled her close, and she slid her hands beneath his shirt and up his muscular back, memorizing the feel of him. The temperature was warmer with the crowd blocking the breeze from the bay—or maybe it was from Pete's body pressed against hers. His hands slid to the curve of her butt and pressed lightly. Jenna's nerves were on fire. She wanted to kiss him and touch him until she had her fill. She felt herself breathing hard, and when he gazed down and searched her eyes, pressing his hips to her, she was as aroused as he was.

He was so much taller than her that lifting up on her toes would never get her close enough for a kiss, but oh, how she wanted to kiss him. Years of wanting him rushed forward. She might not be able to reach his lips, but she could damn well give him the signal he was searching for. She slid her hands around to his rock-hard abs and then ran them up his chest. His skin was hot, and his heart thundered against her palm. When he lowered his cheek to hers and whispered, "Let's get out of here," she had to stop herself from thanking him.

They hurried along the beach hand in hand, closing the distance toward Pete's house and stopping every few feet to kiss. Pete's kisses were like a force unto themselves. His arms engulfed her, making her feel feminine and safe, as he explored every bit of her mouth with deep, lush strokes of his tongue. He didn't just kiss her; he consumed her, claimed her with kisses that held promises of so much more. She'd never felt so desired in all her life.

Waves crashed against the rocks along the shore by his house. Jenna had known that he lived in Eastham, but she'd never been to his house, and when they'd dropped off the truck, they'd gone straight down the beach toward the music. Now, as they followed the sandy trail up the bluff to his house, she took it all in. The dark shingled home and enormous barn were outlined with white trim. Set against the backdrop of the night sky, his property felt welcoming. Pete's hand tightened on hers, big as a bear paw, and if the way he'd held her when they were dancing and kissing was any indication, just as lethal.

When they reached the door, the bay breeze tousled Pete's hair, and his eyes bored into her. His full lips curved up, and he pulled her into another deep kiss. A shiver ran down her spine at the realization of where they were heading. She hooked her finger into the waist of his jeans to keep her legs from wobbling. He didn't say a word, and it was a good thing, because she was sure her nerves would have silenced her voice.

He opened the door and Joey bounded out, climbing Pete's legs and whimpering with excitement.

"Hey, girl." He crouched beside her and loved her up. Joey rolled onto her back, and Jenna joined him, petting Joey's belly as she tried to lick her hands. Her nerves eased, until she glanced at Pete and their eyes locked. The space between them heated with unspoken desires. He reached for her hand, and Joey bounded away as Pete led her inside.

"Joey?" she said.

"Doggie door." His voice was raspy and deep.

They walked through a tidy kitchen and into a warm living room. Sheer curtains billowed around open French doors that overlooked the bay. The breeze carried the crisp, salty scent of the bay, and when Pete drew her into his arms, it picked up his masculine scent and lust clutched her again. A whisper of worry floated through her mind. *Erotic, sensual.* It faded as quickly as it had come. She felt safe with Pete, and she knew he'd never force her to do anything she didn't want to.

He swept her hair from her face. "You're so beautiful, Jenna. I haven't been able to think of anything but you for days."

She felt her cheeks flush as he lowered his lips to her neck and trailed kisses to the sensitive skin just beneath her ear. She closed her eyes and slid her hands beneath his shirt again. Jesus, his kisses spread heat through her body like an inferno, and she went a little wild, plucking at the buttons on his shirt until it fell open, exposing hard planes of tanned flesh. She ran her hands up his ribs to his pecs and felt his nipples pebble beneath her fingers. His mouth was working magic on the curve of her neck, sending goose bumps down her arms. She had to taste him. As if reading her mind, he cupped her ass and pulled her against him. Her lips pressed against his chest, and she followed the arc of his pectoral muscles with her tongue, earning her a low groan from him as he lifted her dress and took hold of her ass with both hands. His mouth moved lower, and she arched back, opening to his advances, wanting, craving, more of him. When his lips touched the crest of her breast, she sucked in air. He ran his tongue along the crease of her cleavage, sending a shiver through her. She clutched his waist at the shock of need that rushed through her. Her hand slid to the front of his pants, and she cupped his hard shaft through the rough material. His lips met hers again as he adeptly untied the top straps of her halter dress, freeing her breasts. Standing before him with her breasts exposed, while he was still dressed, shirt open, should have made her feel vulnerable and nervous. Instead she felt empowered, and the wanton look in his eyes bolstered her confidence. She tightened her grip on his hard length.

"Jenna," he said roughly.

He was breathing as hard as she was, and when he filled his palms with her breasts and brushed his thumbs over her nipples, she thought she'd crawl out of her skin. When he brought his mouth to her nipple, she dug her fingers into his back to keep from collapsing with the intensity of his hot, wet tongue swirling circles, then sucking until she thought she might fall apart right there in his living room. Her other hand tugged at the buttons on his jeans. In the next breath, she was in his arms, being carried down the hall and into his bedroom. Her lips were so close to his neck, and his scent was so intoxicating, she settled her mouth over his neck in an openmouthed kiss, and it still wasn't enough. She sucked, licked, then nipped and licked some more, until he tore his neck from her grasp with a loud exhalation.

"Jesus. You're driving me insane." Heat flared in his dark eyes.

He lowered her to the bed and came down on top of her, their mouths crashing together. His tongue probed hungrily, and his hips gyrated against hers, hard and eager. She pressed her hands to his lower back, wanting him, needing him. *All of him.* She didn't care that this was their first real date. She'd waited a damn long time, and as she writhed beneath him and he moved his mouth down her body, she was completely, utterly, *his.*

He lowered his forehead between her breasts and just breathed her in. Jenna stilled. *Don't stop. Please don't stop.* When he lifted his head and their eyes met, his desire was layered with hesitation. He moved back up so they were eye to eye.

"I'm sorry, Jenna. I got carried away. You're so beautiful, and when we kissed…" He shook his head. "Do you want this with me? We can stop."

There was no question in her mind what she wanted. She

ran her fingers through his hair. God, she loved his hair. "I've wanted this with you forever."

His eyes darkened and narrowed with an animalistic, possessive look. She pressed his shoulders, urging him to continue the heavenly things he'd been doing before his beautiful conscience took over. He hooked his fingers in the sides of her dress and tugged it off, leaving her naked, save for a white thong. His giant hands came down on her hips, and he lowered his mouth to the curve of her waist and kissed and licked his way south to her belly button. *Ohgodohgodohgod.* One hand slid beneath her ass and lifted her hips; the other grabbed her breast, and he squeezed her nipple between his finger and thumb—hard—sending her hips bucking upward. Jenna gasped another breath, unable to remain still as white-hot sensations raced through her. He licked her through the damp material between her legs, teasing, tasting. The light brushing against her swollen sex filled her with anticipation.

"Mm." He hooked a finger beneath the slim line of her thong and dragged it down one thigh. He slid that hand beneath her ass and held her hips up, freeing his other hand to drag the other side of her thong down her thigh.

She could barely breathe she wanted him to touch her so badly. She desperately wanted to open herself to him, but the tether of the thong bound her thighs inches apart. She fisted her hand in the sheets.

"Off. Take them off. Please." *Oh God!* She couldn't believe she was begging him to strip her bare.

Pete moved above the thong, leaving it in place. He slid his thumb from underneath where he'd held her ass and pressed it to the slick skin between her legs, stroking her into a frenzy. He lowered his mouth to her, licking circles on her sensitive bundle of nerves. She fought against the restraint of the thong, and it amped up her arousal as he took her up, up, up to the edge, then he pressed her hips until she connected with the mattress again, and slid his fingers deep inside. Adrenaline coursed through her as he probed her fast and deep, until her inner muscles clamped down around him and her hips shot off the bed. He sealed his mouth over her center as the orgasm tore through her.

"Peter—" Lights went off behind her closed lids. Pinpricks seared her skin. She didn't think the orgasm would ever end—and, God, she hoped it wouldn't—as her body pulsated around him. Just as it began to ease, he buried his tongue inside her, taking her over the edge again as she flailed her head from side to side, trying to maintain her grip on reality. Every muscle was on fire, until finally, her hips fell, spent, to the mattress and she let out a long, heated breath. She panted for air as Pete pressed feathery soft kisses to her inner thighs and around her swollen, pulsating sex.

"Good…Lord…" She reached for him, her eyes still closed, and she tangled her fingers in his hair, wanting to feel him, to be connected again. She tugged, urging him up to her. When she opened her eyes, Pete lowered his mouth to hers. Her juices were still on his mouth, and the sinful seduction of it all sent her hips rising against his again. She pushed at his shirt, wanting it off. Wanting him naked. Needing him inside her.

Pete's lips never left hers as he shrugged out of his shirt. Then he moved down her body and took her thong off in one move. He slid off the bed long enough to strip out of his jeans. Jenna raked her eyes over his bulging muscular chest, down the fine pattern of his rippled abs, and finally—*holy shit*—to his formidable erection. She felt her eyes widen and bit her lower lip to keep from grinning like a fool. He. Was. Beautiful.

Insanely sexy.

And you're finally mine.

He moved like a panther, sleek and powerful, as he came down between her legs and ran his hands up her hips, along her waist, and under her arms, finally curling his strong hands around her shoulders. The tip of his arousal pressed against her wet center, like a python seeking heat.

"Condom." Frustration flashed in his eyes, as he lifted off of her.

Jenna grabbed his arm and held him still. "I'm on the pill."

His eyes narrowed, frustration replaced with something hot and libidinous. He lowered his mouth to hers again and kissed her sensually, running his tongue slowly along her teeth, exploring the roof of her mouth and meeting each stroke of her tongue with his own as he pushed inside her. Jenna sucked in a breath, his girth stretching her as he buried himself deep. Dear Lord, he felt good. His hands clutched her shoulders, holding her still as he thrust deeper, harder, his mouth still loving hers. She wrapped her legs around his hips, wanting to bring their bodies closer together. He must have read her mind, because he tightened his arms around her, their bodies pressed together, and he stilled.

He slid his lips to the edge of her mouth. "I can't believe I was so blind to us for so long."

"Me either." She giggled at her candor. She couldn't help it, and he looked down at her with a smile so genuine and full of emotion that it stole her breath.

"Pretty sure of yourself." He pressed a kiss to her cheek.

"If I had known a little competition would get your attention, I'd have dated a construction worker years ago."

He tightened his grip until she could barely breathe. "Let's not talk about other guys in the bedroom."

She laughed again, and he took her in a needful kiss as his hips began to undulate, hitting all the spots that turned her brain to mush and made her nerves roar to life. She felt another orgasm teasing her, just out of reach, as his hips pressed in deep and moved from side to side. He arched his back and angled his hips, thrusting in hard, buried so deep she held her breath. He breathed air into her lungs, then thrust faster, harder, until they parted with the need for air. With the next thrust, his teeth clenched and her nails dug into his back; they grabbed and groped for leverage. Their hips rocked, bodies slick with sweat, as release tore through them and their eyes caught and held, and they spiraled over the edge together.

CHAPTER ELEVEN

PETE LOVED THE sound of Jenna's hampered breathing as she tried to calm down from their lovemaking. He loved that he had that effect on her—they had that effect on each other. He came up on one elbow and she smiled up at him. He loved her mouth, her eyes, the softness of her skin. He loved that she was in his bed, finally, where he felt she belonged. Pete traced a line down the center of her body, took her hand in his and brought it to his lips.

"This doesn't feel like a first date, Jenna. It feels like you've been with me all my life."

"If I'd been with you all your life, your closet would be organized."

He glanced into his closet, which was neat and orderly, but not color coordinated, and the thought that her mind had gone there so soon after making love made him laugh.

"You have a point." He lowered his forehead to hers. "I'm serious, though. All these years we've known each other, and this. You being here with me. It feels so right." He kissed her cheek and loved the way she closed her eyes the second his lips touched her skin, like she was savoring his touch.

"In my heart I *was* with you all these years; you just never noticed."

"I noticed, but you confused the hell out of me." He searched her eyes for a reaction, hoping he didn't annoy her with his honesty, but it had been on his mind, and he wanted to get it out in the open, because so many other things needed to fill that space. Images of Jenna trying to catch his attention flashed into his mind, but he couldn't hold on to them. They were overpowered by her other confusing reactions.

She laced their fingers together. "You made me nervous, but you don't anymore." She looked down at their naked bodies. "Obviously." Her cheeks pinked up again.

"Why did I make you so nervous?"

"Because I was so damn attracted to you." She shifted her eyes.

"Jenna, talk to me."

She looked at him with a serious gaze. "You made me all flustered, and the harder I tried to get your attention, the less attention you paid to me, so I got nervous."

"And then you gave up and went out with that guy."

"Charlie."

"*That guy.*"

The side of her lips cocked up. "You know, you come across as this quiet, well-mannered, slightly mysterious guy. But you're much more aggressive and possessive."

He pulled her closer, so her legs were pressed against his, her hip against his groin.

"That's because I wasn't dating you."

"Which begs the question…Why weren't you interested in me?" She blinked up at him expectantly.

"Because I was stupid." He smiled and she rolled her eyes. Of course she wouldn't buy his bullshit, and she deserved the truth. He lay back and arced an arm over his head, but he felt too far away from her, so he moved closer again.

"The truth is, when you're with everyone else, you're yourself, but with me, you were so nervous that I didn't know what to make of it. I wasn't sure we'd be compatible. You see how I am. The *real* me. I'm not someone who's terribly gentle or coy. But when I saw you with that guy—" He shook his head. "I don't know, Jenna. I saw you actually pick up a guy. In all these years, I've never seen you do that. And suddenly the threat of losing you was real. I realized how much I looked forward to seeing you every summer, and…" He flopped back on the bed again and threw his arm over his forehead and groaned.

"Go on. I'm liking this whole alpha Pete gets embarrassed thing you've got going on."

He rose over her again and kissed her nose. "Be careful or I'll show you just how alpha I can be. We're friends, Jen. Pretty damn good friends, and I didn't want to jeopardize that. I didn't want a fling with you, but seeing you with him at the bar and then again on the boat…I lost sight of right and wrong, and all those years crashed together." He looked deeply into her eyes, needing her to understand what it had taken him forever to grasp. "I realized how much you meant to me and how stupid I'd been. Then we kissed, and holy hell, Jenna. There was no turning back. At least not for me."

She narrowed her eyes. "So, this is a fling?"

His chest tightened. Is that what she wanted? "Hell no. Not for me it's not. Is it for you?"

"I just thought when you said—"

He pulled her beneath him and pinned her to the bed with his weight. "Let me be very clear. I don't want a goddamn fling, and I'm not into sharing. So if you were looking for a fling, gather your slinky little dress and I'll drive you home."

Her eyes narrowed. "And if I'm not looking for a fling?"

"Then let's get cleaned up and eat some dinner so I can enrapture you with my seductive ways and claim you again and again."

Jenna pushed at his chest. "Would you mind getting off of me?"

Her words sent a sinking feeling to Pete's gut as he moved off of her and watched her scoot to the edge of the bed.

"Did I really misread you?" He wrapped his arm around her waist and kissed the back of her neck—just in case it was the last taste of her he'd ever get.

Jenna hopped from the bed—literally—and turned to face him. Her eyes were wide, her smile mischievous, with every sweet curve on display, making him instantly hard again. "Who are you kidding?" She strutted buck naked to the bathroom. "Get your ass up. Let's rinse off and get you fed. You've got a girlfriend to satisfy."

He followed her into the bathroom, making her laugh as he swooped her into his arms and turned on the shower.

"Girlfriend? So you don't mind that I'm a little possessive?" He kissed her neck as they stepped beneath the warm spray of the water.

"Little?" She arched a brow and dragged her eyes down his body. "There is nothing little about you, and I've been lusting after you for years." She met his gaze again. "I've been *yours* for years. It's about damn time you owned up to it."

"Damn, I like you, Jenna."

"Fair warning. I'll drive you crazy." She held on to his waist and stared at him with a serious look in her eyes. "I'll organize everything in your life, and if you think golden-brown marshmallows are a pain, you should see—"

He kissed her again and brushed droplets of water from her cheek with the pad of his thumb.

"I'll take my chances."

An hour later they were dressed and sitting on his back deck, eating cheese and crackers and sharing a glass of wine, when Pete's cell phone rang with his father's ringtone.

Goddamn it.

"Excuse me." He rose to his feet and grabbed his phone from the living room table. "Hey, Pop." He eyed Jenna on the deck. She kicked her bare feet up on his chair and rested her head back.

"Where is she, Peter?" His father's speech was slurred and slow. Pete's heart ached. No one outside of his family knew about his father's drinking, and just this one night he'd hoped to escape his father's call. Sometimes he went days without calling. Of all the bad luck…

He turned his back to Jenna and rubbed his temples. "She's gone, Pop. But you're okay. Can you get into bed?" He knew his father wouldn't be able to without stumbling, and the thought of him getting hurt worried Pete.

"Gone? What d'you mean gone?"

Pete turned back toward Jenna. "I'll be there in a few minutes. Stay put."

Jenna turned when he opened the screen door. Joey followed him out and rubbed against her leg.

"Everything okay?" she asked.

He ran his hand through his hair and glanced over the bay. "I'm really sorry, Jenna, but I've got to go take care of something." *Fuck.* He did not want to end this night.

"Oh." Her eyes filled with disappointment.

Goddamn it. Jenna had woken up every part of his brain and body. He wanted to protect her, to love her, and damn it, the last thing he wanted to do was leave her. But she didn't need to deal with his father's shit.

He reached for her hand. His jaw clenched tight, and he knew he was being quiet and withdrawn. It was unfair to Jenna that he was acting this way, but he was pissed—at his father, for falling into the bottle night after night, and at himself, for not forcing him into rehab.

"I'm sorry, Jenna. The last thing I want is to end our date, much less end it like this."

"It's okay. Is there anything I can do to help?"

He shook his head. There was nothing anyone could do. Once again he wondered if Jenna would be better off without him—and his father's illness—in her life.

And he knew there was no way in hell he'd ever let her go.

CHAPTER TWELVE

JENNA HUNG UP the phone from talking with her mother and banged her forehead on the table for the millionth time. That seemed to be a theme for the summer.

"I'm the worst daughter in the world. Seriously." It was Monday morning, and Jenna, Amy, and Bella were lying in the sun in the quad behind Jenna's cottage, debating walking the hundred or so steps to the pool or driving to the beach, each too lazy to make a decision, much less get up and go.

"No, you're not. You're dealing with a lot right now. Your mom knows that." Amy shaded her eyes from the sun and reached for Jenna's hand.

"No, she doesn't. I didn't tell her about Pete." Sadness welled in her chest as she thought about her mother, which always brought her mind to her father. Although she wasn't in close contact with him, they talked every few weeks. A brief catch-up phone call, like he was checking off a to-do list, and though she didn't hate him for everything that was going on in his life and he hadn't left her mother for his young bride-to-be, every time she heard the pain in her mother's voice, or saw her mother's emotional turmoil masked by a forced smile and her ridiculous new costumes, it drove an arrow of anger through her, aimed directly at her father.

"Why not?" Amy wore a light pink bikini, and she'd painted her toenails pink to match. She wiggled them now as she waited for Jenna to answer.

"Because. I don't know. She's so in my face these days. She'd ask a lot of questions and want to talk about sex—and there's no way I'm talking about that with my mother."

"Especially sex with Pete," Bella added as she twisted her hair into a pile on top of her head and secured it with a clip.

"I still can't get over our mild-mannered Pete coming out of his shell. How the hell did we not see that side of him? *Ever?*"

"Seriously," Amy agreed.

"If I had seen it, I probably would have been even worse off around him." Jenna sighed, thinking of being in his arms, the sheer strength of him, and the way he looked at her like she was the most delectable creature on earth. "What do you make of the sudden end to our date? I mean, we know he's not married or anything, so what would send him running off like that when I was ready to spend the night? Do you think it was just an excuse? Like he's second-guessing this whole thing?"

Bella slid her sunglasses down the bridge of her nose and looked at Jenna over the enormous brown frames. "You established boyfriend, girlfriend. There's no way he reconsidered."

"He could have. Maybe he thought about it while he was on the phone and realized I am a pain in the ass. Oh God! Bella! What if that call was *his* emergency call?"

Amy gasped and swung her legs over the side of her lounge chair, staring at Bella with worry in her eyes. Bella sat up, and Jenna followed, trying for the millionth time to ignore the worry over her parents. *Is there really such thing as forever for a relationship?*

"You guys?" Jenna's heart raced. "Maybe the connection we felt was momentary for him. Oh my God. I have to know." She needed to talk to Pete, not wallow in her parents' messy lives or let it screw up her hopes and dreams. Jenna jumped to her feet and gathered her towel in her arms.

"Where are you going?" Bella asked as she gathered her suntan lotion and slipped into her flip-flops.

"I'm going to Pete's to see if he's working on his boat. I have to talk to him."

"Jenna, wait." Bella was on her feet in seconds, holding on to Jenna's arm. "If that was his emergency call, you don't want to get upset in front of him. Are you sure you don't want to call first? Maybe find out over the phone so you're not alone? Just in case?"

She looked at her friends, both ready to stand beside her in her pain. She knew they'd both say horrible things about Pete if that was his emergency call. They'd slay him forever in all their minds—and after she got over the devastation of losing Pete, she'd probably thank them for it.

"No, but thank you. I couldn't have misinterpreted our connection. I've never felt so much for a man in my entire life, and I swear, if you could have seen his eyes, you would have thought he felt the same thing, too. I can handle this."

She headed for her house to grab a sundress to throw over her bikini. She turned back and said, "Besides, if I fall apart, I know you guys will be here waiting to put me back together."

"With two full bottles of Middle Sister wine, which Amy and I will go buy right now." Bella dragged Amy toward her cottage. "Come on, Ames. I need to grab my keys and purse."

Twenty minutes later, Jenna drove down the private road leading to Pete's house. The sun streaked through the tips of the tall trees that bordered the narrow road, striping the shaded areas with bright sunlight. It was a strange feeling to know that this time yesterday morning she didn't know exactly where he lived, and just a day later, she not only knew, but had an intimate look inside who Pete really was. It wasn't just the way they'd come together, or the power of his sexuality. She'd seen who he really was, marked by the family photographs all over his house, the masculine style of his furniture—substantial pieces of wood and warm, dark colors—the puppy beds in each room. The thing that lingered in her mind the strongest was that despite so many homey touches and Joey, when she'd first walked in, his house had felt a little lonely.

She breathed a sigh of relief when she spotted his truck parked in the driveway. She parked behind it, and Joey bounded toward her from the barn, a good sign that Pete was in there, too. She crouched to pet Joey, who flopped right onto her back.

"Is your daddy home?" Jenna glanced toward the bay. The tide was on its way out, and the view of the wet sand was calming. She drew in a deep breath and then pushed to her feet.

"Come on, let's find Pete." She followed Joey as she sprinted into the barn. Country music filtered out the oversized doors. Jenna stopped at the entrance, mesmerized by the enormous boat looming above her, propped up by several metal stands that were also much taller than her.

Joey barked and ran around to the far side of the boat.

"Hey there, girl." Pete's voice sent a shiver through her. He was talking to Joey, and obviously hadn't seen her yet. She spied his booted feet and followed them up to his muscular calves. Her view of him was blocked by one of the metal stands and the swell of the boat.

Jenna didn't rush to his side, though she wanted to more than anything. Instead she took in the barn and bided her time, trying to figure out how to handle asking about the way their date had ended. She had much more confidence when she was with Bella and Amy, which was silly, given that she'd been so intimate with Pete.

She looked up at the ceiling. *I can do this. He loves me. I know he does.*

There were windows along the top of the exterior walls of the barn, and a built-in workbench ran along the wall to her left. The barn smelled of freshly sanded wood, paint, and the distinct scent of Pete. She heard a giant fan whirring but didn't see it until she walked around the boat to where Pete stood in a pair of low-slung cargo shorts. His body glistened with sweat, and as he reached above his head, applying something in a long line across the lower section of the boat, his biceps flexed and his abs tightened. Jenna shivered with the memory of wrapping her hands around those muscles. Pete wiped his brow with the crook of his arm and looked down at Joey, wagging her tail at his feet. Pete flashed an easy smile—then his eyes followed Joey as she came to Jenna's side.

Pete's smile widened.

"Jenna." He set down the tools he'd been holding, and in a few determined steps, he folded her into his arms, lifted her up, and pressed his lips to hers, obliterating the worry that the phone call had been a means for escape.

When their lips parted, he still held her against him. Jenna didn't care about the perspiration soaking her sundress, or the fact that Joey was circling them and barking. She was overcome with the love in Pete's embrace.

"I'm so glad you're here. I was going to call you later, but I didn't want to smother you." He kissed her again and then lowered her feet to the ground.

She hooked her finger in his shorts, not wanting to break the connection.

"Okay, that's a lie," he admitted. "I want to consume every second of your time, but I don't want to scare you off."

"You did scare me, but you didn't scare me off." Jenna followed Pete's eyes down to her chest, where two enormous wet spots circled her breasts from being pressed against his chest. "You've marked me."

He pulled her close. "Not well enough, I haven't." He kissed her again, a long, deep kiss, as he had last night.

Heavenly.

He took her hand and walked out of the barn with Joey on their heels. "Come on. We'll talk." They walked to the edge of the bluff, where Pete pulled her down by his side on the large rocks. "I'm so sorry about last night. It was a struggle not to show up at your cottage when I was done."

Done? She didn't want to sound like a jealous girlfriend, but…she was. She couldn't help it. "Was everything okay?"

He ran his hand through his hair, and his eyes became hooded. "Yeah, I guess."

"I was worried that the phone call was a setup. You know, from a friend, so you had a way out of our date."

Joey flopped down behind them with a loud sigh.

He laughed. "Do people really do that?"

She wasn't about to admit that yes, she and her friends did do that. Things were so different for guys, she assumed.

They must not worry about escaping. She thought of all of the dates she'd had in recent years, and the ones that went poorly were easily ended without the emergency call. It was a silly idea, but it had been carried forward from their teenage years, and knowing the girls were at the ready had bolstered her confidence.

He slung his warm arm over her shoulder and pressed his lips to her temple. "I thought our date was anything but bad, and I want more time with you, Jenna. The last thing I wanted to do was escape."

She breathed a sigh of relief.

"Hey." He lifted her chin so they were gazing into each other's eyes. "Don't worry about that stuff. You're not a fling. I told you that. I should have kissed you years ago, picked you up and held you tight and made you realize that you didn't have to be nervous around me. Hell, Jenna, I should have forced myself to stop questioning if we'd work or not and push away all the outside influences."

Pete's eyes grew serious, and worry lines appeared on his forehead. He rubbed his hands on his shorts, then settled his hand over hers.

"But in all honesty, Jenna, there are some things that can't be pushed aside completely. I think we need to talk about last night."

Jenna swallowed hard. After everything he just said, she should feel calm and secure, but the tension in his hand indicated how heavy his thoughts were and made her nervous all over again.

He trained his eyes on their hands. "You know my dad."

"Sure. I mean, I've met him a few times at the hardware store. He seems really nice. How's he doing since your mom passed away?"

Pete turned away and drew in a deep breath. When he turned back, he tightened his grip on her hand.

"This is really hard for me to share, Jenna. He's not doing very well, and no one knows about this but my family." He paused, and the muscle in the side of his jaw repeatedly bulged.

"Pete, you don't have to tell me—"

"I want to tell you, Jenna. I don't want any secrets between us, and if we keep seeing each other, this will definitely have an impact."

"If?" The word slipped out like a whisper. She closed her mouth tightly against the insecurity.

He took her cheeks in his hands and searched her eyes. "I want to be with you. Don't ever think otherwise. I spent years second-guessing, Jenna, and I realize we've spent only one night together. I get how crazy that seems. But we've known each other for years, and last night felt like we'd somehow put a label on us, and all those previous years, when we liked each other and were too blind to come together, were building a foundation of friendship and trust that we never realized we were building."

"I thought it was just me. I feel all those things, too.

That's why I came over. I didn't want to believe that you didn't feel the same."

"I definitely feel the same, but you might change your mind when you hear what I have to say." He let out a loud breath. "After my mom died, Pop's drinking spiraled out of control. He's a functioning alcoholic, Jenna, and it's not an easy situation for any of us."

"Oh, Pete. I'm sorry." Here she was worrying about her mother being too clingy and he had *real* issues he was dealing with. "Have you tried to get him help? What about your brothers and sister? I guess they're too far away to help?"

Pete nodded. "My brothers staged an unsuccessful intervention a few months after we realized what was going on, but all that did was piss him off. Sky doesn't know, or at least I've tried to protect her from all of this. She and our mom were really close, and Sky had such a hard time when our mom died that I worry what seeing our father like this would do to her. She's just starting to find herself again." Pete ran his hand though his hair, and pain flashed in his eyes.

"So she has no idea?"

Pete shook his head.

"Pete, I don't know what Sky is like, but if I had siblings and they kept something like this from me, I would probably be pissed. I mean, he is her father, too."

When he spoke again, his voice was deep and serious. "Sky was twenty-two when our mom died and Pop started drinking. She bounced from job to job; she was barely keeping her head above water. We were all very worried about her. I went and stayed with her for a couple weeks, dragged her out of bed each day, made her face her feelings and life without our mom. I tried to get her into therapy. I thought talking would help, but she refused to go. But she opened up to me. She's still open with me." He shook his head again. "I did the right thing, Jenna. I did the only reasonable thing. I'll tell her, eventually."

"And what about your dad? Does he admit he has a problem?" She had no idea Pete was dealing with such a tremendously difficult family problem, or had been for two years. Now, as she looked back, she wondered if his being quiet or more reserved was driven by his being sidetracked. Who wouldn't be?

"When Pop's sober and I try to talk with him about his drinking, he's adamant that he doesn't have a problem and that he just misses my mother, which I know he does. Then I feel guilty for trying to push him into AA meetings or rehab. And honestly, I think he's past the AA stage. He's worried about people in town finding out and losing business because of it. To be honest, I think he needs real, full-time help to beat this."

"I can't imagine how hard this has been for you. What happens when he's drinking?"

Pete scrubbed his hand down his face. "He's consumed with my mom. He doesn't remember that she died, so he asks where she is. It's pretty heartbreaking."

"He's right about people finding out, but the alternative is not good for either of you." Jenna slid her hand around the back of his neck and kneaded the tension from his muscles. "I'm sorry you've been going through this alone."

Pete pulled back. "I can handle it, but—" He looked away again.

Jenna realized how deeply this was impacting him, and she wasn't sure how to help, but she desperately wanted to. "Well, the next time that happens when we're together, please don't feel pressure to leave me behind. I'll go with you. Maybe I can help."

He shook his head. "No. You don't need to see what he's like."

"Is he violent?" She began to imagine all sorts of awful situations.

"No. He's just the opposite. He's kind of pathetic."

Jenna saw sadness in Pete's eyes, but it was the tension and maybe even embarrassment rolling off him that made her chest constrict. Had his father's alcoholism even allowed for Pete to grieve for his mother, or had it begun immediately after his mother's death? Was he embarrassed for his father, or for himself? And his choice of words rubbed her the wrong way. *Pathetic?* That could only come from years of pain.

"Pete, your parents were married a long time. He probably does feel lost without her, but that doesn't make him pathetic."

Pete pushed to his feet and paced. His hands fisted, and the muscles in his jaw bunched. "What does it make him, Jenna? She died. She's not coming back. So you deal with that, right? You say to yourself, *Okay, the woman I loved died, but I can't die right along with her.* It sucks, and yes, his life is enormously different. Empty, without her in it. But he's killing himself, and that would have killed my mother if she were alive to see it."

Jenna was struck by his words—and his anger. They were so similar to her own, toward her mother. *She just needs to get over it and move on.* She realized how unfair those words were. She pushed the thought away so she could focus on Pete.

"Pete, I think it makes him a man who loved a woman so deeply that when she died, she took too much of him with her." She rose to her feet and reached for his hand. His fingers were tense, but she held tight. "She was the glue that held him together. People don't just become alcoholics. He was probably drinking all along, but her presence kept him in check."

"Yeah. No shit." He pulled his hand away, and Jenna flinched at his spite. He turned back quickly, his eyes heavy with sorrow. "I'm sorry. That was a shitty thing to say. I know you're right, Jenna. I get it. He was always a drinker, but this…The way he's throwing in the towel is just not like him. He's always been the guy who made things happen.

The one who made me and my brothers stand up and be men. You know, face your faults and your fears and overcome them. His famous goddamn words to us were, *Men don't run from hard times. They conquer them.*" Pete set his hands on his hips and looked over at the bay.

"Wait a minute. Pete, do you think he's doing this on purpose? Do you blame him for this?"

He narrowed his eyes. Then his gaze softened and he reached for her hand. "I'm sorry, Jenna. I didn't mean to take you down with me. I know he's not doing this on purpose. But that doesn't make it any easier to accept, and it doesn't make his calls any easier to deal with."

Jenna closed the distance between them and reached up to touch his cheeks. She felt the tightness in his jaw and wanted to ease that tension and take away the sadness in his eyes. She wondered if her friends saw the same sadness and tension when she spoke of her mom.

"Pete, I know you feel like you can, or you should, handle this alone, but I'm going through something with my mom right now, and I've been trying to deal with it on my own. It's hard. It's damn hard. Listening to you talk about your dad made me realize that I was wrong. I don't need to try to deal with my mom by myself or deal with her by keeping my distance. I need to be closer to her and let her grieve for her marriage in whatever way she needs to, *with* my support." She moved closer to him.

"I don't know if you want me to be there or not, but I

want to be here for you. What your father is going through isn't a reflection on you. It's a reflection of how much he loved your mom. So what if her death weakened him? He's already raised you and your siblings. He's done his job. He's allowed to fall apart."

"He's killing himself," Pete hissed out.

"Right, which is why you can't feel guilty about getting him the help he needs. He's allowed to fall apart, as I was saying, but he can't be allowed to kill himself in the process. I think you should talk to him more. Make him understand where you're coming from."

Pete turned away. His shoulders rounded forward and he put his hands on his hips again. "I've talked so much that now when I open my mouth he has a rebuttal out before I even finish. Besides, he's right about the store. If word gets out, it'll affect his business, and none of us wants to run it."

Jenna wrapped her arms around him from behind and pressed her cheek to his back. He covered her hand with his own and exhaled; then he turned in her arms. She loved being close to him, and the more they shared, the closer they became. It pained her to know he'd been carrying this burden alone for so long.

He brushed her hair from her shoulders and ran his thumb over her cheek. "I'm a selfish bastard, aren't I?"

Jenna was gaining a better understanding of what was really going on, and it was hitting home. If they posed an intervention, it would clearly come down to Pete running the store, since his siblings lived out of town. He had his own businesses to think about. She felt bad for his family, and at the same time, Jenna realized how selfish she had been not to give up her vacation time for her mother, when her mother obviously needed her. How could she fault Pete, if she couldn't fault herself?

"We're all selfish, Pete. But after going through these last few weeks with my mom, and listening to what you're going through, I think it's safe to say that we expect our parents to set aside their own needs and be there for us, maybe even rescue us, for the first eighteen years of our lives. They put that energy into raising us well and teaching us responsibility and empathy for a reason, right? All those years of caring for us, putting up with our teenage shit, our ignorance, and putting the rest of their lives on hold, it's got to count for something. I think for some of us—me with my mom and maybe you with your dad—we have to learn to be just as selfless as our parents were. Maybe now it's our turn to rescue them."

CHAPTER THIRTEEN

JENNA STAYED WITH Pete for the rest of the day. She went with him to take care of a small boat repair at the marina, and then they had lunch at the Wellfleet Pier. It had been the most enjoyable day that he could remember in a very long time. Gone was the nervous energy that used to trail Jenna like a shadow around him and the uncertainty of his thoughts of their compatibility. He realized that even if she had remained nervous around him, it wouldn't have hampered his feelings for her one iota. He loved being with Jenna, and even her need to line up the silverware at the café and organize his workbench in the barn didn't bother him. It endeared her to him even more.

Late afternoon found Pete caulking the seams along the bottom planks of the schooner, and he realized that he'd finish refitting the boat very soon. That should have thrilled him, but instead it gave him a sinking feeling in the pit of his stomach. This was supposed to be the project he and his father completed together. A joint effort. More importantly, it was supposed to be the project that pulled his father from his internal hell and brought him back to Pete as the man—

and the father—he used to be.

He wiped the edge of the caulking with a rag, then set to work on the next plank. Jenna had been sitting in the grass talking on the phone with her mother for the last half hour. She was inviting her to visit for a few days, and damn if the first thing that entered Pete's mind was of how it would affect their time together. He knew it was a selfish thought, and between his father and that thought, he was mired in guilt. A moment later, his thoughts shifted to what Jenna had said about *rescuing* their parents. He'd never thought of what he was doing with his father in those terms, but the more he thought about it, the more he realized that he *wasn't* rescuing him. He was enabling him, putting a Band-Aid on a much larger problem. And what made it worse was that he hadn't realized that part of the reason was probably that he wasn't sure he was selfless enough to take over the hardware store and set his life aside for however many weeks it might take for his father to get the help he so desperately needed. Then again, the reality of his father drinking himself to death was a fear that gripped Pete every time he walked into his father's dark house. The silent battle between them must have been warring in his subconscious.

Even though he wasn't running the store, hadn't he already put his father's life ahead of his own and set aside his freedom? Wasn't he still?

Yes, he realized, he was.

He heard Jenna laugh softly, and it was so different from

her normal loud, halting laugh that it pulled him from his thoughts. She was sitting just outside the barn with her legs stretched out in front of her. She wiggled her toes, and when Joey licked them, she laughed. Pete loved listening to the cadence of her voice and seeing her smile as she listened to her mother on the phone, then responded, and then listened again. It made him long for the relationship he once had with his father. He hadn't realized how alone he'd felt dealing with his father's drinking until he and Jenna had spent the day talking about their families.

Jenna ended her call and jumped to her feet, reading a text on her phone. She tugged at her bikini top as she hurried across the grass toward him. Bo Derek had nothing on Jenna Ward. Jenna was the sexiest woman he'd ever met. Her shirts were always too tight on her breasts and too wide on her waist. Her dresses clung to every delicious curve. She couldn't hide her body if she tried, but Jenna's mannerisms that Pete thought might make them incompatible were the very things that softened her and made her even more alluring.

"Bella texted. They're having a barbecue tonight in the quad." She reached for his hand and began swaying to the music. "Do you want to be my date?"

He shoved the rag in his pocket and wrapped his arms around her. "That depends. Can I bring Joey?"

"Always. I love Joey." She went up on her tiptoes and puckered her lips.

Pete pressed his lips to hers. "You love Joey, huh?"

"Yeah. She's the perfect dog. Sweet, cute, and not too demanding."

"So you don't like demanding?" He lifted her into his arms, and Jenna wrapped her legs around his waist. She was light as a bird, and he loved the way she buried her hands in his hair and held on. Her skin was hot from the sun, and when he nuzzled against her neck, she smelled so good he had to kiss his way across her collarbone. "I can be pretty demanding." She tightened her grip on his hair and he pressed openmouthed kisses down her breastbone and along the edge of her bikini top.

"I like..." Jenna's words came out as one long breath. "Oh God, Pete."

"Too demanding?" He leaned back and looked at her. Her eyelids were heavy. She had a foggy, sexy look of wanting to be kissed.

"I like your demands." She returned his kiss with hunger, loving his mouth with hers and pressing her breasts against his chest. She felt so damn good that he wanted more of her. He had no control when it came to Jenna; he always wanted more. He wanted to be closer, wanted more of her heart, more of her love. He slid his hands beneath her bikini bottom and grabbed her bare ass. Jenna tore her lips away and eyed the boat.

"Have you christened it?" She raised her brows with a mischievous glint in her eyes.

Holy hell. "No, I haven't christened it, you dirty girl."

Jenna shot her arms straight up in the air. "Lift me up, baby. We've got lovin' to do."

Pete took her in another greedy kiss. "Where the hell have you been all my life?"

"Trying to get your attention, silly." Jenna kissed his chin and reached her arms up again. "Come on."

She was so damn cute, but there was no way he could hoist her into the boat. It was too tall. He set up the ladder with her clinging to his neck like a monkey. She kissed his chin, his jaw, his neck, driving him out of his freaking mind. Finally, when he had the ladder set up, he lifted her by her waist and turned her around, then grabbed her ass as he followed her up the ladder.

She stood in the middle of the boat, and he watched her eyes dance over his workmanship. He'd refinished all of the wood, stained and painted it, and worked his fingers to the bone, which he now realized he had done to work out his frustrations over his father's drinking.

"Pete, this is stunning. It's beautiful."

"*You're* stunning, Jenna. I don't mean that as cheesy as it sounds." He folded her into his arms and kissed the edge of her mouth. "You have the biggest heart of anyone I've ever known, and it comes through with everything you do and say."

He kissed her softly, loving the feel of her hands as they traveled up his chest, and he deepened the kiss. He pushed away the thoughts of his father and what the boat was supposed to signify and allowed himself to get lost in Jenna, in the taste of her lips as he dragged his tongue over the bow of her upper lip and followed it around to the swell of her lower lip. The feel of her breasts against his chest as he stripped away her bikini, and later, her softness beneath him as he lowered himself down on top of her.

"Pete."

She reached for him, her eyes full of pleasure and desire, her body ready to receive all that he had to give. Pete reveled in the sound of his name coming off her lips, and when their bodies joined together for the second time, his heart swelled and his whole body became hot with emotions. He'd shared his most intimate secret with Jenna, and as he lowered his cheek to hers, he barely contained the three words that he wanted to say. Their relationship was years in the making, and there was no stopping his heart from pouring out, one word at a time. He had to tell her, had to let her know, even if he withheld the words he really wanted her to hear.

"I can't even begin to conceive of a single night without you in my arms."

CHAPTER FOURTEEN

THE NEXT MORNING Jenna lay on her side watching Pete's chest rise and fall as he slept in her bed. She'd been watching him since before the sun came up, partially because she was still in shock that he was finally *in her bed* and partially because she couldn't fathom a time when they weren't together. They were so in sync with each other's thoughts and desires. Not only in the bedroom, but even at the barbecue last night. It was like Pete instinctively knew when she was chilly, and he wrapped his arms around her and held her close. When she was talking to Bella and Amy about her mother arriving in two days for a visit, he'd rubbed her shoulders, as if he knew the conversation was stressful for her. She'd never felt so comfortable with anyone, or with herself.

She cuddled up against his warmth, trying to move quietly so as not to wake Joey, who was sleeping on a doggie bed that Pete had brought with them. Pete was wearing only a pair of black boxer briefs, with the sheets bunched up around his hips. Jenna took full advantage, drinking in every inch of him while he was unaware. His shoulders and chest looked enormous as he lay on his back with his heels hanging off the end of the bed. She'd always known her cottage was small, but last night they'd begun making love in the living room and had to move into the bedroom for lack of space. He somehow magnified how small three hundred and fifty square feet really was.

He draped an arm over her back and pulled her against him. "How long are you going to stare at me?"

"Your eyes have been closed. How could you possibly know I was staring at you?"

"Babe, I can feel the heat of your stare almost as sharply as I can feel the heat of your body." He kissed her and pulled her on top of him. "That's better."

"How am I supposed to stalk you if you can tell when I'm doing it?"

"Stalk me?" He arched a brow, and he looked so damn sexy all sleepy she could barely stand it.

She kissed his chest. "Yeah, sneak peeks at you, take my fill of all these glorious muscles." She moved farther down his stomach and traced the ripples of his abs with her tongue and felt his hard length against her belly. She rolled down the edge of his skivvies, revealing the tip of his arousal. "And all this pleasure." She licked the tip of him, then drew down his skivvies and took all of him in her mouth, drawing a groan from Pete.

"Babe, you can take your fill..." He sucked in a breath. "Holy shit, Jenna."

His reaction spurred her on, and when he fisted his hands in her hair, she nearly scaled his body and mounted him like she'd said she'd wanted to do that afternoon in the library, but his reaction was too enjoyable to give up.

"Fair's fair," he said. "Believe me...Holy Christ...I'm going to take my fill when you're done."

Those were promises she couldn't wait to collect on.

AFTER PETE AND Jenna showered together, Jenna made coffee and toast while Pete scrambled eggs. The radio was on in the bedroom, and Jenna danced as she moved around the kitchen, humming as she spread Luscious Leanna's watermelon jam on the toast. Jenna tried to bump his hip with hers, but their height difference was too great. She nearly gave him a charley horse. He pulled her into a hug and laughed.

"Are you always this chipper in the morning?" He'd wanted to spend the day with Jenna, but he worried about smothering her.

"Most of the time, but I think this is the Pete afterglow." She pressed her hands to his waist and kissed his solar plexus, then pushed away to retrieve mugs and plates from the cabinets. She smiled up at him with so much warmth in her eyes that smothering didn't seem like it would be an issue.

Last night he'd seen the worry in her eyes, and he'd

heard it in her voice when she was talking about her mother coming to visit. Despite what he knew must be eating her up inside, she was humming and smiling like her life was peachy. Her mother was arriving tomorrow, and he wanted nothing more than to take her mind off of it for a while.

"I have a great idea. How about if we spend the day in Martha's Vineyard? I can reschedule the boat repair I have scheduled, and you said you weren't planning much today anyway."

Jenna turned with wide eyes. "Believe it or not, I've never been to Martha's Vineyard."

"I know. That's why I asked."

"You know?"

"Just because we weren't dating doesn't mean I didn't pay attention to the things you did and said."

"See? Just one more reason I'm drawn to you like fish to water. I'd love to go, but are you sure you can delay a boat repair? That sounds pretty important."

Her hair was still wet from their shower. He moved a few strands that were clinging to her chest over her shoulder and tucked her hair behind her ear.

"*You're* important, and we have a lot of years to make up for. I need to clean the pool here—it is Tuesday, after all—but then I'll clear my schedule and we can go." He wrapped his arms around her waist and kissed her again.

"Can we bring Joey?"

She and Pete had taken Joey for a walk earlier, after

they'd finally pried themselves from each other's arms and gotten up for the day. He loved that she thought of his adorable pup. "We can, but if you'd rather not, I'm sure I can wrangle someone to keep an eye on her."

Jenna crouched beside Joey and petted her head. "Aw, poor Joey. Look at her. She doesn't want to be pawned off on someone else." She kissed the pup's nose. "Do you, Joey? You want to come with us and spend the day in the sun, walking around, sniffing strangers and being too cute for words." Jenna tilted Joey's face up toward Pete. "Tell him, Joey. Tell Daddy you want to come with us."

As if on cue, Joey barked.

Pete lifted Jenna to her feet and kissed her. "Nothing would make me happier than spending the entire day with my two best girls." Pete didn't tell her that tonight was the annual Illumination Night on Martha's Vineyard, a night where all the lights in a neighborhood called the Campground were turned off and paper lanterns lit the streets and cottages. He knew Jenna would be blown away by the magical evening, and he couldn't wait to experience it with her.

Almost four hours later, after a forty-five-minute drive to Woods Hole and a ferry ride that took equally as long to reach the Vineyard, they parked Pete's truck and meandered through the crowded streets and quaint shops. Like many Cape towns, the shops were mostly shingle sided, and they were decorated with an island feel. Most boasted aged wooden floors, and some had narrow staircases that led up to a second floor. No matter what the store, Jenna wanted to explore every inch. Pete wasn't a big shopper, and he didn't care for crowds, but as they walked hand in hand beneath the summer sun, moving in and out of stores at Jenna's whim with Joey trotting happily by their side, he realized that it didn't matter where they were or what they were doing. Being with Jenna felt good.

Her eyes lit up as she inspected everything from knick-knacks to kitchen items. He took pleasure in the little things that were unique to Jenna—the way she squeezed his hand when she saw something she loved and how she slipped one finger into the waistband of his shorts and pressed her other hand to his abs when she wanted his attention. It felt like they'd been a couple forever, and he wished they had.

He wished he'd looked past everything else, and they'd come together before his mother had died, so Jenna could have known her. Hell, he wished for that time back so he and Jenna could have had time together before his father lost himself to the disease that changed both their lives.

Jenna sifted through sarongs in an eclectic little clothing shop, swooping one after another around her neck with dramatic flair as she pranced a short path in front of Pete, batting her eyelashes and putting her palms up toward the ceiling.

"Blue? Green? Yellow?" She fingered the edges of the colorful sarongs.

"I love the green."

She frowned. "I like the blue."

He laughed. Only Jenna would ask and then dispute the answer. "The blue is beautiful. It sets off your eyes."

Jenna wrinkled her brow. "But the yellow will go with my yellow bikini."

Pete reached for her hand and led her to the cashier. "We'll take all three." He pulled out his wallet.

"Oh, no." She began unwinding the vibrant material from her body. "I can't afford—"

Pete unwrapped the sarongs, folded them neatly, and set them on the desk beside the cash register. He handed his credit card to the cashier, a gray-haired woman with bright blue eyes and weathered cheeks.

"Pete, you can't buy all of them."

He draped an arm over her shoulder. "I think I just did."

"Petey…thank you." She hooked her finger in his shorts.

The nickname no longer struck him as out of place. It claimed him as *hers*, and he liked that.

THEY WALKED AROUND until the sun went down, and then they got takeout to eat in the park with Joey. It was intimate and romantic. Pete had ordered dinner for the two of them, and as he handed Jenna her dinner, she was surprised by what he'd chosen for her—oysters on the half shell and a chicken Caesar salad. Two of her favorite foods.

"How did you know exactly what I'd want?" She watched a smile curl his lips.

"I told you before, just because we weren't dating didn't mean I wasn't paying attention. I adore you, Jenna, and I guess that my mind must have known that before my heart caught on, or the other way around. You know what I mean." He leaned in for a kiss.

She thought she must have died and gone to heaven. All those years she thought he hadn't paid much attention to her, and meanwhile he was memorizing her likes and dislikes?

"What do you think of the Vineyard?" he asked.

"Amazing, but I'm glad this was my first time. Now we have something that's ours. Or at least in my memory it is." She put her hand on his thigh, worrying over the question she couldn't keep from asking. "Have you…taken many women here?" *What is wrong with me?*

"Eh, I guess I bring a different woman about every other week or so." He sipped his drink, and Jenna's heart sank.

He set his drink down and cupped her cheeks in his hands. "You're a goof. Do you think I'd take you someplace I made a habit out of taking other women? What do I have to do to prove how different you are?" He kissed her, and the *zing* Jenna had come to love warmed her all over. "The last time I was here was a few years ago with Sky. I brought her the summer after she graduated from college."

She poked him in the side. "Don't do that to me. In fact, if I ever ask you something stupid like that and the answer is not something I would want to hear, lie to me, okay?"

He shook his head. "No can do. I'm not a liar."

She loved that about him. They poured more water into Joey's water bowl and watched families stroll around the park.

"So, when are you going to fess up to turning off your hot water so I'd come over and fix it?"

She nearly choked on her drink. She swallowed the liquid and blinked away the surprise. "Excuse me? I didn't turn off my hot water."

He arched a brow. "Jenna, I was there, remember? I fixed it?"

"I swear I didn't do that. I even checked the fuse box to make sure it hadn't flicked off."

"Tripped." He flashed a sweet smile.

"Whatever. Do you really think I'd take a shower at Bella's if I could have—Oh my God." She narrowed her eyes. "We've been had."

"We have?"

"I didn't do it, but I'd bet a million dollars that Bella and Amy did. Or at least Bella. They were less than pleased when I asked Charlie out."

"Well, then, I'll have to thank them."

She remembered her towel falling and the way Pete had looked over her ass, all the while causing her entire body to catch flames. She thought she might just have to thank them, too.

"*I* wasn't pleased about you asking him out either."

She snuggled into his side. "Who are you kidding? If I hadn't asked him out, you might never have been interested in me."

"That's where you're wrong. I have always been interested in you. If I wasn't interested, would I know that your favorite color is orange? Or that the dinner we're eating is your favorite? Would I know that on Tuesday mornings you peek at me from around the side of your cottage? Or that you're afraid of sharks? Would I know that you secretly wish you could go out on the sand barge with the seals when they gather at low tide on the beach near P-town—regardless of the ten-thousand-dollar fine if you're caught?"

Holy cow. "Pete? How do you know all that?"

He ran his finger down her cheek. "Because during all those get-togethers, the only thing that interested me was you. I might look like I'm a million miles away, but my mind has always been on you, Jenna. Just you." He pressed his lips to hers in a sweet kiss.

"I never knew." Oh, how she wished she had. Maybe she wouldn't have been so nervous around him. "You said, *just me*, but at the Beachcomber you were all over that blonde."

Pete smiled and turned away.

"Oh God, this is one of those times when you should lie to me." Jealousy sliced through her.

Pete moved closer and set their food aside; then he pulled Jenna's legs over his and wrapped her in his arms. "Babe, I have some fessing up of my own to do, and it's a little embarrassing."

Jenna braced herself for a blow. "If you slept with her, please lie to me." She heard the fear in her own voice.

He shook his head. "She's only a friend, babe. But I did something that I probably shouldn't have. You were with that guy, and it made me jealous as hell."

"I like where this is going." Jenna smiled and ran her finger along his lower lip.

Pete's eyes went dark.

"Keep going." She could tell by the way his mouth twitched that he was embarrassed about whatever he was going to reveal, even if he was staring at her like he wanted to devour her.

He touched his forehead to hers. "I feel like a stupid teenager." He shook his head. "Here goes. I asked her to make you jealous so you would want me as badly as I wanted you."

Jenna threw her head back with a loud laugh. Her hand flew to her mouth. "*You* tried to make *me* jealous? Me? The woman who has been trying to get your attention forever?"

He looked away. "I'm not proud of it."

"Well, it worked. She basically told me that you were an animal in bed. I thought she'd slept with you, and between that and your comment about erotic, sensual sex…"

A coy grin curved his lips. "Promises, not comments. I got your attention."

She kissed his chin. "Petey, you had my attention the first time you cleaned the pool in that white tank top and black board shorts, with your John Lennon sunglasses."

Pete laughed. "You remember my round sunglasses?"

"There are so many things about you that I'll never forget. And the list just keeps getting longer and longer."

AN HOUR LATER they were standing at the edge of the crowded Tabernacle in the Campground neighborhood of Oak Bluffs, where Illumination Night was taking place. The Tabernacle was surrounded by small cottages decorated elaborately with flowers and brightly colored paper lanterns hanging from their eaves and off the porch railings. The cottages were built very closely together, boasting vibrant colors, peaks adorned with gingerbread, and decks complete with fancy balusters. Children played on the lawns, light sticks glowing like sabers in the darkness, as people of all ages sang and moved to the melody beneath dozens of paper lanterns that hung from the rafters and on the railings of the Tabernacle.

Pete watched Jenna's eyes widen as she took in the enormous wooden Tabernacle. A band played on a stage beneath the high ceiling, and the crowd began to sing "I've

Been Working on the Railroad." She gasped an excited breath, and he was glad that he hadn't ruined the surprise by telling her about it ahead of time. Her hand flew to her chest, and she opened her mouth to say something to Pete, who could do little more than beam at her delight. She didn't say a word. Her eyes shifted back to the crowd, and a few minutes later she joined the crowd in singing, "Someone's in the Kitchen with Dinah."

Jenna wrapped her arms around Pete's waist and gazed up at him. Joey wagged her tail at their feet. "What is all of this?"

"It's called Illumination Night. It's an annual event put on by the Camp Meeting Association. They don't publicize it to try to keep crowds to a minimum." He watched her as she turned slowly around, taking in the interesting architecture of the two-story cottages. "Back in the 1800s, when the Tabernacle was first built, Methodists gathered here and held their annual meetings. They camped back then, and over the years they replaced the campsites with these cottages."

"Why are the roads so narrow?"

"Because they were made to fit horse-drawn buggies."

The crowd sang "Yankee Doodle," and then the din of the crowd quieted, calling Jenna's attention back to the Tabernacle. The band silenced, and all eyes were drawn to the stage, where two men, one older and one about Pete's age, lit a paper lantern. As if the lighting of the lantern controlled the electricity in the entire neighborhood, as soon as the lantern was lit, all of the lights in the neighborhood went off. A collective gasp rose from the crowd as the paper lanterns bloomed to life, illuminating the Tabernacle, cottages, and streets in bubbles of color and magic.

Jenna inhaled loudly, her eyes opened wide as she tugged on Pete's shirt. "Petey, take a picture. Quick, before the lights go back on."

He already had his cell phone in hand, clicked a picture, and captured Jenna's excitement. He bent down so their cheeks were pressed together and snapped another picture; then he kissed her lips. Joey crawled up their legs and they crouched beside her, getting her in the shot. Jenna laughed and made faces as he snapped a few more; then her eyes grew serious and she pressed her small, soft hands to his cheeks.

"It's not this place that's magical, Pete. It's you. It's always been you."

CHAPTER FIFTEEN

THEY TOOK THE last ferry back to Woods Hole, then drove back toward Wellfleet. Joey was sprawled across Jenna's lap, and Jenna had a dreamy look in her eyes. Pete reached for her hand.

"Did you have fun today?"

She smiled and stroked Joey's back. "I had the most amazing day. You know how sometimes you want to savor every second of something? Sear it into your brain so ten years from now you remember more than just what you did, but how it smelled, the sounds around you, and the way the air felt? That's what I'm trying to do. Only instead of memorizing the heat of the sun, I keep feeling the brush of *us* whispering across my skin. I can't describe it, and I know it sounds strange, but…" She lifted a shoulder, as if that explained it all.

He brought her hand to his lips and kissed it. "It's not strange. I feel it, too. We're creating our own private history. Then years from now we'll look back and remember how it felt."

His cell phone vibrated, and Pete tensed. He reluctantly

released Jenna's hand and pulled the phone from his pocket. His father's name flashed on the screen. *Of all the goddamn nights.*

"I'm sorry, Jenna. It's my dad, and there's a good chance it's not going to be pretty."

She set her hand on his thigh. "History is rarely all pretty. Why should ours be any different?"

They drove the rest of the way to Pete's father's house in silence. His father lived on a quiet street of Cape-style homes, most of which were dark, as it was closing on ten thirty.

"Is this where you grew up?" Jenna asked as Pete parked the truck in his father's driveway.

"Yeah." Pete stepped from the truck and came around to open Jenna's door. Joey jumped out and ran up to the porch. Jenna turned to get out of the truck, and Pete stood blocking her way. He leaned forward and kissed her, despite the worry in his eyes. "Babe, you don't have to come inside. I appreciate your support, but really. It's okay if you stay here."

Jenna touched his cheek. "I'm dealing with a mother who dresses like she's twenty and acts about the same. There's no difference, Pete. Your situation might be more dire, but part of being in a relationship is helping each other, and if that meant only when times were good, then we'd never grow together as a couple."

He searched her eyes, as if he was debating if he should move out of her way and allow her to go inside. "It's embarrassing for you to see him this way."

"Then I'll stay in another room. I just want you to know I'm there with you."

Pete touched his forehead to hers. "I don't know what I did to deserve you, but I'd gladly do it again and again."

Jenna followed him and Joey inside. Pete led her into a dark living room and turned on a lamp, revealing a well-loved sofa, fireplace, and a room full of family photographs.

"Do you mind waiting in here?" Pete's shoulders rode high, knotted with tension.

"Not at all." She watched him leave the room with Joey on his heels.

Some houses smelled of home cooking, baked goods, or cleaning agents, while others smelled of warm family memories. Pete's father's house smelled of sadness. The air was heavy, not stale, but on its way there. It felt empty and lonely, and on top of that, Jenna felt pain hanging in the air. She listened to the sound of Pete's voice coming from somewhere down the hall. She couldn't make out what he was saying, but she caught his empathetic tone. She perused the photographs on the wall. Although she'd met Pete's father in the hardware store, she'd never met Pete's siblings or his mother. The family resemblance was strong among the boys, each tall, dark, and chiseled, with brooding eyes and broad chests. His sister, however, looked different from the others, less serious—probably because she was so young—with large, round eyes and a soft chin. She had full lips, and her hair was a shade lighter than Pete's and hung to the middle of her back.

She followed a trail of pictures that marked the boys' journey from lanky and hairless kids to thickly muscled stalks of power, while Sky remained lithe and feminine. The boys had their arms slung over one another's shoulders in one picture, and in another Pete and another brother each held up fish, still attached to their fishing lines, proud grins on their lips. The other boys were in the background, hip deep in a pond, fishing rods in hand. Sky was sitting on the sand off to the right behind a woman whom she resembled and could only be their mother. Pete had her eyes, and the way she was smiling at Sky spoke of her love for her.

Jenna turned at the sound of footsteps on hardwood and Joey's nails tapping across the floor. She peered down the hall and saw the back of the two men, Pete's arm securely around his father's thick waist, his head bowed, as he helped him toward another room.

"Come on, Pop. That's it. I've got you." Pete's voice was compassionate and quiet.

"Bea? Where's she, Peter?" His father's words slurred together, and Jenna's heart squeezed.

Joey padded toward Jenna, and Pete turned, his eyes catching hers with a heartbroken expression. She wanted to go to him, help him, and tell him it was going to be okay. She wanted to help tuck his father into bed and rub a damp cloth over his father's head, assuring him that he, too, would be okay. A chill ran down her spine at the immense struggle she saw in Pete's eyes, and she knew she could make no such promise. This was a battle his father had to *want* to win, and no matter how much she wanted to help Peter get his father the help he so desperately needed, this struggle was between father and son. She felt love fill the hallway, bonding Pete and his father in a way that could only come from years of love and respect—and she felt the pressure of the alcohol forcing its way between them, doing everything within its power to create an even greater divide between father and son.

They left a while later and drove to Seaside in silence. Pete's forehead was etched deep with worry. When Jenna reached for his hand, he blessed her with a try at a smile—it faltered as quickly as it had been forced to appear.

"I'm sorry you had to see that, but I was glad you insisted on being there. Thank you." Pete parked in her driveway and came around to open her door. Joey jumped out of the truck and sniffed around his feet.

"Don't be sorry for me, Pete. I feel bad for you."

They went inside, and Joey ran straight to her puppy bed, walked in circles, then flopped down on her belly with an exhausted huff. Pete sat on the sofa, his long, powerful legs stretched across the floor. He reached for Jenna's hand, and as she lowered herself beside him, he lifted her onto his lap. She circled his neck with her arms and ran her fingers through the back of his hair. Their foreheads touched, and

Pete's hand slid from her waist to her cheek. He tilted her head and brought his lips to hers, angling her jaw so they could each take more of the other in a kiss that somehow felt loving and tender at the same time. She wanted, *needed*, to take away his pain and replace it with the feel of her body, the sense of her love, if only for a while. To be his in any way he wished, to love, cherish, possess, until there was no room for sadness or worry.

A deep moan escaped his lungs, filling hers, as he pulled her dress over her head and bared her of all but her lacy black lingerie. Pete unhooked her bra and tossed it aside. Jenna arched back, giving him full access to her breasts, her heart, and he was quick to find the respite he needed. Pete's hands moved frantically over her heated skin. When his mouth met her breast, Jenna gripped his shoulders, clawing with the need to erase the bad memory of what he'd just gone through. His teeth grazed over her sensitive flesh, and in the next breath, his hands gripped her waist and shifted her beneath him. He tore off her panties with a dark, possessive look in his eyes as he stripped himself bare, then came to her side. Jenna reached for him, wrapping her fingers around his hard shaft as she took him in her mouth. Pete tangled his hands in her hair and helped her efforts. She took him deep, felt him swell, ready and eager for her.

"Jenna." A plea, as he tore her lips from him and shifted her onto her back.

He came down upon her and took her hands in his as his

thick, powerful thighs spread her legs wide and he thrust into her. His fingers laced hers, holding them beside her head as he buried himself with one deep thrust after another, sending hot streaks of lust through Jenna's body. Her insides coiled like a snake itching to strike. His lips crashed down against hers, taking their love deeper, pinning her beneath him in a way that should have felt too rough, but instead felt all-consuming, passionate, and thrilling. Jenna could barely breathe—Pete breathed for her, long breaths from his lungs to hers, as her mind lost its grasp and her thoughts webbed together in a mash of elicit thoughts. She drew her head back, panting, needing to free her emotions.

"Pete…Oh God, Pete. I love you."

She slammed her eyes shut as her body bucked and thrust beneath him, taking him deeper, pulsating, squeezing him into his own fierce release. He spoke, but her mind was numb with lust. His words circled around her.

"Love you…Whole life…"

Every fiber of her body was on fire, and she wasn't done. She needed more of him, and as he came down from his own release, he moved slowly, lovingly inside her, until he was potent and desirous once again.

He loved her slowly, deeply, his hands pressed against her sides, slipped to her hips. He stilled them both as he arched up and drank her in. "You're beautiful, but you're so much more, Jenna. I love making love to you. Not just your body—*you*."

He wrapped his arms beneath her, holding her as tight and as close as two beings were physically able. His cheek pressed to hers, his hot breath stroking her need.

"I love you, Jenna. I love you so damn much."

A whisper in her ear, a promise, a confession.

Her throat thickened as his admission vibrated through her, rooting itself deep in her heart.

CHAPTER SIXTEEN

PETE HADN'T EVER thought much about love or marriage. He'd attended friends' weddings over the years, and he'd still never given the idea a second thought. He watched Jenna standing with her hands on her hips, her face pinched into a scrutinizing leer as she stared into her closet Wednesday morning. *How did I go so long without you?* With Jenna, he was possessive and jealous. She had her own quirks, but somehow they worked well together. He might think he was nuts if they hadn't been silently courting each other for years, but during those years their emotions took hold and finally had the space to bloom.

"How can it be that difficult to pick a pair of sandals?" he said with a tender smile as he touched her cheek. He loved that she went to such great lengths to make sure things were just as she liked them to be. He knew she was nervous about her mom's arrival, but he also knew that she took great pains like this every time she dressed. Bella and the others often teased her about it, but watching her in action gave him a whole new appreciation for Jenna and what she needed to feel comfortable, and he loved her even more for her Jennaisms. He couldn't believe he'd almost let her slip away. It killed him to think he could have lost her before they'd ever had a chance, and he'd do anything—everything—within his power to ensure she knew how much he adored her.

Jenna slid her eyes to Joey, lying on her doggie bed a few feet away. "How can I explain this to a man?" She wore her green bikini and a pair of cutoffs, and she looked amazing. Her lower lip came out in a little pout that drew his arms around her. "I need to match my cover-up to my flip-flops. And it's very important. If I pick the wrong ones, I might realize it when it's too late and I won't be able to change them."

"Why won't you?"

She sighed, with the cutest pout on her lips. "Because what if we're already out?"

He wrapped his arms around her. "So we come back for them. I will never understand how that brilliant mind of yours works, but I love how you see things that no one else does. The beauty of rocks, the way you pull things together until they calm your obsessions. I want to be your obsession, Jenna." He smiled—though he was only partially teasing.

"You have been for years." She went up on tiptoes, and he met her halfway for a sweet kiss. "So you don't think my OCD will drive you crazy?"

"Never."

"I'll make us late to get-togethers."

He shrugged. "Being on time is for losers."

"I'll make you come back home if I decide my earrings aren't the right ones, even if we're already late."

He kissed her forehead. "And I'll turn the truck around and come back without hesitation. Right, Joey?" He leaned down and pet the pup's head. Joey rolled over so he could scratch her belly.

"I'll organize your entire house and you won't be able to find anything." She bit her lower lip, her cheeks plumping with her smile.

"I'll make you a key today." He planned on paying a visit to his father's store today, and he'd make her a key while he was there. He sealed his promise with a kiss.

Jenna took his hand and led him into the living room. Sun streaked through the window, warming the room. Pete's chest tightened with the memory of their lovemaking on the sofa and their admissions of their feelings.

She took her keys from the hook by the door and removed the key to her cottage. "Make one of these for you, too. But I will warn you, there's a price to pay."

He arched a brow.

"Darn it. I wish I could think of something sexy to say."

"Baby, you don't have to *say* anything. You're always sexy." After another heart-thumping kiss, Jenna returned to her closet to choose a pair of sandals while Pete cooked breakfast.

She came out of the bedroom wearing a white tank top

over her bikini. She flung her arms up in the air and thrust her hip to the side.

"Ta-da!" She lifted each foot and wiggled her toes.

His eyes never left her face. "Sheer perfection."

She swatted his stomach, then reached into the cabinet for plates. "I meant the sandals, not me."

"Wait, you have feet?" He dodged another swat and glanced at her tan leather sandals with white embellishments. "They're perfect, too." He filled their plates with scrambled eggs and toast.

"What time is your mom arriving?"

Jenna's smile faltered. "Soon."

He reached for her hand and felt tension in her movements as he held her against him. She took a deep breath and melted against him. Tension relieved. He loved that he could have that effect on her.

"Babe, if you want me to stick around for the morning, I'm happy to." He'd planned on talking to his father this morning with the hopes of convincing him to get help without having to force the issue, but if Jenna needed him, he'd remain by her side.

"I'm fine. Really." Her words were stilted.

She was definitely not fine.

He kissed her forehead. "Every time I've seen you with your mom, you got along well. Is she really that different now?" He'd met her mother several times over the years. She tended to dote on Jenna, and her pride in her daughter was apparent in the things she said and the look in her eyes. He couldn't imagine how much things had changed for Jenna to look so conflicted. Then again, he never would have imagined his father changing so much, either.

"We still get along."

"Why do you look so worried? I know she's going through a hard time, but you were so sure of how we needed to be there for our parents." He ran his hands along her hips, letting her know she wasn't alone with her worries. "What are you *not* telling me?"

Jenna lowered her eyes to his chest. "She's acting really weird. She talks about things I definitely don't want to talk about with my mother, it's…nothing. Forget it. It's nothing."

That *nothing* was filled with *everything*. He lifted her into his arms and set her on the counter, then stood between her legs so they were eye to eye. "Babe, you don't have to tell me what's bothering you, but I'm here if you want to. Whatever it is, it can't be that bad."

Her brows drew together. "I'm fine. Really. She crosses lines these days, so I'll just be careful how much I tell her." She picked up a fork and filled it with egg, then offered it to Pete with a smile that didn't quite reach her eyes. "Let's eat before she gets here."

They took their breakfasts onto the deck, and within minutes, Bella, Amy, and Leanna appeared, mugs in hand, wearing their bathing suits under sundresses. Amy dropped to her knees and loved up Joey.

"It's about time." Bella sat across from Pete. "Usually Jenna's up early." She wiggled her eyebrows.

Amy swatted her leg and then went back to petting Joey. "Ignore her. She has no manners."

Pete met Bella's teasing stare with one of his own. "She *was* up early." Jenna's cheeks pinked up as she set her hand on his thigh.

"Finally, a man who can give it right back to you, Bella." Leanna sipped her coffee and smiled at Bella from behind her mug.

"Ha-ha. I'm so glad you two are finally together. I swear, Pete. I thought we were going to have to hang a banner out front spelling it out for you." Bella held her palms up, pressing them forward with each word. "Jenna. Likes. Pete."

He laughed and finished his breakfast.

"Jenna, I was thinking that we should take your mom over to the library with us today." Amy glanced at Jenna's plate with an arched brow. "You cooked?"

"Petey did."

"If I call you Petey, will you cook for me, too?" Leanna asked.

"No." Jenna leaned in to his side. "I told him that I wasn't the best cook around."

He draped an arm over her shoulder. "But you're the best at a million other things. Teamwork." He shrugged to make it seem like he was well versed in relationships, when the truth was Jenna made everything feel natural. They'd fallen into sync so easily that he was beginning to think he wasn't meant to have a meaningful relationship until they came together.

"Aw, you guys are so cute." Amy sighed.

Pete rose to carry their empty plates inside, and Jenna reached for his hand.

"I'll get them. You cooked; just relax."

He smiled down at her. "It's okay. Visit with your friends. This will only take me a few minutes, and then I need to take off." He glanced out at the road. "I was hoping to see your mom before I left, but I can catch up with you guys later." Joey followed him inside the house.

Pete glanced out the window above the sink as he washed the dishes. Jenna tucked her feet up under her as she leaned forward and whispered to Amy and Bella. He couldn't hear a word they said, but the smile on Jenna's lips told him that she was as happy as he was. After he washed the dishes, he went into the bedroom to gather his things in his overnight bag. Joey trailed his every step. Jenna had made the bed with hospital corners, and it made him laugh a little under his breath. *Jenna.* Several paperbacks were stacked neatly, and upon closer inspection, alphabetized by author, on the bedside table, and he noticed that even the rocks she kept on the floor by the door were perfectly lined up. He grabbed his bag and went into the bathroom to collect his toiletries.

Jenna was on the deck with her mother when he went

outside, bag in hand, Joey on his heels. Gina was taller than Jenna by a few inches. She wore her hair shoulder length, and she wore a tight red dress that barely covered her thighs. Jenna had mentioned that she was going through a hard time and dressing younger, and still Pete had to mask his surprise with a fake cough. If the short dress wasn't enough to tip him off, the heavy makeup on a face that he'd always seen almost bare would have.

"Pete? I didn't know you were here." Gina embraced him, and her smile lit up when she noticed Joey sniffing around her feet. She crouched to pet her.

He shot Jenna a look over her shoulder. *Didn't know? What the hell is going on?* It never dawned on him that Jenna wouldn't tell her about them.

"Were you fixing something?" Gina's eyes bounced between Jenna and Pete as she ruffled Joey's head.

Jenna nibbled on her lower lip and set a pleading gaze on Pete. Bella and Amy had the same look in their eyes. He got the hint, but it pissed him off—and confused the hell out of him.

"Yeah. The sink." He touched Jenna's arm. "You should be all set now. Call me if you need anything."

Jenna let out a breath. "Okay. Thanks, Pete."

He nodded and hoped like hell her mother didn't see the confusion or the anger he felt. He climbed into his truck after Joey jumped in, and a minute later Jenna was standing at the window of his truck.

"Pete," she whispered. "I'm sorry. I didn't plan on not telling her, but she started right up with, *Where are the hot men?*" Jenna let out a frustrated breath. "I didn't want her getting into our business."

He didn't know what to say. He was hurt and angry, but the sincere, worried look in Jenna's eyes softened his annoyance. He glanced at Amy and Bella ushering Jenna's mother into the cottage.

"You could have warned me, babe." He stroked her cheek.

"I'm sorry." Jenna put her hand on his. "It was a split-second decision. I just…She talks about sex and stuff, Pete. She's not like she used to be, and I don't want her in that part of our lives."

"Babe, I get it, but I'm not a liar or a sneak. I can't look into your mother's eyes and pretend I'm not falling for her daughter. You're either all in or you're not. I'm all in. Can't you just define boundaries? Tell her what aspect of our lives are off-limits?"

Jenna nodded, but the worry in her eyes seemed to magnify with his words.

"Jenna, is there something else going on?"

Her mother came back outside laughing with Bella and Amy. Jenna took a step back from the truck. He had half a mind to step from the truck and tell her mother himself, but again, Jenna's pleading look kept him in line.

He ran his hand through his hair and spoke quietly. "Do

whatever you need to, but after all this time, the last thing I want to do is pretend you're not everything to me."

JENNA SPENT THE day with her mother and Amy at the beach. Her mother wore enormous sunglasses and a bathing suit with cutouts at the waist. Gina Ward was petite like Jenna, without the mammoth-sized bust, and Jenna had to admit that she looked great for a woman in her late fifties. But she lowered her sunglasses and leered at every guy who walked by, and Jenna was mortified. She'd tried to dissuade her, but her mother's retorts came quick and sharp. *Oh, please. They know they're hot.* Or, *I'm not doing anything more than looking. Maybe you should look, too.* Or the one that grated on Jenna's nerves the most. *I settled for years with your father. He never looked that good a day in his life. No more settling for me.*

Her mother's comments about her father put Jenna on the defensive. It was a struggle not to snap at her and remind her that she'd once loved everything about him, from his paunchy stomach to his dry personality and silver hair. But she knew from experience over the weeks before she came to the Cape that comments like that would only feed her mother's venom toward him and put Jenna in the middle of an even more uncomfortable situation.

Jenna had been mulling over what Pete said all day, and

she knew he was right. She needed to tell her mother about their relationship, and she could define boundaries with her mother. She had to, and she wanted to, but every time she tried to bring up Pete, her mother would point out another twentysomething guy on the beach, or bring up a memory of a guy she dated before she'd met Jenna's father, and Jenna held back.

When they arrived back at Jenna's cottage in the afternoon, Jenna promised herself she'd say something.

"That was such a fun afternoon," her mother said as she carried her beach bag to the deck. "Jenna, you're here with all these available men. I just don't get why you never seem to date."

"Mom, I have to—"

Her mother set her bag on the table on the deck and interrupted her. "And Peter?" She fanned her face. "He's a doll, baby. If one of you ladies don't go after him, I will."

Amy choked on her water, and Jenna elbowed her.

"Mom! He's at least twenty years younger than you." *And he's mine!*

"That didn't stop your father." Her mother took her bag and went into the cottage, leaving Jenna to stew on her words.

"I thought you were exaggerating about her," Amy said. "But she was like a woman in heat on the beach. I swear she said something about every man who walked by."

"No shit." Jenna's insides were simmering. She felt as

though she was on the verge of blowing up, and it took all of her efforts to remain calm. She stomped back to the car with Amy by her side and grabbed the beach chairs from the trunk. She reminded herself that what her mother was doing was a hundred times less painful than what Pete was going through with his father.

"How am I going to tell her about Pete? You heard her on the beach, talking about all those guys. I don't even want her *thinking* about Pete that way."

Amy laughed. "Too late. She clearly has thought about him in that way already, so if I were you, I'd nip it in the bud."

"Right. I'll get right on that." Jenna rolled her eyes. "Library in an hour?"

"Sounds good."

PETE HELPED HIS father stock the shelves with a shipment of paint. His father had been busy with customers when Pete arrived earlier in the day, so Pete had gone to work on a boat repair at the marina. He'd needed the time to calm down anyway, as he was still upset over Jenna keeping their relationship from her mother—even after he'd confided in her about his father. And the fact that she hadn't told him she'd done it made it even worse. He knew she had her reasons, and by the time he returned to his father's store a few hours after lunch, he was pretty much over it, but he worried about her. Whatever she wasn't sharing with him about her mother was obviously eating away at her, and he could only hope she'd grow to trust him enough to open up. He sent her a text before heading into the hardware store. He knew she didn't carry her cell phone, but she'd promised to check her messages when she was back at the cottage.

Hey, babe. Sorry I was upset. Do whatever you feel is right. I'm not going anywhere. Miss you.

He noticed that his father was moving slower than normal, an indication that he'd had very little sleep last night. That was okay. Pete hadn't had a lot either, and he was thankful his father hadn't called in the middle of the night. He treasured the night he'd had with Jenna. His mind drifted to making love to Jenna in her cottage, and his body went hot. He struggled to push the lustful thoughts away, scrubbing his face, focusing on Joey as she sniffed around the store, and finally turned his attention back to his father.

"Pop, can we sit down for a minute?"

His father looked at him out of the corner of his eyes while he lifted a can of paint to the shelf. "I've got work to do."

"Yeah? So do I. It'll only take a minute." He knew this wasn't going to be easy, and he hated how his stomach clenched tight at the prospect of bringing up his father's drinking, but he had to try.

"I've got three more boxes in the back to unload." His

father wouldn't meet his gaze. He rubbed his hands on his faded jeans and pulled at his leather belt. It was the same belt he'd worn for as long as Pete could remember. His father was a creature of habit—and Pete hoped his drinking was a habit he could break.

"Luckily you've got enough paint on the shelves for the next hour. Come on, Pop. Five minutes." Pete arched a brow and set a hand on his father's shoulder. He felt his father exhale. A reluctant acceptance of the inevitable.

"Fine. Five minutes," he grumbled under his breath as he ran his eyes over Pete's face. "You look different."

"Yeah, so do you."

His dad laughed. "Nothing different in this old man, but you? You've got a spark in your eyes."

He was surprised to hear that when he felt like his body was on fire and every nerve was strung tight.

"Sky called me last night," his father said.

Pete drew his brows together. "Yeah? What did she want?" They'd never discussed the fact that Pete protected Sky from his father's drinking, and Pete wondered if his father had figured it out. He'd have to be blind not to notice how many times Pete had swept Sky away to his house under the pretense of wanting to spend more time with her rather than have her spend the night at his father's house.

"She said she's thinking of coming for a visit." His father rubbed his chin.

"It'd be nice to see her," Pete said to assuage his father,

and made a mental note to call Sky again. He thought he'd taken care of this little visit.

"Well, looks like we may have company." His father's eyes drifted to the photograph of Pete's mother beneath the counter, pushing Pete's mind back to the reason he'd come.

He'd thought about how to bring up his father's drinking a million times throughout the morning and finally decided the best tactic was indirect.

"Pop, I met someone."

Neil smiled and lifted his hands in the air. "Finally. I was getting worried about you."

Pete shook his head, agitation dulling his father's jest. "I go out with women all the time." *I just don't see them more than a few times.* "I didn't just meet her, but we just started dating. You know her. Jenna Ward."

"Oh." His father raised his brows. "Jenna Ward. I always liked Jenna. What took you so damn long?"

"My life isn't exactly conducive to long-term relationships." He held his father's gaze and saw discomfort skate across his face as he shifted his eyes away. "Pop, we need to talk about this. I really like her, and I can't keep coming over at all hours of the night to take care of you."

"I don't need you to come over." His father waved a dismissive hand and stepped away.

"Pop." He followed Neil back to the paint aisle and watched as his father began stocking the shelves again. Pete put his hand on his father's arm, stopping it in midair. "Pop, this isn't going to go away by ignoring it."

His father pulled his arm from his grasp and set his eyes on the paint can, his jaw set firm. Pete knew he was raging his own silent battle, and he felt guilt grip him again. When Neil raised his eyes, they were narrow, determined.

"I love you, Pete, but why can't you do as your brothers and sister do and go live your life and let me live mine?"

"Let you…Pop, really? Is that how you see this? As me messing with your life? You know why they let you live your life? Because it's easier, and because you call me, Pop, not them. *Me*." Anger brewed in Pete's gut. "The last thing any of them need is to have their lives fucked up by this nightmare."

His father fisted his hands, and his cheeks reddened. Those were the only visible indications that he'd heard Pete's words. With a deep exhalation, he calmly went back to shelving the paint.

"You've always been afraid to commit to a woman, Pete. It sounds like I'm a good excuse for you not to."

Pete ground his teeth together to keep from yelling. "You know what, Pop? I'm not afraid to commit to Jenna. I already have, but I can't live a normal life when I have to come drag your drunken ass into bed every night. Mom's gone, Pop. She's not coming back, and this double life you're living? She'd be ashamed of it." *Fuck*. They were the last words he'd expected—or wanted—to say, even if he meant every word.

The color drained from Neil's face. He set a hand on a shelf, as if Pete's words hit with the impact of a bullet and he needed the shelf to remain erect.

Pete grabbed his arm. "I'm sorry. I didn't mean that."

His father shook his head, and when he looked up, his eyes had turned to liquid steel, but his tone was calm and even. "Son, I think you'd better leave."

Like hell. The can of worms was open and Pete wasn't about to stop there. "No, Pop, I'm not leaving. We need to talk about this, even if it's difficult. I worry about you."

"You have no idea what it's like to lose the person you loved most in this world, and I pray to God that you never do. I know you worry about me, and God knows I love you for it. But do yourself a favor, Peter. Go live your life, and stay the hell out of mine." His voice was as icy as his words, and when he walked away, Pete felt his heart split down the middle. Living his own life sounded easy, even doable. But he could no sooner turn his back on his father than he could walk away from Jenna.

"This isn't the end, Pop."

His father stilled.

"She was my mother, and she'd be ashamed of me if I didn't try to help you. And whether you choose to remember it or not, you have kids who love you, and you owe us more than this."

His father's neck bowed, but he didn't turn to face Pete. He stood still, staring at the floor, and Pete couldn't imagine what was going through his head.

"I'm not giving up on you." The promise sailed heated and honestly from Pete's lips. "You have a lot of years left. Years to refit boats with me, years to meet your future grandchildren. Mom died, Pop. You didn't."

CHAPTER SEVENTEEN

WHEN JENNA WAS young, her mother volunteered in the elementary school library, and later, in the town library. Now Jenna watched her mother sorting through books and chatting with the other men and women library volunteers who were closer to her mother's age. She pictured her mother as the person she'd been before her father had sent her world spinning with the news of his impending marriage. She missed that person, and she hoped like hell she wasn't gone forever.

Amy sidled up to Jenna, her eyes on Jenna's mom. "Even though she's acting weird, it's really good to see your mom. I missed her."

"I still miss her," Jenna admitted.

"Aw, Jenna. She'll be back to her old self in no time." Amy patted Jenna's shoulder. "This is a phase, like when a man goes through a midlife crisis. Did you tell her about Pete yet?"

Jenna sighed. She'd received a sweet text from Pete saying to do what felt right and that he wasn't going anywhere, but she knew it was wrong to keep their relationship a secret.

"No, but I need to. She's talking about going to drag queen karaoke tonight in P-town, and I want to ask Pete to join us. Is that awful of me? Should I give her all of my attention? I'm so torn. I know she's only doing this because she's hurt over my dad getting remarried—speaking of a midlife crisis." She rolled her eyes. She had no idea if her father was going through a midlife crisis or if he really loved the woman he was marrying, and she didn't really care either way. She just wanted her parents to be happy, and she didn't want to be part of defining how that happened.

"I wish your father would just wake up and realize he's made a mess of things and fix it," Amy said.

Jenna crossed her arms and narrowed her eyes in her mother's direction. "You don't really think she'd take him back? After all this time? I think she'd feel humiliated after he's been with someone so young."

Amy shrugged. "Love's a powerful thing."

You're telling me. Jenna thought of waking up in Pete's arms, and the intimate things he'd shared with her and said to her over the past few days. It wasn't fair to Pete, or to herself, to act as though they weren't in love. *In love.* She was definitely, one hundred percent, in love with Pete, and as she watched her mother heading in their direction, she drew in a deep breath and prepared to do what she should have done at the cottage.

"Speaking of love." Jenna nodded to her mother. "I guess I better come clean about Pete."

"That's my cue to take off. Good luck." Amy hurried to another table and went back to sorting and pricing books.

"Well, that was nice. It was refreshing to be with people my own age and not feel like I had something to prove." She looked fondly at the group she'd just been talking with. "Thanks for bringing me with you today. At home I feel like I have to prove something to my friends because, before they were my friends, they were *our* friends. There's a whole different dynamic."

Something to prove? She'd never considered that her mother might be facing such pressure. "I'm sorry you're going through that, Mom."

Jenna's mother patted her hair. "How are you, sweetheart? You look a little worried."

You could say that. "I'm good."

She brushed Jenna's hair from her eyes. "I do love your hair this way. It's less severe. Sexier."

"Mom. It's weird to hear you talk about things that are sexy."

"Oh, honey. Please. You're a grown woman."

"Yes, but you're still my mother." *And Dad's still my father. And Pete's the man I'm in love with.* She didn't know what was worse, knowing her mother was comparing young men to her father or worrying her mother would say things about having sex with Pete. Jenna took a deep breath and took her mother's hand in hers.

"Can we go outside and talk?" They went out the back

door and walked through the lush, flowering garden behind the library. Jenna's stomach fluttered nervously. She sat on an iron bench and patted the seat beside her.

"Sit with me, Mom."

"It's lovely back here, isn't it? I miss coming up during the summers, and I really enjoyed working in the library. Maybe I should think about going back to work."

"That would probably be good for you, Mom. Then you'd get your mind off of…" *Shit.*

"Your father?"

She said it so matter-of-factly, without the venom that usually laced anything having to do with him, that Jenna had to take a second look at her.

"Yeah. Dad."

Her mother patted her leg. "Sweetie, I wanted to talk to you about that whole situation. I'm thinking of selling the house."

Jenna's eyes opened wide. "Your house?" Jenna wasn't sure *she* was ready for her mother to sell the house she grew up in. Selling the house would signify the end of what was. *Or maybe the beginning of what is yet to come.*

"Well, I can't exactly sell your house, now, can I?" She smiled, and it was sincere and reminiscent of the genuine smiles Jenna knew so well and missed so much.

Gina's smiles had changed dramatically over the last few weeks. They'd become a little conniving, and it was disconcerting. This smile softened the discomfort that Jenna had begun to associate with spending time with her mother.

"No, I guess you can't. But where would you live?" Jenna watched a car drive by, then turned her attention back to her mother. She had a solemn look in her eyes, and instead of the bright lipstick she'd been wearing lately, her mother's lips were natural, her cheeks pink from lying out in the sun. Without the mask of heavy makeup, fine lines were evident around her mouth and puckered around the creases of her eyes. Despite the signs of age, she looked beautiful.

Her mother shrugged. "I'm not sure, but your father is moving on, and being in the house we shared makes it terribly hard for me to do the same." She smoothed the front of her shorts. "I know I've been…different lately."

Jenna arched a brow, wondering why, if she knew she'd been acting different, she didn't stop herself.

"This whole thing has been an eye-opener, Jenna. I was so shocked by your father getting remarried. Somehow even this long after the divorce, it really threw me for a loop that he's replacing our marriage with a new one. Our relationship was *replaceable*. That's a big pill to swallow. I guess I went a little nutty. I'm still going a little nutty."

Jenna set her hand on her mother's hand. "You're not nutty, Mom. You're just confused."

"That's just it. I'm not at all confused." Her mother pulled her shoulders back, and her eyes became serious. "I know you think I am. I even know I'm driving you crazy with the way I'm dressing and the way I'm acting, but honestly, it's the only way for me to move forward."

Jenna covered her face with her hands. "Ugh." She dropped her hands and had to laugh. "You know you're acting weird and you think it's a good thing? And you knew you were driving me crazy and you didn't tell me that you weren't losing your mind?"

"Oh, honey. I'm not sure how to explain this to you. But the best way I can is that sometimes we put ourselves into these molds when a period in our life requires it. Like when you're deep into the throes of motherhood and your personal life gets put on hold. Or when you're building a career and nothing but climbing that silly ladder matters. And then we wake up one day, and we realize that we had no idea who we were *before* we got into that mold. It turns out, it's not so easy to move between them, only no one warns you of that when you're young." A breeze swept through the garden, rustling the purple, yellow, and white flowers beside them.

Gina set her eyes on Jenna. "This is your warning, honey. We have to adapt to certain phases, but it's not easy to keep from getting lost in them. This attitude adjustment of mine is my way of kicking myself in the rear to try and remember who I really am."

"But aren't you embarrassed by...?"

"By how I dress and how I act? No. I'm not embarrassed. *You* are, and I understand that, but I never realized *how* embarrassed you were until this morning."

"This morning?"

"Oh, honey. Do you really think I'm blind? Pete had an overnight bag in his hand, not a tool box, and last I looked, you didn't have a dog, but you have a dog bed in your bedroom." She smiled and touched Jenna's hand. "I also saw how upset it made him when you tried to cover up whatever is going on between you two, and that's when I realized that while I was busy finding myself, I was losing you."

"You're not losing me." She hadn't realized how true the words were until she refuted them. She'd been putting distance between her and her mother, not returning her texts and calls right away. Her mother was right; she was losing her.

"Yes, I was. I was pushing you away by trying to be something I wasn't, and I understand that, but I need you to understand that I'm not trying to be someone else. I'm trying to figure out who I really was, who I am, and trying out lots of things. But, baby girl, the last thing I want to do is to ruin things between us. I know I've been leaning on you a lot lately, and I'm sorry. It isn't fair. You were so damn willing to be there for me before the summer, and as awful as it sounds, I was broken, Jenna. I needed that."

Jenna's throat thickened with guilt. "It's not awful. You're my mom. I'd do anything for you."

"I know you would." She put her arm around Jenna and pulled her closer. "But you're my daughter, not my parent, and you have a life to live, too."

"I'm *finally* living my life." Thinking of Pete, Jenna

couldn't repress her smile.

"Oh, Jenna. You've always been living your life. You're just living your life with the man you've been crushing on for years on end. I was afraid he'd never come around."

"Crushing on?" Jenna laughed. Dreaming of. Fantasizing over. Both were more accurate. "I wasn't sure he ever would either. I asked out another guy, and that got his attention."

"Why is it that men need a threat to realize what they have?" Her mother's eyes saddened.

"Mom, I'm sorry about Dad."

She squeezed Jenna's hand. "So am I, honey. I loved him. I *love* him. I'll never stop loving him, and I'll never replace him. You know what I said about it being hard to break out of the molds from different phases of our lives?" She didn't wait for Jenna to answer. "Well, I knew things weren't good between your father and me for a very long time. I just didn't know how to fix them. I was comfortable in our life, and your father wanted to travel and see the world. It's like one day he woke up and realized that we were on the downhill side of our lives, and he wanted to experience more of what life had to offer, not just wait for it to end." She shrugged. "I was too content. I was afraid to break out of the mold."

"So that's why you're doing it now? Breaking out of the mold?"

"I guess. I don't really know. I know I say things about your father that I shouldn't. I'm just hurt, and I'm brokenhearted, and it's not fair to you. You love your father, as you should, but it hurts to know that I could have changed things and I lost my chance." Her mother looked away, but not before Jenna noticed her damp eyes.

"Mom, have you talked to Dad about this? Does he know you're trying to change now?" Could they reconcile? It was a strange idea to ponder, since her father was about to be married to Cara, but Jenna felt a flutter of hope in her chest.

"Your father and I are close, Jenna. We talk often."

"You do?" How could she not know that?

"True love doesn't just wash away because you're bored."

"But you got divorced. It's been two years."

"True. Your father is happy with his new tart."

"*Mom*."

"Sorry. She's actually a nice woman, and she makes him happy. We'll never lose what we had. They're great memories, but he did the right thing. He took control of his life, and now it's time for me to move on."

"So…you're not going to try to reconcile with Dad? I feel like I'm on an emotional roller-coaster ride."

"Oh no, honey. I didn't mean to give you that impression. You can't go backward in life. Only forward. Which is why after tonight I'm going to get out of your hair and let you move on with your life." Her mother hugged her, and held her against her while she spoke. "Thank you for being there for me. It was your kick in the pants that made me wake up."

Jenna pulled back. "What do you mean? What did I do?"

"When you came down to the Cape, you said you wouldn't come back until the end of the summer, and you implied that I needed to deal with life on my own. You were right. I was hiding behind you, trying to fit into whatever you had going on in your life, like I was a girlfriend. I knew I couldn't hide anymore. I just had to find the strength to stop, and when you didn't return my texts and you hesitated about me coming to visit, it was the eye-opener that I needed."

"Then what was up with the tight dress? And the comments on the beach? And the comments about Pete?" *Especially the comments about Pete!*

"The dress? Because I've still got it." She patted her hip. "The comments? Because they were hotties. I'm old. Not blind." Her mom sighed. "Don't worry, honey. I'm kidding. But as far as Pete goes, sweetheart, I was egging you on, trying to get you to stake claim to your man."

"Could have fooled me. I thought you were becoming a cougar."

"Meow." Her mother reached out like her hand was a bear claw.

They headed back into the library arm in arm.

"Hey, Mom? Can you please not ask me anything sexual about Pete? *Ever?*"

"You never let me have any fun." Her mom laughed. "There's no need to ask. The way you looked at each other left nothing up to the imagination."

Jenna groaned, but her insides were doing a happy dance—for both the understanding that her mother wasn't losing her mind after all and at the notion that others could see how much she and Pete cared for each other. She felt like she wanted to stand on top of the Wellfleet fire tower and yell, *I'm Jenna Ward, and I love Pete Lacroux!* It was a relief to share that love with the woman who had been there for everything from skinned knees to career issues. Her mother had never shooed her away the way that Jenna had done to her the last few weeks. As she held the library door open for her mother, she realized that she had to come clean about something else. Something equally as important.

Jenna touched her mother's arm. "Mom, before we go in." She let the door close and reached for her mother's hand.

"What is it, honey?"

"Two things, really. I have a hard time when you say bad things about Dad. I just wish you wouldn't, because it makes me feel like I can't be close to him—despite all the things you just said." She lowered her eyes, then forced herself to meet her mother's gaze again. "I'm sorry, Mom, but can you please not say things about him, or compare him to other men?"

"I'll try, Jenna. I've told you how I feel about him. How I really feel about him. The rest is just a defense mechanism—and a very bad one at that." Her mother embraced her. "I'm glad we raised you to speak your mind, and I'm glad you feel as though you can be honest with me."

Jenna drew back. "There's one other thing. I'm sorry that I tried to avoid your calls and your texts. I'm sorry that I judged you instead of being there for you this summer. I feel really bad about that."

"Oh, honey." Her mother shook her head and hugged her again. "You have your own life to live, and I have mine. You did exactly what we raised you to do. You spoke your mind and took care of yourself. You can never go wrong when you do that, and you know what that means…"

"I don't know what it means, but it feels selfish."

Her mother smiled, and in that smile Jenna saw the mother she knew and had loved for her entire life. "Sometimes you have to be a little selfish to make things right. It means that your father and I did something right, and that makes everything okay."

It was nice to hear her mother say something nice about the time when she was married to Jenna's father. *Progress.*

WHEN THEY ARRIVED back at the cottage that afternoon, Jenna felt more relaxed. She was glad to know that her mother wasn't going through a crazy midlife crisis that might end with her owning a Corvette and having her lips plumped.

Jenna was putting away the new books she'd taken out from the library when her mother came into her bedroom and sat on the bed.

"I think I'm going to pack up and take off this afternoon. You have a life to lead, and God knows I have to start pulling mine back together. Today was a real eye-opener for me. I've missed seeing you look at me like you're not afraid of what I'll say." Her mom smiled up at her.

Selfishly, Jenna couldn't help but think that if her mother left, she and Pete would have tonight alone together, but her mother was trying to mend the bridge between them, and there she was trying to jump over it. She pushed away the selfish thought and focused on her mother.

"This weekend is the book sale. Why don't you stay and help us with it? You're enjoying being here, and it's nice to have you around."

Her mother looked around the bedroom with a thoughtful gaze and smoothed her dress over her hips.

"As fun as that would probably be, there's someone waiting for me at home." Her mother's mouth quirked up into a mischievous smile.

"Someone?" *Oh boy.* Jenna's nerves became inflamed again. *Please don't tell me he's a twentysomething guy.*

"Do you remember Carlos? The butcher?"

Jenna's eyes widened.

"Of course I remember him. He's only been flirting with you since you and Dad split up. But you never pay any attention to him. You do realize he's probably not any younger than dad?"

"Yes."

"Or particularly fit," Jenna reminded her.

"Yes, he does have a bit of a belly, doesn't he?" Her mother put an arm around Jenna's shoulder. "I've been thinking about everything as we've been talking. Maybe who I am really is the person your father left. It's fun to act young, but honestly, it's exhausting. Carlos is kind, he's stable as a rock, and we have a lot in common."

Jenna was relieved to hear her mother say that, and now, more than ever, she didn't want her to get hurt.

"How do you know that Carlos will still want to go out with you?"

Her mom blinked her eyes in a dramatic fashion. "Because your mama isn't a fool, baby. I might have been playing around with my clothes and how I acted, but inside I think I always knew who I was. I can't compete with your father's *young thing*."

"That isn't making any sense. What does that have to do with Carlos seeing how you've been acting and wanting no part of it?"

"Because while I have been feeling things out with you, and with some of my girlfriends back home, outside of those who love me no matter what I do, I've remained the same boring person I've always been."

"But I thought your closest friends had gotten tired of

how you were behaving." Jenna was totally confused.

"Yes, they have, and I'll make that right when I go home. And I hope we're okay now. I'm sorry things got so weird."

"Me too, Mom. I was afraid we'd never get back to normal."

"Honey, we survived your teenage years; we can survive anything."

CHAPTER EIGHTEEN

THE NEXT THREE days passed without any middle-of-the-night calls from Pete's father, but Pete wasn't jumping to any hopeful conclusions. He was sure nothing had changed. Pete called Sky and urged her to delay her visit. *I'm swamped and want to be available to see you when you come out.* Thankfully, Sky had bought the excuse.

Pete spent his days dealing with boat repairs and working through refits for his clients, while Jenna spent mornings with her girlfriends, enjoying the beaches or the pool, and early afternoons tooling around nearby towns. They came together in the late afternoons, usually when Pete was working on his schooner. Jenna read or walked on the beach with Joey. Sometimes she sat in the grass reading, stealing glances at Pete when she thought he wasn't looking. She did that a lot, and he realized he was just as guilty of stealing peeks at Jenna while he worked.

He wiped his hands on a rag and took a deep breath. He'd done as much of refitting the boat as he could before the final step. He'd been waiting to add the final coating of the antifouling paint to the bottom of the boat, with the hopes of his father joining him. His chest tightened as reality settled in. His father wasn't going to be helping him with the boat this summer; that much was clear. Once the sun went down, his father wasn't even equipped to help himself.

"Hey, are you okay?" Jenna hooked her finger in the back pocket of his jeans.

He hadn't heard her approach. "Yeah, babe. Fine." He folded her into his arms. Jenna never minded that he was sweaty or his hands were gritty from working, and he loved that about her.

"I'm almost done. A day or two of painting the bottom, and then she goes in the water."

Jenna ran her finger along his abs. "And you're thinking about your dad?"

She knew him so well already. He didn't want to talk about his father. It was Saturday night, and he hadn't heard from him since they'd had the blowout on Wednesday afternoon. Pete was trying to convince himself that meant his father was making a change, but no matter how hard he tried to believe it, he knew it wasn't so. They'd had blowouts before, and this was what his father did. He could go a few nights without needing help, or maybe he couldn't. Pete didn't know what his father did during those silent nights, but his father always went back to the same old habits, and Pete knew his uninterrupted evenings were limited.

"Yeah. Let's go inside and clean up. We can have dinner out on the patio."

They'd spent most nights at Jenna's cottage so Jenna could be closer to her friends, but they'd spent last night at his house, and when they walked inside, the scent of Jenna's body lotion surrounded him. When he pulled open a drawer next to the sink and found all of the dishtowels neatly folded and color coordinated, he knew Jenna had made herself right at home.

"Sorry," she said with a sweet smile.

"Don't be. I like seeing traces of you here." He wiped his face with a towel, then scrubbed it down his chest and over his arms as Jenna pushed his hands aside and snuggled against him, her cheek pressed tightly between his ribs.

"Babe, how come everything around you needs to be in order, but you take me as I am? I'm not exactly a guy who matches my clothes and shoes; my hands are always covered in grime or wood dust, and—"

"I like things organized because they make sense to me that way. You make sense to me just the way you are." She pressed her hands to his stomach and gazed up at him with love in her eyes.

With all the guilt and worry he carried over his father, Pete wasn't sure he made sense to himself most of the time, but Jenna's love made him feel like the luckiest guy on the planet. He couldn't wait to experience fall at the Cape with Jenna, then winter, when they could snuggle up by the fire and—*Oh shit.* Jenna was only at the Cape for the summer, and they'd gotten so serious so fast that they hadn't slowed down enough to talk about their future—and he wanted a future with Jenna. A shiver of worry rushed through him.

They ate dinner out on the deck, surrounded by the sounds of the bay, and later, they walked down the beach with Joey happily trotting alongside them. As the night progressed, thoughts of the summer ending played in his mind. Jenna lived only a couple of hours away, in Rhode Island, but the thought of not being with her was twisting his gut into a tight knot.

Jenna found a stick and tossed it for Joey to chase. She laughed when Joey tumbled nose first, diving for the stick. God, he loved her laugh.

"Hey, Jen, would you ever consider moving to the Cape full-time?"

Jenna stopped walking and gazed out over the water. Her hair blew back from her shoulders, and a few strands whipped across her cheek. She reached up to clear her hair from her face, and Pete took her hand in his and pressed a soft kiss to the back of it. Then he brushed her hair away from her cheek and smiled down at her.

"Like give up my job and my house and move here?" Her eyebrows drew together.

Not exactly the reaction he'd hoped for.

"I guess. I'm just wondering what we'll do when the summer's over."

Jenna bit her lower lip. "Would you ever consider moving to Rhode Island?"

He folded her into his arms and pressed his hand to the back of her head. He couldn't leave his father, and he knew she wasn't asking him to. She was throwing the ball back into his court so he could feel the same impact of the question as she did.

"Maybe," he finally managed. "I have a lot to work out here, so maybe we should both think about it."

Jenna pressed her lips to his stomach. He lifted her chin, and his stomach clenched at the sadness in her eyes.

"Hey," he said softly. "We'll figure this out. I didn't bring it up to worry you. I just…" He thought about how to explain what he was feeling without putting pressure on her. She was gaining solid ground with her mother again, which was wonderful, but it also made him realize that he had a long road ahead of him with his father. Honesty came before he could process a way to cushion his thoughts.

"I don't want to lose you, Jenna, and just the thought of not seeing you seems impossible. But I know you have a job, and a life, in Rhode Island, and I have both here, not to mention a fucked-up father who needs looking after."

She clenched her fists in his shirt. "In all these years of wanting to be with you, I've never fallen short of seeing forever in my mind. But I never really worked out the particulars, I guess. How can I organize everything in my life except this?" Jenna's voice was laced with worry.

Pete draped an arm over her shoulder. "Maybe because it all made sense to you, like I did. It wasn't a project, or a thing. It was *us*, and you can't figure out us all by yourself."

The issue of their future expanded with every breath as they walked back the way they'd come, their path illuminated by the moonlight, the porch lights of Pete's house beacons of their destination.

The house was quiet, save for the curtains billowing around the living room windows. They went into the bedroom, and Jenna set her sandals beside a pair of her flip-flops in the bottom of Pete's closet. She went to the dresser and squeezed a dab of her body lotion into her hands, then set the bottle beside Pete's cologne. The room instantly smelled like Jenna. With one hand, Pete reached over his back and pulled his shirt off. Thinking of Jenna, he laid it carefully over the chair rather than dropping it to the floor. Everything he did, he did with Jenna in mind, and he liked it that way.

Jenna untied the shoulder straps of her long cotton dress, and it puddled at her feet. She crossed her arms over her bare breasts. The thin line of her taupe thong was barely visible against her tanned skin. Jenna rarely went without a bra, but at night, when it was just them, she felt comfortable enough to do so, and the flush that crept up her neck made her sexy and sweet at once, and utterly irresistible. Pete drew her body against him.

"Love the worry away, Petey." Her whisper brushed over his skin.

He lifted her in his arms, cradling her against him, and

kissed her deeply. Her arms circled his neck as he lowered her to the bed. After divesting himself of his pants, he came down beside her and kissed her again, loving her mouth with all the tenderness and all the desire that consumed him every moment they were together. He slid his lips along the smooth line of her jaw and took her earlobe between his teeth. Jenna sucked in a breath; her fingernails dug into his back.

"I love when you do that," she whispered.

He released her lobe and laved the tender spot with his tongue. Jenna arched her hips against his.

"This isn't bigger than us, Jenna. We'll figure it out," he whispered.

Jenna tightened her arms around his back and buried her face in the crook of his neck, inhaling loudly. She held him so tightly that he felt a nervous trembling in her limbs. She drew back and looked at him with wide, trusting eyes.

"It took so long to find us. I don't see an easy answer." She searched his eyes, and the vulnerability he saw in hers cut him to his core.

"I'll take care of this, Jenna. I promise you, I'll always take care of us."

I'LL ALWAYS TAKE care of us. Pete's hands slid down Jenna's sides, gripping her tightly, his mouth trailing in the wake of his certainty. She knew he would always take care of them. He'd always taken care of everyone. His siblings. His father. Seaside. He'd fixed her pipes, her closet, her roof, and now he'd keep her heart safe, too.

His touch sent shivers through her body as he kissed a path along the edge of her panties. He gripped her hips, holding them strong and sure as he teased and taunted her. She clenched the sheets as he pressed light kisses down her thighs, around the outside, and close—*oh so close*—to her inner thighs. She wanted to feel his mouth on her inner thighs. He knew just how to make her squirm and beg, and she cherished every second of being loved by him. He took her panties off and grazed her thighs with his lips, making Jenna's entire body shudder with need. His stubble scratched her sensitive skin, and when he pressed his thumbs just inside her hipbones, she couldn't suppress a desperate plea for more.

Pete lifted his eyes; a crooked smile curved his lips. He hesitated just a second before settling his teeth over her inner thigh and sucking, sending her hips flying up from the mattress. He pressed her hips back down, driving her out of her mind. She tangled her hands in his hair, urging his mouth higher. He pushed her legs farther apart with his broad shoulders and moved his hands to her thighs, splaying his long fingers across them, his thumbs dangerously close to her center. She felt his thumbs graze her slick skin, and she closed her eyes. His breath swept across her wetness, hot and tantalizing as his thumbs made another teasing pass.

"Pete…Unfair…"

He kissed along the crease in her thighs, then back down to the edge of where she needed him most. *Finally*, his tongue stroked her lightly, pulling another needful moan from her lips. Then deeper, harder. He drove the worry from her mind with every lap of his tongue, every tease of his fingers as they dipped into her and expertly found the spot that made her entire body clench tight and her breathing become jagged.

"Come for me, baby." A heated whisper against her center.

Her entire body shuddered as he swirled his tongue against the bundle of nerves that sent her hips bucking, her fingers digging into his shoulders, and Pete's name sailing from her lips. Her head fell back and the world careened around her as tingling sensations prickled her limbs. She panted hard, and before she could regain control, Pete was on top of her, thrusting into her and sending her into the clutches of another mind-blowing orgasm. Pete buried his hands in her hair, clenching his muscles tight with his own mounting release.

"Open your eyes, Jenna. Look at me."

Jenna tried, but her eyes fluttered closed as her body pulsed and the orgasm claimed all of her muscles.

"Can't…open…eyes," she managed. "Come with…me."

He pushed in deep and stilled, his back muscles coiled tight, and with the next thrust, his head fell to her neck as he groaned through his own magnificent release.

Both fighting for air, they clung together in a tangle of slick body parts and sporadic flinches and thrusts as they calmed from their frenzied state.

Jenna felt Pete's muscles relax and his breathing become even, calm. She sighed contentedly, and her mind drifted to his earlier question. She wanted to be with Pete. She'd always wanted to be with him. She knew family was as important to him as it was to her, and she loved that about him.

"Petey."

Pete lifted his head, his eyes were sleepy and satisfied.

"If you were serious before, I would definitely consider moving to the Cape full-time. Rhode Island is way too far from you, and I'd never ask you to leave your father."

"Aw, babe. You can't begin to imagine how much that means to me."

A vibrating noise sounded. Muffled and short, like a fleeting thought. Jenna glanced across the room at the same time that Pete's head shot up, his brows pinched together.

Pete groaned. "For Christ's sake."

She knew by the look in his eyes, and his angry words, that it was his father calling.

"It's okay, Pete. We'll rinse off and go right over."

He pushed up on his palms and smiled down at her. "Do you have any idea how much I love you?" He pressed a kiss to her lips. "Maybe this was sort of okay when it was just me, but this is definitely not okay now." He pushed off the bed and reached for her hand. "This is going to end. I promise you, Jenna, our lives will not be spent dealing with this."

CHAPTER NINETEEN

SUNDAY MORNING PETE and Jenna sat on the couch drinking coffee, neither wanting to leave before the other.

"Want some toast?" Jenna's leg bounced nervously.

"You're stalling." Pete kissed her neck. "You have to be at the book sale in half an hour."

"Do you blame me?" She set his coffee cup on a coaster and climbed onto his lap. Pete was bare chested, wearing just a pair of Levi's. His skin was still warm and moist from his shower, and he smelled like heaven. Jenna nuzzled against his neck.

"I'm getting used to this whole wake-up-to-Petey thing." She ran her hands through his wet hair and kissed each cheek.

He cupped her butt in one hand and rested his head back. She knew he loved when she stroked his cheek, and she did so now. He had shaved this morning, and his face was smooth and soft. Jenna ran her thumb over his lips and then kissed them lightly, feeling the effect of her love beneath her.

"Careful, or you'll be late." He opened his eyes and resituated Jenna so she wasn't sitting fully on his erection, then kissed her deeply. "I'm getting used to us, too, Jenna. In fact, I never want to go back to not being us."

PETE'S WORDS CARRIED Jenna through the chilly morning. By midafternoon the sun had burned through the clouds and crowds of people milled around the annual book sale—and Jenna was still smiling like a schoolgirl in love. Cars lined up along Main Street waiting to pull into the public parking area behind the church. The parking lot had been packed tight since eight o'clock in the morning. Churchgoers came decked out in their Sunday best, and families rode their bicycles through the quaint town, stopping to check out the titles, which were lined up three boxes deep in the alley, covering the tops of long tables and spread on blankets on the lawn.

"Everyone here is going to know you're a dirty girl if you don't get that stupid grin off your face," Amy teased.

Amy and Jenna sat on metal chairs in front of Abiyoyo, a specialty shop with upscale toys, gifts, and clothing. Behind them was a waist-high brick wall with a New England garden boasting colorful flowers and verdant foliage of varying heights and types.

"You'd be smiling, too, if it were you and Tony." Jenna handed a red-haired woman change for her purchase, and Amy bagged the books she bought for her two young children, who were tugging on her shorts.

"Thanks for stopping by." Jenna watched them walk away and turned her attention back to Amy.

"So, anyway, it looks like I might be moving to the Cape!" She and Amy squealed and hugged for the hundredth time that day. No matter how many times she said it aloud, it still didn't feel real.

"I'm sickeningly jealous, but so happy for you." Amy had on a pair of shorts and a light blue tank top. Her hair was pulled back in a ponytail, and as she spoke, she tightened the elastic band, lifting her ponytail higher. She sat back with a sigh. "I can't get over that you two are finally a couple. And when I see you two together, it's like that's how it's always been."

"That's how it feels to us, too."

"Have you told your mom you might be moving yet?" Amy asked.

Jenna's pulse kicked up a notch. She took a deep breath and reminded herself that her mother was figuring out her own life, and that she wasn't losing her mind. Relief came quickly as she recalled her mother's confession. "Not yet. But I will. He just brought it up last night, and we didn't make any final decisions. He just asked if I would consider it. If, or *when*, I move, my mom and I will still live close enough to see each other often."

"If? I would stick with *when*." Amy smiled and eyed a handsome guy in bike shorts flipping through a box of books. "It's not like you have any obstacles. You rent your house, and you're an art teacher, so you can work anywhere. Or maybe you can start painting again." Amy raised her brows.

"That would be like two dreams come true. Me and Pete *and* painting on the Cape. God, Amy, who would have guessed that our lives would turn out like this?"

"Oh no. I just realized that if you move here, I'll be the only one of us not living here." Amy's eyes filled with worry. "If you guys are always together and I'm the only one who's not, I'll start to feel like a fourth wheel."

Jenna draped an arm around her shoulder. "Ames, you already *are* our fourth wheel, and I'm our third. We need all four wheels to make the girlfriend bus go. That will *never* change. Besides, I can't just quit work this close to the beginning of the school year. That would be irresponsible. Who knows when I can really move here?" The pieces of her life suddenly began swimming before her. She couldn't leave the school without an art teacher, and she'd have to give her landlord notice. Neither was an insurmountable obstacle, and when she compared them to Pete's declaration this morning, that it was time to put a stop to his father's drinking, they paled in comparison.

Amy rolled her eyes and lowered her voice as she rose to help a customer. "You'll make it happen, or I'll make it happen for you."

Jenna didn't want to breach Pete's confidence and tell

Amy about Pete's father, but she was having trouble holding it in, and Amy was one of her most trusted friends. She'd never kept secrets from Amy or their other friends before, and as she thought about sharing what Pete was going through, she realized how her priorities had shifted. How her heart had shifted. She hadn't thought she could ever love anyone more than Amy, Bella, and Leanna, but as she ferreted away Pete's secret, she realized that he'd moved to the head of the line. She waited for guilt to pump her to share the secret that was weighing heavily on her, and when it didn't come, she knew she was making the right decision.

She turned her attention to a woman holding a stack of books and helped her set them on the table. "Wow, that's an armful. I'm glad you found some you liked."

"I always do." The petite, gray-haired woman pulled a leather wallet from her purse. "I time my vacation around the annual sale, believe it or not. Pathetic, I know." She shrugged with a smile.

"Not pathetic at all. Thrifty and smart." Jenna bagged the books as the woman paid Amy. "Enjoy your vacation."

"I'm in Wellfleet. How could I not?" The woman waved as she walked toward the parking lot.

"See? Everyone knows Wellfleet is the place to be. I still can't believe I've gone all summer without seeing the man I wait all year to see. *That* shows me how little I mean to Tony."

Although Amy hadn't said much to Jenna about Tony

not being there this summer, Jenna knew how upset she was. If the tables were turned, and she hadn't seen Pete all summer, her heart would have been broken, too.

"He's been texting you, and I think that tells you what he thinks of you more than his stupid work schedule," Jenna offered, but she knew it wasn't enough, not when Amy wore her love for Tony on her sleeve.

"I know, and it's not his fault, but being stuck in the friend zone was a little easier when you were there with me."

Jenna put her arm around Amy again. "I'll always be there with you. That, you can count on. It sucks that you haven't seen him, and I'm really sorry. I wish I could fix it for you."

"You have your own life to figure out." Amy sighed loudly, her brow wrinkled. "Besides, everyone says absence makes the heart grow fonder, so my fingers are crossed." She crossed her fingers and held them up.

Jenna crossed her legs, toes, and fingers. "I'd cross my eyes, too, with the hope that absence really does make the heart grow fonder—especially since Pete and I will also be separated for a while. I'll have to go back home for some period of time to work things out there."

Amy crossed her eyes. "There. Now we're both covered."

PETE RAN HIS thumb over the rehabilitation and

treatment counselor's card for the millionth time in the past few weeks. He'd done it so often that the card stock was beginning to fray. Calling his brothers had been difficult, and listening to Grayson tell him it was *about goddamn time* had touched a nerve, but he knew Grayson was right, and Grayson's anger had also confirmed that talking to his father alone this time in an effort to get him to seek help was the right way to handle the situation. Even though his siblings weren't dealing with the effects of their father's drinking on a near-daily basis, like Pete was, it had taken a toll on all of them, and it had definitely driven a wedge between them, even if everyone but Grayson pussyfooted around the topic. If they were going to heal as a family, it had to begin with his father's recovery.

Pete considered calling Sky, but he'd protected her this long, what was another couple of weeks? He'd tell her everything once their father was on the road to recovery.

His cell phone vibrated with a text from Jenna. He wondered how long he would have let his father's drinking ride if they hadn't finally come together. Like most uncomfortable thoughts, he shoved it away, thankful that Jenna hadn't turned tail and run when she found out.

The book sale is crazy busy and I miss you tons. How are you holding up? Talk to your family? I found a few books on surviving recovery written for the families of alcoholics. Want me to pick them up?

He never realized how much he could love a person, but

he lived and breathed for Jenna. She'd not only supported his decision to take a firm stance with his father, but she'd also offered to skip the book sale to be there with him. *And now she is spending the time she should be focusing on customers finding books for me.* It was time for him to deal with this head-on. Jenna deserved a life free from his father's disease, and he would do everything he could to ensure that she had it. Hell, he deserved a normal life, too, and he wanted that life with Jenna.

He sent her a text. *I miss you, too. Talked to everyone except Sky. Calling the counselor now. Thanks for finding the books, and sure, please get them. Can't wait to see you.*

Pete patted his thigh, and Joey bounded to his side. Together they walked out to the barn. Pete pulled open the doors, inhaling the pungent smell of old wood, varnish, and paint. The aroma that he'd hoped to associate with his father's recovery now left him a little empty. He ran his hand along the bottom of the boat, calculating the time his father would be in the rehab center if he agreed to go. The rehab counselor had said to plan on three to five weeks of inpatient care, depending on his father's progress. His father had been in complete denial when his brothers had staged a full-on intervention, and he could only hope that with enough love—and enough one-on-one pressure—this time would be different. He had to believe that somewhere in his father's heart he wanted Pete to have a chance at a full life with Jenna, just as he'd had with Pete's mother.

His cell phone vibrated again, and he withdrew it from his jeans pocket and read another text from Jenna.

I know this is hard. Your mom would be proud of you, and one day your dad will realize all you've done and he'll be proud of you for it, too. Xox.

He had his doubts about his father being proud of this particular effort, but with Jenna's encouragement, he held on to a shred of hope that one day they'd both look back and the past two years would be history. A glitch in an otherwise warm and loving family history.

Pete took another long look at the boat—*I'm not giving up on you, Pop*—pulled the barn doors closed, and headed down the sandy path to the rocks overlooking the bay. He and Joey sat side by side on a large rock as he called the emergency number for the counselor and left a message. As the minutes ticked by, Pete's anxiety mounted. He felt like a traitor, turning to the counselor behind his father's back. Someplace deep inside, he knew he wasn't a traitor. He was probably saving his father's life, and he was definitely saving his own, but that knowledge didn't quell the tightening in his gut.

Joey laid her chin on Pete's lap and he stroked her fur. Since day one, Joey had trusted he'd feed her, care for her, and keep her safe from harm. She trusted him like he used to trust his father. Jenna's words whispered through his mind. *I think for some of us—me with my mom, and you with your dad—we have to learn to be just as selfless as our parents were.*

Maybe now it's our turn to rescue them.

He turned her words over in his mind, and his perspective began to change. He rose to his feet as he pushed the guilt aside with a sense of finality, and by the time the counselor called back, Pete was bound and determined to get this done, but first he had one more phone call to make. Being worthy of someone's trust meant more than protecting them from the life's brutal realities. He dialed Sky's number.

"Hey, big brother. What's up?" Sky's smile came through in her voice.

"Hi, sis. Do you have a sec, or are you busy?"

"You sound so serious. Is everything okay?"

Not even a little. "I always sound serious, don't I?" He tried to laugh it off, and knew he failed when she remained silent. "Are you someplace you can talk or are you out?"

"Actually, I just pulled up behind Dad's store. I know I told you that I'd wait to come out, but my hours got canceled at the co-op this weekend, so I figured, why not go see Dad? Besides, it's Mom's birthday. I thought he'd be lonely."

Shit. How could he have forgotten? So much for Pete's plan of heading over to the store after talking to Sky and getting this thing over with.

"Really? You're in town? Great." *Fuck.* He eyed Joey. "Come to my place. I have a new puppy who's dying to meet you, and I'd love to catch up."

"Okay, let me stop in and see Dad. Half an hour sound

good? I just want say hi to him and then I'll come over."

"Perfect." Pete never thought he'd count himself lucky that his father was a functioning alcoholic during the day, but knowing that Sky wouldn't see anything different from what she'd seen during any other visit drove the thought home.

Sky showed up thirty minutes later and ran across the grass toward Pete and Joey. She was wearing a long patchwork skirt, a tank top, and an enthusiastic smile as wide as Julia Roberts's. She dropped to her knees and smothered Joey with kisses. Joey pawed at Sky's hair and licked her cheeks.

"Pete! She's so cute! I love her."

Pete crouched beside Sky and hugged her. "Looks like she loves you, too, sis."

Sky sat cross-legged on the grass as both she and Joey calmed down. Joey nipped at her fingers, and Sky was all too happy to lavish her with more love. Pete's chest was tight at what he had to tell Sky, and as the day wore on and closing time for his father's store neared, he knew he had little time before his father would hit the bottle and there would be no reasoning with him.

He noticed new ink on Sky's shoulder and brushed her hair to the side. "New tat?" She'd begun getting tattoos after their mother died, and though most of them were easily hidden beneath her clothing, Pete wished he could get to the root of what caused her to wear her hurt in colorful, permanent ink, and help her heal.

"Yeah." She craned her neck and looked over her shoulder.

Upon closer inspection, Pete made out the trunk of a tree, with deep roots that spread along her shoulder blade.

"It represents you and my other dork brothers. Roots? Get it?"

Pete arched a brow. Yeah, he got it, all right, and it was a great metaphor.

"I know it looks funny without the top of the tree, but when I was designing it, I realized that I have no idea what my life will be like, so I left it like a blank canvas. I'll fill it in some other time."

"Well, I'm honored." He couldn't help but wonder what type of tattoo his father's alcoholism might incite—and he hoped that was the only thing it incited. He'd kept this from Sky for so long that he'd thought of a million ways she might react, the worst of which was spiraling right back down a dark and lonely tunnel, as she had after their mother died.

"Come on. Let's go hang out on the deck and talk." Pete reached for her hand.

Sky jumped to her feet. "Come on, Joey. He sounds serious. I might need reinforcements." She took Pete's hand, and they headed down the sandy path toward the house. "Are you going to lecture me about finding my niche?"

"I wasn't going to. Although, now that you bring it up…"

She bumped him with her shoulder as they stepped onto the deck. He watched her settle into a chair and gather her long hair over one shoulder. She sighed and stretched her arms out on the armrests.

"You are so lucky to live on the water."

"Yeah. I am pretty lucky, I guess." Every second that passed made it more difficult for Pete to begin explaining. He leaned forward in his chair and took her hand in his once again, hoping the connection would ease the blow of his words.

"Sky, I need to talk to you about Pop."

She smiled. "He looks great. You should have seen his face when I walked in. He was so surprised. Totally worth the drive."

"Good. I'm glad."

"Oh God, Pete. You look like you have something really bad to tell me. Your face has that *oh shit* look." She drew her eyebrows together and pinched her mouth into a tight line, mocking him. "Whatever it is, it can't be worse than when you told me about Mom—" Her hand flew to her mouth. "Oh no. Is Dad…?"

"No. No, Sky. Dad's not dying." *Yet*.

She let out a loud breath. "Oh, thank God. Then what is it?"

"This is really hard to say to you. I know how much you love Pop and that you look up to him."

"Who wouldn't? He runs his own business, he's always

in a good mood, he went to every one of my track meets and to my graduations, and he totally loved Mom with all his heart. Still loves her with all his heart." She shrugged. "He's the best father anyone could ever have."

Pete looked down at his hands, then met her gaze with a serious one. "Sky, Pop has a drinking problem, and I've kept it from you, but it's gotten out of hand."

"Oh, please. He's always had a few drinks, but that doesn't mean he has a problem." She crossed her arms over her chest.

"I know it doesn't, but the fact that he drinks himself into a stupor every night does." He paused, letting his words sink in.

Sky's brows drew together again; then they relaxed and a smile began to curve her lips. "Right," she said tentatively. A second later her eyes filled with worry. "Wait. What? You aren't kidding?"

"It's true, Sky. It started right after Mom died, and it's only gotten worse."

"No. You have to be wrong." She shook her head. "No way."

"Sky—"

She rose to her feet and paced the deck with Joey on her heels. "No way, Peter. You're overreacting. What happened? Did he have too much to drink one night? Two? You have to be overreacting."

"I wish I was." Pete rose and touched her arm.

She shrugged him off.

"Sky, every night it's the same thing. He drinks in Mom's sewing room, same chair every night. He calls me so drunk off his ass he can't do more than ramble about Mom."

Sky's lower lip trembled, and it was all Pete could do to give her the space her body language told him she needed.

"I'm sorry. I thought it was best to shield you from it."

Tears streamed down her cheek. "Why are you doing this? Dad would never get that drunk night after night. Why are you trying to get me to believe this? Do you think it's going to make me suddenly figure out my life or something? Because that's all you care about."

Pete had expected this reaction, but it still stung. "No. I'm telling you this because I am going to talk to him this afternoon and try to get him into rehab before he drinks himself to death. Sky, I don't care if it takes you years to figure out your life, or your career, as long as you're safe and happy."

She scoffed and turned away.

"If you don't believe me about Pop, just think about it. When's the last time you saw him after dark?"

She spun around and snapped, "Last..." She looked away, then turned back and pointed at Pete. "Easter."

"No, you stayed here on Easter, and on Christmas, and during every visit for the last two years." He kept distance between them and fought the urge to reach out to her again. He knew Sky too well. Cornered, she'd strike like a viper.

She needed to come to him on her own terms. She'd always been like that. Even as a little girl she'd refused to hear the things that she didn't want to, until she had time to process them and found them to be true.

"That's because you always have something going on and you invite me and Matt and Hunter, and…Wait. If that was true about Dad, they'd know about it." She pulled out her cell phone and pressed a speed-dial number. "Hunter. I'm with Pete, and he…" She flashed a heated look at Pete while she listened to their brother.

She and Hunter had always been close. While Pete was her protector, Hunter, the second eldest, was more like a best friend to them all, especially Sky. Hunter was the ultimate peacemaker. Pete knew he'd never tell Sky the truth about their father without asking him about it first.

"Yes, I'm in Wellfleet." She listened again. "Why?" Her nostrils flared as she listened to Hunter on the other end of the phone. "Wait, he says Dad—" She quieted again and thrust the phone at Pete. "He wants to talk to you."

Pete took the phone from her trembling hand. "Hey, Hunter."

"Dude, you're telling her?" Hunter spoke a little louder than a whisper.

"Yes."

"Everything?"

"Yes." Pete looked at her damp eyes and felt his stomach sink. "Let me give you back to Sky." He handed her the phone. "I'm sorry, Sky."

She pressed the phone to her ear. "Is it true? Is Dad an alcoholic?" Her hand flew to her mouth and she turned away from Pete. "Mm-hmm. 'Kay. Love you, too." She set the phone on the table and wept softly.

Pete moved behind her, aching to comfort her. "Sky, he's still the same father you know and love, and he loves you to the ends of the earth."

"Why…Why didn't you tell me sooner?" Her shoulders shook with her sobs. "Why is he doing this?"

"Best I can figure is that losing Mom was too much for him."

She turned to face Pete. "He looked fine when I saw him."

"He does look fine during the day, honey. He's a functioning alcoholic. I honestly don't know if he drinks during the day, but he holds himself together somehow. At night, in his house, it's a different story." Pete opened his arms, giving her the option of stepping into the safety of his embrace.

Sky turned away again. "So everyone knows but me?"

"Yes, and that was my doing, not Hunter's, Matt's, or Grayson's. So be mad at me, not them. You were so torn up after Mom died that I didn't want you to worry."

"I'm not a child, Peter." She faced him again, red faced and puffy eyed. "You need to stop treating me like I am."

He nodded. "You're right, and I'm sorry."

She stepped forward, just a few inches from him. "I have

a right to know. I'm part of this family."

"You are, and I'm sorry. I didn't want you to worry about him when you were just getting your life back together." He had been so sure that protecting her was the right thing to do, and now, watching his sister's pain and hearing the anger and hurt in her voice, he reconsidered everything he'd believed.

She took another step closer and punched his chest with the side of her fist. "You should have told me. How can he do this? Every night? Are you sure?"

"I should have, and yes, I'm sure."

"Damn it, Peter." She banged her fist on his chest again and again.

Pete folded her into his arms, and she struggled and pressed against his chest to break his hold, until finally, her sobs took over and she collapsed against him, drenching his shirt with her tears. Pete stroked her back, as he'd done during those treacherous weeks after their mother died.

"I'm sorry. I'm so sorry, Sky." His eyes welled with tears for the harsh reality he'd just revealed. "It's going to be okay. I promise you it will. I'm going to take care of it."

"How can it be okay?"

"Because this isn't who Pop is. I didn't give up on you after Mom died, and I won't give up on him." Flashes of the weeks after their mother's death came rushing back to him. Sky had been so distraught that she'd stopped going to work every day and communicated less with Pete and their brothers. He'd gone to New York and spent two weeks with her. They'd talked about their mother and he'd offered to pay for a therapist, but she insisted that *big brother therapy* was all she needed. He'd kept close tabs on her after returning to the Cape, and thankfully, she'd come out of it okay. He only wished he could have the same effect on his father.

She pushed away from his chest and wiped her eyes. "What now?"

"Now I'm going to talk to Pop and make sure he goes into rehab. I'm involved with someone now, and I can't be running out every night to drag him into bed. I can't worry that one day I'll walk in and he'll be dead. This needs to happen."

"Every night? Dragging him into bed? You've been taking care of him? Alone? All this time?" She searched his eyes.

He shrugged. "Someone had to."

She gulped a breath and punched his chest again. "Why do you always take care of everyone?"

He caught her next punch midair. "Whoa. Why are you beating on me?"

"Because if you're taking care of him every night, you're not taking care of yourself every night. I want to hate you for not telling me. You always take care of everyone, but you don't have to, Pete. You could have let me grieve on my own, and you could have told me about Dad. Hell, you could have let Dad deal with his own mess."

Pete laughed. "Do you think, even for a minute, that I'd let you suffer on your own? Or let Pop disappear into the bottle for good? This is what love is, Sky. This is what family does."

"No, this is what *you* do. Matty and Hunter aren't here taking care of him. Grayson sure as hell would never do it." Her tears had stopped, and every step she took was determined as she paced a path across the deck. "You've been doing this for two years? Two years, Peter? What does your girlfriend think of all this?"

"Her name is Jenna, and she's all for me getting him into rehab."

"That's good. At least someone is looking out for your interests. I want to be there when you talk to Dad."

"No way." Pete dug his keys from his pocket.

"Peter! I'm not a kid anymore. Yes, I was devastated when Mom died, but that was two years ago. I want to help Dad. I want him to know I know what he's doing. Maybe that will push him into getting help." She paced the deck, her long skirt swishing against her legs. "Maybe this is why I haven't found my niche. I've been looking in the wrong places. I was thinking about coming home for the summer next year. I'll come home now. I'll help you with Dad."

Pete couldn't even begin to think of Sky giving up whatever dreams she might have to deal with their father, but he couldn't push her away, either. She was right that she wasn't a kid anymore, even if in his eyes she'd always be his baby sister. He lifted serious eyes to her and saw compassion and love—and something he hadn't seen often enough. *Conviction.* At that moment, she resembled their mother more than she ever had before, and it gave Pete a shiver, and then a sense of pride in how far his sister had come.

"Mom would be proud of you, sis. I'm proud of you. We'll talk about it. If Pop goes into rehab and you feel the same way a week from now, after you've had time to process all this…" He waved his hand in the air. "Then we'll figure it out."

CHAPTER TWENTY

PETE CALLED JENNA on the way to the hardware store. She offered to join them a hundred times, but Pete felt it was best if she didn't. He was worried enough about how his father was going to react to Sky being there, much less someone outside of their immediate family. Although to Pete, Jenna was already part of his family. If all went well, he'd call Jenna after they took his father to rehab. If it didn't, he'd call her when they were done trying. He hoped like hell for the first outcome.

The bell above the door rang out when Pete and Sky walked into the hardware store. Pete locked the door and hung the CLOSED sign in the window. Sky had been quiet on the ride over, but before she got out of Pete's truck, she'd reached for his hand and said, *I know I scared the hell out of you after Mom died, but I'm okay, Pete. I promise. Thank you for letting me come with you to talk to Dad. I want to help.* He looked at her now, standing strong and tall before him, waiting for him before walking to the back where their father was. He'd protected her for so long that having her here in the pit of the mess with him sent a stroke of guilt slicing through him. He forced himself to see her as the woman she was, rather than the scared girl she'd been when their mother died.

He draped an arm over her shoulder. "Let's do this."

Their father turned as they neared the counter in the back of the shop. "Now, this is a pleasure. Seeing Sky twice in one day? Pete usually whisks you away and I don't see you until the next day."

"Hi, Dad." The strength in Sky's voice surprised Pete.

"Hey, Pop. How was your day?" Pete came around the counter and embraced his father. He inhaled out of habit, and when he didn't smell alcohol, he had a fleeting thought that maybe he was overreacting. Then his mind traveled to the image of his father passed out in his mother's sewing room.

"Fine, fine. Can't complain. Did you guys come by to go to dinner?" He set his hands on his hips and smiled at Sky.

"Actually, Pop, we came to talk to you." Pete tried to sound lighthearted, as if he were talking about the weather, boats, anything other than the issue that clawed at his nerves, but he heard the seriousness of his own voice and knew he'd have no chance of masking a damn thing during this conversation.

"Aw shit. There's that tone again." His father walked past him toward the front of the store. "I've got to close up the shop."

"We already did," Sky said. She reached for his hand as

Pete had reached for hers.

"Pop, there's no easy way to say this, so I'm just going to lay it out there." Pete ran his hand through his hair, buying time as his father grumbled under his breath. "Last night was the last time, Pop. I'm done."

"Done with what?" His father smiled nervously at Sky, as if he had no idea what Pete was talking about.

Pete saw the glimmer of worry in his eyes and shot a look at Sky, whose gaze softened. *Shit.* Was she buying into this charade? In an effort to make this as painless as possible for all of them, he avoided defining the elephant in the room.

"You don't need me to spell it out. You know damn well what we're talking about. I've spoken to Tatum Rehab, and I've arranged for a three-to-five-week program—"

"This horseshit again, Peter?" His father shook his head, then shot a look at Sky. "Your brother needs someone to save."

Sky's eyes darted between the two men.

"No, Pop. That's where you're wrong. I'm done saving you. It's time you saved yourself." Pete stepped closer to his father, and the years rolled back, playing in his mind like a movie. Tossing baseballs in the backyard, learning to sail on the bay, his father holding him too tightly the day he went off to college, and holding him just as tightly the day he graduated.

Pete drew in a breath and gathered his determination like armor. "I love you, Pop. I want you to be around for a lot of years."

"Listen to you." He laughed under his breath, then pointed his thumb at Pete and spoke to Sky. "Do you believe this guy? Do you have any idea what he's talking about?"

Pete watched uncertainty float across his sister's face. He held her gaze, hoping she had enough faith in him to trust what he'd told her.

"I do, Daddy." Her voice was thin and shaky.

His father's face aged ten years with her words. His jowls sagged, and his eyelids drooped heavily. "Sky?"

She stepped forward. "I know, Dad. I know about your drinking." Her eyes watered, and again Pete fought the urge to go to her, to put an arm around her and let her know he was right there with her. He didn't want this to be her fight, and he hated seeing her take it on—but it was, really. It was their whole family's battle.

"Sky." Their father reached for her.

She allowed him to take her hand, and she held it in silence for a beat. "I don't want you to die, Dad." A tear slipped down her cheek. "With Mom gone, you're all I have left."

He opened his mouth to respond, but no words came.

Pete's chest constricted as he closed the gap between them. "We all love you, Pop. This ends now. No more burying your grief in alcohol. No more looking for Mom to come back." He glanced at his sister and saw fresh tears fill her eyes. "It's a month of your time, and it'll save your life—

and ours."

His father grumbled something under his breath again.

"Daddy, please? Please get help?" Sky's plea sounded like she was a little girl again, scared and fragile.

Pete couldn't help placing his hand on her lower back to comfort her, allowing her to soak in his strength while hers faltered.

"I have the shop to mind," his father said gruffly.

"I'll run it while you're in rehab," Pete assured him.

"I'll run it," Sky said. "Pete has his own business to run."

Pete shot her a questioning look.

"It makes sense. I go from job to job, and you have clients who rely on you. I can do it, Peter. Have as much faith in me as I have in you."

Well, hell, how could he say no to that? "We've got it covered, Pop. What do you say? There's no more hiding. It's this way, or you're on your own, because I'm done enabling this double life you're living. I've let this go on for two years too long, and I love you too much to let it go on any longer."

His father huffed a breath. "I don't need rehab. So I have a few drinks every night. Big deal."

Pete shrugged and stalked toward the front of the store.

"Peter? Where are you going?" Sky's voice was rattled and high-pitched.

"I'm done. If he wants to kill himself, so be it. I have a life to start living." Pete heard Sky's footsteps hurrying toward him.

"You're just going to leave?" She grabbed his shirt. "You can't just let him keep doing this. You said he could die."

He turned and locked eyes with his sister's terrified gaze and said the hardest thing he'd ever had to say.

"Yes, he could die, and at this point that's his choice. I'm not going to be part of it. This is his choice, Sky, and if he chooses to keep drinking, then I'm out of his life from here on out. He's on his own." He glanced over her shoulder at their father. His head was buried in his hands, his red ears and jowls visible through his fingers. Pete was finally getting through to him. He hated playing hardball without first warning Sky, but he had no choice.

"Damn it, Peter." His father's voice boomed through the shop, loud and tremulous. "Don't you walk out on me."

Pete held his hands up in surrender. "I'm done, Pop. We lost Mom to something she had no control over. I won't watch you willingly kill yourself."

"Peter." Sky's eyes darted from Pete to their father, then back again.

"You're a goddamn stubborn mule, you know that? You got that from your mother." Neil stomped up the aisle to where Pete stood and pointed at his face. "If one single person finds out that I'm in rehab, I'll have your ass."

Pete bit back tears that fought to come. "I've already spoken to the counselor about anonymity, and as far as Sky and I know, you're visiting your cousin in Miami while his wife recovers from surgery." He pulled that out of his ass on the spot, but it sounded plausible.

"Don't expect me to thank you for turning your sister against me." His father narrowed his eyes. "Jackass."

Music to Pete's ears.

CHAPTER TWENTY-ONE

LATER THAT NIGHT Pete, Jenna, Sky, and Joey sat on a blanket on the beach. The bay lapped at the shore, bringing a gentle breeze across the hibachi with each lick of the waves. Stars peppered the sky like glimmers of hope, and Pete couldn't remember a time when he'd felt so settled.

"I still can't get over everything that happened today." Sky wore a hoodie over her tank top, and as she drew her knees up to her chest, her skirt billowed around her bare feet. She rested her head on her knees and sighed.

"I'm sorry, Sky. I should have told you sooner, but—"

"Don't, Pete. Even if you should have, you never would have. You'd protect me until I was a hundred years old if I didn't speak up. I appreciate you taking care of me. I really do." Sky smiled at Jenna and petted Joey. "But now you can focus on Jenna."

Jenna and Sky had bonded over a pint of ice cream while Pete called each of his brothers and gave them the good news. By the time he was done with the phone calls, Jenna and Sky were laughing like best friends—and the ice cream container was empty.

"He always focuses on me." Jenna leaned over and kissed Pete; then she turned back to Sky. "But if you think he'll stop taking care of you, I think you're sorely mistaken. One thing I've learned about Pete is that his love knows no confines, and once it finds you, it never lets go."

"Yeah, I guess it could be worse," Sky teased.

"Hey. I'm sitting right here." Pete reached behind Jenna and playfully pushed his sister's shoulder. "I'll damn well protect both of you as much as I please, so shut the hell up and pass me that pack."

Sky handed him a black backpack. He loaded up two sticks with marshmallows and handed one to Sky. Joey sniffed at the sweets.

"Hey, what about mine?" Jenna wrinkled her brow.

"That's what I'm here for, remember?" Pete began cooking Jenna's marshmallow. So little time had passed since their first date, and it felt like a lifetime. "Sixty-seven seconds on each side, five inches from the fire, twenty seconds with the tip of the marshmallow aimed directly at the flames. I've got this, my little marshmallow princess." He smiled at Jenna.

"Wow, that's quite a process." Sky ate her marshmallow without cooking it. She licked her fingers. "Best thing ever. Besides ice cream, that is." She rose to her feet. "I'm going to go inside and settle in for the night. I guess I'll see you two in the morning?"

You two. It was a given, and one that Pete was ready to

solidify. "Take Joey with you. I don't want you to be alone."

"Oh my God. Are you going to do this all the time?"

"What do you think?" He nodded at Joey.

"Fine. Come on, Joey." Sky patted her leg, and Joey trotted along beside her.

"See you in the morning, sis." Pete blindly fished around in the backpack, watching Sky and Joey walk inside the house. He knew he was overprotective, but he also knew he wasn't about to change, and he was okay with that. Annoying his sister was a small price to pay for peace of mind.

"Here you are, princess." He handed Jenna her marshmallow. "There are very few times in a woman's life when she can don a tiara." He gently placed a plastic tiara on Jenna's head and moved a few strands of her hair over the band. "When you're royalty, of course, but we might be waiting a while for that one. When you're five years old and it's your birthday, if you're lucky, and when you are the marshmallow princess and your prince presents you with golden-brown marshmallows. Not golden, not brown, but golden brown."

Jenna touched the tiara and smiled. "You got me a tiara?"

"I would have bought you diamonds if they sold them in the novelty section of Stop & Shop. Every marshmallow princess deserves a tiara."

"That's almost as romantic as the rock you gave me on our first date." She pulled him down beside her.

Pete waited for her to finish eating the marshmallow, and

then he put her finger in his mouth and sucked the sticky sweetness from it.

"Mm. I like where this is headed." Jenna leaned forward and kissed him again, a passionate kiss that tasted of sugar and love.

Pete lowered her to her back and lay beside her, drawing one thigh over her legs. He caressed her cheek with his thumb.

"Today marks the first night in two years that I won't have to worry about my cell phone going off in the middle of the night and having to race out to check on my father." He paused, letting the weight of that settle into his own mind. When he'd taken his father to the rehab center, Neil had given him a condescending look and followed it up with one of the tightest hugs they'd ever shared. That look cut Pete to his core, and the hug shored him up again. "And it marks the first night of the rest of our lives. Jenna, I don't want to just consider moving in together. I want your face to be the first thing I see in the morning, and I want you safe in my arms when you fall asleep at night. It took us a long time to come together. Let's not wait any longer."

"I have to give notice at my work and let my landlord know I'm moving out, and get all my stuff. I can't just leave the school hanging."

He knew this, of course. He'd never expect Jenna to be irresponsible. He touched his forehead to hers. "I don't mean to rush you, but what are you waiting for?"

Jenna laughed and pushed him onto his back. She climbed him like a mountain, her legs straddling his waist. "I was waiting for you to do more than ask me if I'd *consider* it. I thought that might take another five years."

Pete wrapped an arm around her waist, and in one swift move he rolled her onto her back and pinned her to the blanket beneath him.

"Jenna Ward, will you move in with me? Now? This second?"

She laughed. "No."

He dropped his head to her shoulder. "You're killing me here."

"If you think I'm getting up from beneath you to move stuff into your house, you're totally wrong."

He lifted his head and saw the tease in her eyes.

"Yes, I'll move in with you, but I'm not missing one second of making out in the moonlight with my hunky hero. So moving will have to wait."

"Baby, we might never get you moved in." He sealed his lips over hers and disappeared into luscious Jenna.

EPILOGUE

GONE WERE THE hot afternoons of summer, replaced with the crisp coming of fall. It was the end of September, and Jenna had moved in with Pete three weeks earlier. The school where she'd worked in Rhode Island had thrown her a lovely farewell luncheon, and her landlord was able to find a new tenant quickly and relieved Jenna of the last two months that remained on her lease. Her mother had been excited about Jenna and Pete's news. She'd come full circle and was more like the mother Jenna had always known. Jenna would miss her today, but her mother and her new boyfriend, Carlos, were on a cruise to the Bahamas, and Jenna was happy that her mother had settled down and seemed happy again.

Pete's father had done well at rehab and he'd been home for almost a week. Sky was living with him now and running the hardware store until he was ready to go back full-time. He'd spent the last few afternoons helping Pete put the final coat of antifouling paint on the bottom of the schooner. Today they were taking it out for the first trip on the open water, and all their friends returned to the Cape to celebrate with them.

Jenna leaned against Pete's kitchen counter, watching Leanna pull a tray of warm muffins from the oven. The kitchen smelled warm and inviting and felt like home with Leanna and Bella tooling around as they waited for Amy, Jamie, and Tony to arrive. After a summer of not seeing the guys, they were all excited to spend the afternoon together. Amy was over the moon. She'd talked Jenna's ear off on the phone last night, gushing about seeing Tony again, and Pete was excited to show off his handiwork to the men of Seaside. Unfortunately, Kurt was in New York for the weekend meeting with his editor, Caden had to work, and Evan was working at his part-time job.

Jenna's stomach got all fluttery when Pete walked into the kitchen looking sinfully sexy wearing nothing but his favorite pair of Levi's. Bella and Leanna called Jenna's reactions to Pete, and his to her, their *honeymoon stage*, but as far as she could tell, Bella and Leanna were still in that stage, too, with Caden and Kurt, and she hoped it never ended for any of them.

Pete folded her in his arms and kissed her.

"Hey, you have guests here," Leanna teased.

"Sorry, Leanna, but I don't think Jenna would approve of me kissing you, too." He kissed Jenna again. "Hey, babe. I noticed that you made your way through my drawers, and I appreciate it, but where can I find my white tank tops?"

She hooked her finger in the waist of his jeans and raised

her brows. "I love making my way through your drawers."

Pete pressed his hips to hers. "You have free rein to my drawers anytime you want it," he said against her lips before stealing another kiss. "Tank top?"

"On the closet shelves, with the rest of your white shirts. You had too many whites for the drawer, so I took over a shelf."

"Your house will never be the same," Bella said.

"I knew what I was getting into," Pete said. "And *our* house has never felt more like home."

Our house. Jenna hugged him tightly and shot a cheesy grin in Bella's direction. She watched Pete walk away, embarrassed when a dreamy sigh—the kind Amy was known for—escaped her lips.

"Careful, swoongirl. You're going to burn a hole in the man, looking at him like that. I can hardly believe that all three of us are living at the Cape now. You and Pete will still stay at Seaside during the summers, right?"

"Of course. We'll live here the rest of the year. The same way you and Leanna have done with Caden and Kurt."

"Good. Now we need to work on Amy. And you know, if Amy and Tony ever do get together, we'll have to find a woman for Jamie, too. He's too great to be without a woman." Bella reached for one of Leanna's muffins, and Leanna swatted her hand. "You're so testy."

"I want there to be enough for everyone," Leanna said. "And you always pick at the tops and leave the rest."

"First we have to get Jamie away from his computer. Good luck with that," Jenna said.

Leanna turned to set the hot pad on the table, and Bella snuck a muffin. Without turning around, Leanna said, "I saw that."

Bella laughed. "Hey, they're here!"

They hurried out the door in one mass, pushing past one another on the way to greet Amy, Tony, and Jamie. It was a chilly morning and, as if they'd compared notes before dressing, the girls wore hoodies and jeans, and the men wore jeans and T-shirts. It might set women back fifty years, but Jenna secretly loved that men could brave the cold while women needed warmth.

Pete walked outside in his tank and jeans as Jamie hugged Jenna.

"Hands off my woman," Pete said with a smile.

"I believe that's, *hands off my princess.*" Jenna touched her tiara, because who wouldn't wear one if she had one?

Pete embraced Jamie. "Great to see you, man."

"It was a long summer, but the new project is off the ground with a great management staff in place, so I'm on track to spend more than just weekends here next summer." Jamie pulled Bella into his arms. "I missed everyone."

Pete went to greet Tony, who was still hugging Amy. Jenna gently touched Pete's hand.

"Give them a sec," she whispered.

"They're just friends, Jenna," Pete reminded her.

"So were we." She smiled up at him, and he draped an arm over her shoulder and pulled her close.

"What's with all the touchy-feely stuff?" Pete's father and Sky had taken a walk together on the beach, and judging by their smiles, it had done them both a world of good. Joey trotted along beside them. Joey and Pete's father were as close as Pete and the lovable pup.

Pete's father had looked relaxed in the days since he'd come home, and now his eyes had a sparkle in them that Jenna hadn't seen when they'd visited him in rehab. He had a long road ahead, but he was working closely with his counselor to ensure his transition into living a sober life went as smoothly as possible. Pete, Jenna, and Sky attended weekly meetings for families of alcoholics to learn how to support him in ways that would make sobriety easier for him, and it had brought all three of them closer together.

Sky smiled at Pete, and Jenna saw a silent message of something positive pass between them. Pete had told Jenna that Sky had grown up over the past six weeks. The hardware store customers loved her, and although Pete visited her daily and helped her with shelving supplies and handling the books, she was already putting her own touches on the shop with plants on the counter and in the window and colorful knickknacks that should look totally out of place in a hardware store but somehow warmed it instead. Pete must have told Jenna a hundred times in the last few weeks how proud of Sky he was, and Sky seemed to flourish with his praise.

"Mr. Lacroux, how was Florida?" Jamie asked.

Jenna had kept Pete's secret about his father's rehab. He hadn't asked her to, but she'd known it was the right thing to do. Even friends could make a mistake and let something slip out in the wrong company.

Pete's father slung an arm over Pete's shoulder. "It wasn't what I expected. You know, helping my cousin care for his wife and all. It was touch and go for a while, but they pulled through and were even stronger than they'd been before the whole nightmare arose."

"Glad to hear it." Jamie held a hand out to Sky. "We've never officially met. I'm Jamie Reed."

"Oh gosh." Jenna ran over to Sky. "I'm sorry. It feels like you guys all know each other. Sky, this is Jamie, and the guy glued to Amy is Tony." Jenna hoped that the endless hug was a sign of more to come for Amy and Tony.

Tony set Amy on the ground and they joined the group.

"Hi. Pete's talked about you guys forever. It's nice to finally meet you." Sky crossed her arms over her long-sleeved cotton shirt. She looked like she'd walked out of a summer clothing magazine with her long skirt, sandals, and layers of bangles on her thin wrists. "I'm going to grab a sweater." She headed for her car, and both Tony and Jamie watched her walk away.

Amy swatted Tony. "She's too young for you."

"*Pfft.* What's age but a number?" Tony bumped her with

his elbow and winked.

Amy rolled her eyes.

They took two cars over to the marina. The boat looked picture perfect in the water with a bright red ribbon running along the railing. It had leaked for the first few days until the wood swelled into place. Jenna had fretted over the leaks, imagining the boat sinking while they were at sea, but both Pete and his father had assured her that minor leaks were normal in older wooden boats that had been out of the water as long as his had.

She stood on the deck of the schooner, watching Pete and his father talk on the dock. Pete's head kicked back with a loud laugh, and his father's shoulders moved up and down with a chuckle.

"I missed your whole courtship." Jamie leaned on the railing beside Jenna.

"No, you didn't. Pete still courts me every day." She smiled at Jamie as their other friends gathered around them.

"I'd say you're a pretty lucky lady, then, Jenna." Jamie glanced at Sky, talking with Amy and Bella. "At least now Bella and Amy can stop sneaking into your cottage to break things."

"Yeah, as much as I'd like to bonk them on their heads for turning off my hot water, I can't."

"And the dishwasher last summer. And the roof the summer before…"

Jenna's jaw dropped open. "What? Are you shitting me?"

"Nope. They've been working their magic for years." Jamie laughed.

Jenna narrowed her eyes and glared at Bella. "Nope. I still can't be mad at them. They deserve medals for not giving up on us."

Jamie draped an arm over her shoulder. "You know better than that. Seaside friends never give up."

"Jesus, Jamie. Get your own girl already." Pete's smile told Jenna he was kidding. He knew how close she and her friends were, but she also knew that Pete had at least one jealous bone in his body, though he hid it fairly well most of the time. She didn't mind, as she felt the same pangs of jealousy when other women ogled her man.

"Ready to christen this baby?" Pete asked. He helped his father onto the deck of the boat and stepped on behind him.

"I thought we already did that," Jenna whispered.

Pete patted her butt and leaned in for a kiss. "How about we name it, then?"

Pete hadn't even revealed the name of the boat to Jenna yet, and she was dying to know what name he and his father had chosen. His brothers had come to visit the day his father came home from rehab, and even after hours of brotherly pressure, Pete hadn't caved.

His father came to Jenna's side and placed his hand on her elbow. "Son, can I have a moment with you and Jenna before we do this?"

"Sure, Pop." Pete said something to the others and followed Jenna and his father to the far end of the boat.

Jenna had gotten close to Neil over the past few weeks, and she saw Pete in many of his mannerisms—the way he ran his hand through his hair when he sighed, the dichotomy of his soft tone to his masculine breadth when they were having a private conversation, and maybe the most striking of all, his protective nature toward his family. The last one struck her, because he seemed to have forgotten that one when he was drinking. Luckily, Pete had a long memory, and he'd never given up on his father finding it once again.

"I have spent six weeks trying to figure out what I wanted to say to you," his father began. "At first, I was pretty pissed at you, Pete, and at you, Jenna. I figured that Pete's demand for me to go into rehab was because of you."

Oh shit.

"Pop, please." Pete reached for Jenna.

His father drew in a breath and set a serious stare on Pete. "Peter, I'm going to have my say, so settle down and have a little faith, will you?"

Pete tightened his arm around Jenna's waist.

"*Into rehab.* I can say that now without feeling like I want to choke someone." He smiled at them. "When you lose someone you love, you have two choices. Handle it like a man, or run like hell from the pain. I ran. Straight into the bottle. Pete, I know I put you through the type of hell that no son should ever have to experience, and God only knows how, but you managed to keep our family together, and you never gave up on me." He slid his gaze to Jenna. "I know now that it was your relationship with Jenna that finally pushed you to give me that ultimatum."

Jenna swallowed hard, unsure of what was coming next.

He continued and held Pete's stare. "And I'm damn glad she did." He turned a soft gaze to Jenna. "Jenna, I owe you my life as much as I owe it to Pete, and in the end, to Sky, too."

Pete had told Jenna that when Sky and Pete were working together one morning at the hardware store, Pete had come across his father's stash of alcohol. He hadn't even realized he'd had one there at the store, but he wasn't surprised. By then he'd read the books Jenna had bought at the book sale and he'd spent time with his father's therapist and learned of the many ways alcoholics hide their drinking. Finding a box marked VARNISH full of bottles of alcohol was par for the course. Pete, Jenna, and Sky had scoured every inch of the store after that. Turned it upside down and cleaned out every hateful reminder of the two years that nearly ruined their family. Sky had gone through every emotion in the book—anger, sadness, guilt—and finally settled on not taking apart what she felt, but honoring each of those feelings until she came back to her normal self. She spent most evenings with Pete and Jenna, talking through her feelings, which had been good for all of them. She and Pete had become even closer right before Jenna's eyes.

"I didn't do anything other than fall in love with Pete. It

was his efforts that made the difference." Jenna smiled up at Pete and he kissed her forehead.

"No, Pop's right. It was my love for you that made the difference. You were my eye-opener, Jenna."

"And you were mine, Peter," his father said. "I guess I just wanted to take a moment to say that I love you both, and, Peter, your mother would be proud of you for standing up to an old, stubborn goat like me." He embraced Peter, then extended that embrace to Jenna.

"I haven't had a chance to say it before this, but welcome to the family, Jenna. You deserve a hell of a lot more than a plastic tiara."

"I love my tiara." Jenna reached up and touched the accessory she cherished the most.

His father nodded at Pete and headed back toward the others.

Jenna took a step to follow him, and Pete gently pulled her back to him.

"We should join them."

"We will. I just want a second to say *my* two cents." Pete pressed his hands to Jenna's cheeks—she loved when he did that, and smiled in response.

"Jenna, you changed my world. You opened my heart and my eyes, and Pop's right, you do deserve more than that tiara." He kissed her forehead. "That's why I've gotten the permits to add another structure to our property, a smaller one. An art studio. For you."

"Pete. That sounds expensive, and I don't even have a new job yet." *Holy cow.* Jenna was used to living on an art teacher's salary, a shoestring budget. She had enough savings to help with a few household expenses—which he continuously told her was ridiculous, but still she offered. She was enjoying settling into their new life together, and she'd planned to start looking for a job the following week.

"Shh." He kissed her. "This is my gift to you. You can get another job if you want, but you don't need to. I make enough money to take care of us, and Kurt hooked me up with his friend Blue Ryder, the guy who renovated his cottage for Leanna. He gave me a great deal in exchange for my refitting his brother's boat. That'll be mine and Pop's next project."

"I...I don't know what to say."

Pete dug his hand into his pocket and reached for Jenna's left hand. He sank to one knee, and suddenly she felt like she was in a vacuum, her eyes fixed on Pete's. The sound of the water splashing against the boat, the din of their friends, and the heartbeat that had been thundering in her chest—silenced.

"Say you'll marry me." Pete's eyes never left hers.

Ohgodohgodohgod. She couldn't breathe. Her legs turned to wet noodles, and it was all she could do not to cry. She placed her hands on his shoulders for stability.

"Say you'll let me love you forever in the ways you deserve. Say you'll bear our children and raise them in ridiculous matching outfits and shoes. Say you'll fill our house with rocks that speak to you, and—"

"Yes! Oh God, Pete. Yes! Yes! Yes!" She launched herself into his arms as he rose to his feet and covered his face with kisses as he stumbled backward.

"Oh my God." She kissed him again. "I never expected…" Their lips met again. She hung from him like a monkey, arms locked around his neck, legs dangling a foot off the ground. With his help, she moved down his muscular body until her toes hit the ground, and she clutched the waist of his jeans for support as Pete slid the sparkling ring on her finger.

"This was my mother's. If you don't like it, then we'll pick one out that you love."

Tears of joy streamed down her cheeks. "Your mother's? Is your dad okay with this?"

"I love that you're worried about my father instead of yourself, but yes; Pop gave it to me. I asked him to come with me to pick out your ring and he offered Mom's. I asked Sky, of course, in case she had hoped for it, and she said Mom would have wanted you to have it as her first daughter-in-law."

"Oh, Petey." Jenna looked at the gorgeous square-cut diamond surrounded by several smaller rubies and was powerless to stop the flow of tears spilling down her cheeks. "I'm honored to wear your mother's ring, and there's nothing I want more than to be your wife."

Their lips met again, and the sounds of the morning came rushing back in.

Sky ran toward them with Joey on her heels. She squealed with delight. "You gave it to her! I'm going to have a sister-in-law!"

"We can have a triple wedding!" Bella hugged Jenna.

Jenna glanced at Amy, her smile genuine, her eyes alit with sincere excitement, but Jenna knew her heart must be aching at the idea of not being included in the wedding.

"I don't think a triple wedding works," Jenna said as she pulled Amy into her arms. "Either we wait for a quadruple wedding, or we each have our own."

"No, have the triple. It will be fun," Amy said.

Tony moved to Amy's side. Jenna wanted to smack him into loving Amy, but as she felt Pete's hand touch her lower back, she knew there was no rushing love.

"Jenna's right. Sorry, Ames. I wasn't thinking." Bella hugged her while Jamie and Tony congratulated Pete, and his father stood off to the side, taking it all in.

After being passed around from friend to friend, Jenna joined him.

"Thank you for allowing me to wear your Bea's ring. I'll cherish it forever."

"I wish she were here to be part of this." He glanced at Pete, and Jenna saw a worried look flash in Pete's eyes. She knew that look. She'd seen it many times over the past few weeks. Pete was worried about his father turning back to the bottle. Every day took renewed commitment from his father, and they were all bound together, equally committed to helping him through it. She realized how this emotional time could be overwhelming for him and send him spiraling backward and was relieved when Pete came to his father's side.

Two men with a world of worry between them—and a world of love to pull them through.

"You okay, Pop?" Pete placed a hand on his shoulder.

"Fit as a fiddle. Now, get that worried look out of your eyes. I want to be sober every second of the rest of my life. I missed two years. I'm not going to miss another minute. Let's name this boat."

Pete and his father had nixed the idea of breaking a bottle across the bow or holding a traditional naming ceremony. Instead, they stood arm in arm before the group, with the sun shining down upon their shoulders and smiles on their lips.

"We never had any doubt about *what* we should name this boat. It was just a matter of when it would happen." Pete glanced at his father.

"Christ. Let's not get all sappy," his father grumbled. He handed Pete one side of a vinyl banner and they stretched it out between them. "Without further ado, we give you *New Beginning.*" The banner read, NEW B-E-A-G-I-N-N-I-N-G.

"Uh-oh. I think they spelled *beginning* wrong," Bella said with a furrowed brow.

Jenna's heart swelled with the value that Pete placed on family and the thoughtfulness of the name they'd chosen. She didn't think it was possible to love him more than she did, but in that moment, when their eyes met, the pride in his was palpable, and love blazed an unyielding connection between them.

Pete mouthed, "I love you," and Jenna knew that he would always honor their love, and the family they were bound to have, with the same conviction as he did his nuclear family.

"No," Jenna said. "They spelled it just right."

Ready for more Seaside Summers?

Fall in love with Jamie and Jessica in SEASIDE SUNSETS

CHAPTER ONE

JESSICA AYERS COULD hold a note on her cello for thirty-eight seconds without ever breaking a sweat, but staring at the eBay auction on her iPhone as the last forty seconds ticked away had her hands sweating and her heart racing. She never knew seconds could pass so slowly. She'd been pacing the deck of her rented apartment in the Seaside cottage community in Wellfleet, Massachusetts, for forty-five minutes. This was her first time—and she was certain her last time—using the online auction site. She was the high bidder on a baseball that she was fairly certain was her father's from when he was a boy.

"Come on. Come on. Come on." *Fifteen seconds.* She clenched her eyes shut and squeezed the phone, as if she could will the win. It was only seven thirty in the morning, and already the sun had blazed a path through the trees. She was hot and frustrated, and after fighting with her orchestra manager for two weeks about taking a hiatus, and her mother for even longer about everything under the sun, she was ready to blow. She'd come to the Cape for a respite from playing in the Boston Symphony Orchestra, hoping to figure out if she was living her life to the fullest, or missing out on it altogether. Finding her father's baseball autographed by Mickey Mantle was her self-imposed distraction to keep her mind off picking up the cello. She'd never imagined she'd find it a week into her vacation.

She opened her eyes and stared at the phone.

Five seconds. Four. Three.

A message flashed on the screen. *You have been outbid by another bidder.*

"What? No. No, no, no." She pressed the bid icon, and nothing happened. She pressed it again, and again, her muscles tightening with each attempt. Another message flashed on the screen. *Bidding for this item has ended.*

No!

She stared at the phone, unable to believe she'd been seconds away from winning what she was sure was her father's baseball and had lost it. She hated phones. She hated eBay. She hated bidding against nonexistent people in tiny little stupid phones. She hated the whole thing so much she turned and hurled the phone over the deck.

Wow.

That felt really, really good.

"Ouch! What the…" A deep male voice rose up to her.

Jessica crouched and peered between the balusters. Standing on the gravel road just a few feet from her building, in a pair of black running shorts and no shirt, was the nicest butt she'd ever seen, attached to a tanned back that was glistening with sweat and rippled with muscles. Holy moly, they didn't make orchestra musicians with bodies like that. Not that she'd know, considering that they were always properly covered in black suits and white shirts, but could a body like that even *be* hidden?

He turned, one hand rubbing his unruly black hair as he looked up at the pitch pine trees.

Yeah, you won't find the culprit there.

His eyes passed by her deck, and she cringed. At least he hadn't seen her phone, which she spotted a few feet away, where it must have fallen after conking him on the head. His eyes dropped to the ground…and traveled directly to it.

Jessica ducked lower, watching his brows knit together, giving him a brooding, sexy look.

Please don't see me. Please don't see me.

He looked at the cottages to his left, then to the pool off

to his right, and just as Jessica sighed with relief, he crossed the road toward the steps to her apartment. His eyes locked on her. He shaded them with his hand and looked back down at the phone, then back up at her, and lifted the phone in the air.

"Is this yours?"

She debated staying there, crouched and peering between the railings like a child playing hide-and-seek, hoping he really couldn't see her.

I've been seeked.

Darn it! She rose slowly to her feet. "My what?" She had no idea what she was going to say or do as the words flew from her mouth.

He laughed. God, he had a sexy laugh. "Your phone?"

He stood there looking amused and so damn sexy that Jessica couldn't take her eyes off of him. "Why would that be mine? I don't even have a phone." *Great. Now I'm a phone assaulter and a liar.* She had no idea that being incredibly attracted to a man could couple with embarrassment and make her spew lies, as if she lied every day.

He looked back down at the phone and scratched his head. She wondered what he was thinking. That it fell from the sky? No one was that stupid, but she couldn't own up to it now. She was in too deep. As he mounted the stairs, she got a good look at his chest, covered with a light dusting of hair, over muscles that bunched and rippled down his stomach, forming a V between his hips.

He stepped onto the deck and raked his hazel eyes down her body with the kind of smile that should have made her feel at ease and instead made her feel very naked. And hot. Definitely hot. Oh wait, he was hot. She was just bothered. Hot and bothered. Jesus, up close he was even more handsome than she imagined, with at least three days' scruff peppering his strong chin and eyes that played hues of green and brown like a melody.

"Hi. I'm Jamie Reed."

"Hi. Jessica…Ayers."

"How long are you renting?" He used his forearm to wipe his brow. She never knew sweating could look so sexy.

"For the summer." She shifted her eyes to her phone. "What will you do with that phone?"

He looked down at it. "I guess that depends, doesn't it?" The side of his mouth quirked up, making his handsome, rugged face look playful and sending her stomach into a tailspin.

Jessica needed and wanted playful in her too prim and proper life, but she needed her phone even more, in case her orchestra manager called.

"Let's say it was my phone. Let's say it slipped from my hand and fell over the deck, purely by accident."

He stepped closer, and suddenly playful turned serious. His eyes went dark and seductive, in a way that bored right through her, both turning her on and calling her on her shit. He placed one big hand on the railing beside her and peered over the side. His brows lifted, and he stepped closer again. She inched backward until her back met the wooden rail. He smelled of power and sweat and something musky that made her insides quiver.

"That's a hell of an accident." His voice whispered over her skin.

Jessica could barely breathe, barely think with his eyes looking through her, and his crazy, sexy body so close made her sweat even more. The truth poured out like water from a faucet.

"Okay. I'm sorry. I did throw it, but it's not my fault. Not really. It's that stupid eBay site." Her voice rose, and her frustration bubbled forth. "I don't know how I could lose an auction in the last ten seconds. My bid held strong for forty-five minutes, and then out of the blue I lost it for five lousy dollars? And it was all because the stupid bid button was broken." She sank down to a chair. "I'm sorry. I'm just upset."

"So, let me get this straight. You lost a bid on eBay, so you threw your phone?" He lowered himself to the chair beside her, brow wrinkled in confusion, or maybe amusement. She couldn't tell which.

"Yeah, I know. I know. I threw my phone. But it must be broken. I hate technology."

"Technology is awesome. It's not the phone's fault you lost your bid. It's called sniping, and lots of people do it."

"Sniping?" She sighed. "I'm sorry. I know I sound whiny

and bitchy, but I'm really not like this normally."

He arched a brow and smiled, which made her smile, because of course he didn't believe her. Who would? He didn't know she was usually Miss Prim and Proper. He couldn't know she never used words like *stupid* or even visited the eBay website until today.

"I swear I'm not. I'm just frustrated. I've been trying to find the baseball my father had as a kid. It was signed by Mickey Mantle, and somewhere along the line, his parents lost it. His sister had colored in the autograph with red ink, and I think I finally found it...and then lost it."

"That's a bummer. I can see why you're upset. I'm sorry."

"How can you be so nice after I beaned you with my phone?"

He shrugged. "I've been hit by worse. Here, let me show you some eBay tricks." He scrolled through her apps, of which she had none other than what came with the phone. He drew his brows together. "Do you want me to download the eBay app?"

"The eBay app? I guess."

He fiddled with her phone, then moved his chair closer to hers. "When you're bidding on eBay, and other people are bidding at the same time, you need to refresh your screen because bids don't refresh quickly on all phones." He continued explaining and showing her how to refresh her screen.

She only half listened. She simply didn't get technology, and she was used to sitting next to men in suits and tuxedos, not half-naked men with Adonis-like bodies wearing nothing but a pair of shorts with all their masculinity on display. She could barely concentrate.

JAMIE COULD TELL by the look in Jessica's eyes that she wasn't paying attention. As the developer of OneClick, the second-largest search engine rivaling Google, he'd been in his fair share of meetings with foggy-eyed people who zoned out when he started with technical talk. But refreshing a screen was hardly technical, which meant that either beautiful Jessica was really a novice and had lived in a cave for the past ten years or she was playing him like a cheap guitar. She sure as hell didn't look like she'd been living in a cave. She was about the hottest chick he'd seen in forever, sitting beside him in a canary-yellow bikini like it was the most comfortable thing in the world. Maybe she was a fashion model with handlers that did these kinds of things for her.

Her light brown hair brushed her thighs when she leaned forward, and her bright blue eyes, although looking a little lost at the moment, were strikingly sexy. She had a hot bod, with perfect, perky breasts, a trim waist, curvaceous hips, and legs that went on forever, but that didn't change the fact that she'd tried to avoid admitting that the phone was hers. The last thing Jamie needed this summer was to be played, even by a beautiful woman like Jessica. This was his first summer off in eight years, and he intended to relax and spend time with his grandmother, Vera, who was in her mid-eighties and wasn't getting any younger. If the right woman came along, and he had the time and interest, he'd enjoy her company, but he had no patience for games.

"Either your phone is new, or you don't use many apps."

"No. To be honest, I don't even text very often. I've been kind of out of the swing of things in that arena for a while. And after this I'm not sure that I really want to dive in."

He handed her the phone. "You can do this on your computer. Some people find that easier."

She closed her eyes for a beat and cringed. "I get along with my computer even worse than I get along with my phone."

He still couldn't decide if she was playing him or not. She sounded sincere, and the look in her beautiful baby blues was as honest as he'd ever seen. Oh hell, he might as well offer to help.

"Then you've met just the right guy. I can give you a crash course in computers and phones."

"I've taken up so much of your time already. I would feel guilty taking up any more on a beautiful day like today. But I really appreciate your offer."

Are you blowing me off?

Jamie rose to his feet. "Okay, well, if you need any help,

I'm in the cottage on the end with the deck out front and back. Stop by anytime." He hesitated, knowing he should leave but wanting to stay and get to know her a little better. If she was playing him, she would've taken him up on his offer for sure.

Jessica rose to her feet, grabbed a towel from the back of her chair, and picked up a tote bag from beneath the table. "I'm heading to the pool, so I'll walk down with you."

They walked down to the pool together in silence, giving Jamie a chance to notice how nice she smelled. It took all of his focus not to run his eyes down her backside—he was dying to see her ass, but why rush things and make her uncomfortable? She'd walk into the pool and he'd have his chance.

Jessica dug through her tote bag. She placed a slender hand on her hip and sighed. "I forgot my key. Why do they keep the pool locked, anyway?"

He had no idea why, but she looked so curious that he made up a reason. "To keep the derelicts out."

"Derelicts? Really? My friend suggested that I rent here. He said there was almost no crime on the Cape."

Jamie wondered who her *friend* was. "We had some trouble with teenagers two summers ago, but other than that, your friend was right. There are no derelicts lurking about."

"Oh, thank goodness. I didn't think my coworker would lead me astray. I guess I'll go get my key."

She turned to leave and—*holy hell*—her bikini bottom

was a thong. A thin piece of floss between two perfect ass cheeks. How had he missed that?

It was all he could do not to drool. "Nice suit," he mumbled.

She looked over her shoulder. "Thanks! I saw the Thong Thursday flyer and thought, why not? I bought this suit when we were overseas and wore it there once. I brought it with me, but I never would have had the guts to wear it here, until I saw that you guys had an actual *day* for one." She waved and disappeared up the steps to her apartment.

Jamie spun around and scanned the bulletin board where the pool rules were posted. A blue flyer had been tacked front and center: JOIN US FOR THONG THURSDAY!

Thank you, Bella.

Jamie jogged up to Bella's cottage. The screen door was open.

"Bella?" Bella Abbascia owned the cottage across from the apartment Jessica was renting. Bella was the resident prankster. Her favorite person to play tricks on was Theresa Ottoline, the Seaside property manager. Theresa oversaw the homeowner association guidelines for the community—including the pool rules, which included a rule that clearly stated, *No thongs on women or Speedos on men.*

Her fiancé, Caden Grant, walked out of the bedroom in his police officer uniform. "Hey, Jamie. Come on in."

Jamie stepped inside. "Hi. I wanted to thank your fiancée for Thong Thursday."

Caden shook his head. "She did it, huh?"

"Hell, yes, she did it, and…" Jamie looked out the window at the *big house* where Jessica was renting. The house was owned by Theresa Ottoline, the property manager for Seaside. The apartment Jessica rented had a separate entrance on the second floor.

"Did you see the new tenant? Jessica Ayers?" He whistled. "Hotter than hell."

"I saw her sitting on her deck the other night when I pulled in, but I haven't met her. Bella's over at Amy's with the girls."

Evan, Caden's mini-me teenage son, walked out of his bedroom. Evan was almost seventeen, and this year he'd cropped his chestnut hair short, like his father's. Over the year he'd grown to six two. His square jaw and cleft chin, also like Caden's, had lost all but the faintest trace of the boy he'd been two years earlier.

"Dude. You went running without me?" Evan, Caden, and their other buddy, Kurt Remington, whose fiancée, Leanna Bray, owned the cottage behind Bella and Caden, sometimes ran with Jamie in the mornings.

"Sorry, Ev. Vera wanted to get a jump on the day, so I went early."

"That's okay." Evan glanced out the window in the kitchen and looked down by the pool, where Jessica was spreading a towel out on a lounge chair. "I was gonna go for a run, but if it's Thong Thursday, I think I'll go for a swim instead, then head over to TGG for the afternoon." Evan had worked with Jamie for one summer, learning how to program computers, and he'd been working part-time at TGG, The Geeky Guys, ever since.

Jamie set a narrow-eyed stare on Evan.

"What?" Evan laughed.

"Behave," Jamie said, before walking out the door and across the gravel road to Amy's cottage. *Christ, now I'm jealous of a kid?*

He glanced at the pool, tempted to put on his own suit and head down for a gawk and a swim. Instead, he headed across the gravel road to Amy Maples's cottage.

"Hi, Jamie. Just in time for coffee." Amy handed him a mug over the railing of her deck.

"Thanks."

Jenna Ward, a big-busted brunette, and Bella, a tall, mouthy blonde, followed Amy out of her cottage. They wore sundresses over their bathing suits, their typical Cape attire. The Seaside cottages had been in their families for years, and Jamie had grown up spending summers with the girls and Leanna Bray, who owned the cottage beside Vera's, and Tony Black, who owned the cottage on the other side of Leanna's.

"Come on up here, big boy." Bella waved him onto the deck and pulled out a chair.

"I owe you big-time, Bella." He sat beside her and set his coffee on the glass table.

"Most people do," she teased.

"I know I do." Jenna had recently gotten engaged to Pete Lacroux, a local boat craftsman, who also handled maintenance for Seaside—and had been the object of Jenna's secret crush for years. Bella and Amy had secretly broken things in Jenna's cottage for several summers without Jenna knowing, to ensure that she and Pete would have reasons to be thrown together.

"Thong Thursday?" Jamie shook his head. "You are a goddess, Bella."

She patted her thick blond hair. "Thank you for noticing."

"Leanna is going to be so mad at you for doing that," Jenna said. "She doesn't think our men need to see butt floss on any of us." Leanna ran a jam-making business out of Kurt's bay-side property.

Bella swatted the air. "She's staying at their bay house for a few days. She'll miss it completely." The lower Cape was a narrow peninsula that sprawled between Cape Cod Bay and the Atlantic Ocean. The cottages were located between the two bodies of water, and both Kurt and Pete owned property on the bay. Caden and Bella had a house on a street around the corner from the bay, and all three couples spent most of their summers at Seaside and the rest of the year at their other homes.

Luscious Leanna's Sweet Treats had really taken off in the last two years, and since her business was run from a cottage on their bay property, she was spending more and more time there.

"I'm sure Tony won't complain," Amy said with an eye roll that could have rocked the deck. Tony Black was a professional surfer and a motivational speaker, and Amy had been hot for him for about as long as Jenna had been lusting after Pete, but Tony had never made a move toward taking their relationship to the next level. Jamie didn't get it. He'd seen Tony eyeing Amy, and Tony took care of her like she was his girlfriend. Amy was hot, smart, and obviously interested—Tony was a big, burly guy with a good head on his shoulders. They'd make a great pair.

"Speaking of Tony, I saw him leave early this morning. He's spending the day at the ocean." Jamie sipped his coffee.

"Good, then maybe he'll miss the thong show, too." Amy leaned over the table and lowered her voice. "Did you guys see the chick renting Theresa's condo?"

"All I know is that she's smokin' hot and she doesn't talk much." Jenna was busy resituating the top of her sundress, pulled tightly across her enormous breasts.

"I don't know what her deal is," Bella said. "But she was yelling at her phone the other day."

"You mean yelling on her phone," Jenna corrected her.

"No, I mean at. She was staring at it, smacking it, and yelling at it." Bella made a cuckoo motion with her finger beside her head.

Nothing new here from the girls. A little jealousy over

the new hot chick. Jamie picked up his coffee mug. "Mind if I bring this back later? I have to get going. I'm running into Hyannis to pick up a few things. You guys need anything?"

The girls shook their heads.

"You're willingly going to miss Thong Thursday?" Bella put her hand to his forehead. "You must be ill."

No shit. "One look at my ass in a thong and she'll be chasing me around the complex. I wouldn't want to subject you three ladies to that. It could get ugly." He smiled with the tease.

"Ha! Yeah, right. Like you'd ever wear a thong." Jenna threw her head back with a loud laugh. "You're just worried about sporting a woody down by the pool."

She had him there.

"You've got woodies on the brain," Jamie said. "Are you guys coming to Vera's concert tonight?" Vera had played the violin professionally when she was younger, and this summer a group of older Wellfleet residents had put together a string quartet and invited Vera to play. They never saw much of a crowd, but it got her out of the house and playing for an audience again, which she enjoyed.

"I wouldn't miss Vera's concert," Amy said.

"Bella and I are going over together because Caden's taking someone's shift and Pete's hanging with his father tonight, working on a boat. I'll ask Sky if she wants to come, too." Sky was Pete's sister. She'd come to the Cape last summer to run their father's hardware store while he was in rehab, and she'd never gone back to New York other than to pack up her things. Now sober for almost a year, their father helped Pete with his boat-refinishing business.

"Vera will be glad to hear it, and she loves Pete's sister." He glanced down at the pool, then headed for his cottage.

"Want to bet who's going to bang the new chick? Tony or Jamie?" Jenna's voice trailed behind him.

Jamie slowed to hear the answer.

A crack of hand on skin told him that Amy had shut Jenna up with a friendly swat.

To continue reading, buy **SEASIDE SUNSETS**

Have you met the Bradens?

Fall in love with Treat and Max in this emotionally gripping love story.

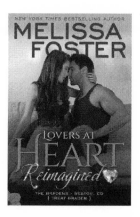

CHAPTER ONE

TREAT BRADEN DIDN'T usually charter planes. It wasn't his style to flash his wealth. But today he needed to be anywhere but his Nassau resort, and missing his commercial flight had just plain pissed him off. He owned upscale resorts all over the world, and he'd been featured on travel shows so many times that it turned his stomach to have to play those ridiculous media games. Lately, the pomp and circumstance surrounding him had begun to irk him in ways that it never had before meeting Max Armstrong. It had been too many long, lonely weeks since he'd seen her standing in the lobby of his Nassau resort, since his heart first thundered in a way that threw him completely off-kilter—and since they'd spent one incredible evening together. Treat wasn't a Neanderthal. He'd known he had no claim on her, even after their intimate evening. Hell, they hadn't even slept together. But that hadn't stopped his blood from boiling or kept him from acting like a jerk the next morning when he'd seen her with another man in front of the elevators, wearing the same clothes she'd had on when Treat had left her the night before.

He hadn't been able to stop thinking about Max since the moment he'd first met her, despite the uncomfortable encounter, but he'd been burned before, and he wasn't into repeating his mistakes. Getting away from resorts altogether and spending a weekend with his father at his ranch in Weston, Colorado, a small ranch town with dusty streets, too many cowboy hats, and a main drag that had been built to replicate the Wild West, was just what he needed.

His rental SUV moved at a snail's pace behind a line of traffic that was not at all typical for his hometown. It wasn't until he crawled around the next curve and saw balloons and banners above the road announcing the annual Indie Film Festival that he realized what weekend it was. He uttered a curse. He wasn't in the mood to deal with crowds.

His cell phone rang, and his sister's name flashed on the

screen. Before he could say hello, Savannah said, "I can't believe you didn't tell me you were coming to town."

"Hi, sis. I miss you, too." The only girl among his five siblings, Savannah was a cutthroat entertainment attorney, but to Treat she'd always be his baby sister.

"When will you get into Weston?"

"I'm here now, sitting in traffic on Main Street." He hadn't moved an inch in five minutes.

"I'm at the festival with a client. Come see me."

All he really wanted to do was reach his father's two-hundred-acre ranch just outside of town, but Treat knew that if he didn't see Savannah right away, she'd be disappointed. Disappointing his siblings was something he strived not to do. Having lost their mother when Treat was only eleven and his youngest sibling, Hugh, had been hardly more than a baby, his siblings had already faced enough disappointment for one lifetime.

"You're with a client. Sure you can get away?" he asked.

"For you? Of course. Besides, I'm with Connor Dean. He can handle things for a little while. Come in the back gate. I'll wait there." Connor was an actor who was quickly climbing the ranks of fame. Savannah had been his attorney for two years, and whenever he had a public engagement, he brought her along. It wasn't a typical attorney-client relationship, but for all of Connor's bravado, he'd been slandered one too many times. Savannah kept track of what was and wasn't said at most events—by both Connor and the media.

"I'll be there as soon as traffic allows." After he ended the call with Savannah he called his father.

"Hey there, son."

Hal's slow, deep drawl tugged at Treat's heart. He'd missed him. Hal had always been a calming influence on Treat. After his mother passed away, his father had pulled him and his siblings through those tumultuous years. But Hal wasn't a coddler. He had instilled a strong work ethic and sense of loyalty into their heads, and that had enabled each of them to be successful in their endeavors.

"Dad, I'm here in town, but I'm going to stop at the festival first to see Savannah, if you don't mind."

"Yup. Savannah called. She misses you, and I'd venture a guess that you could use a little extended family time, too."

He could say that again. Anything to keep his mind off Max.

TREAT PULLED UP to the rear gate behind a mass of media surrounding a number of cars. He rolled down his window and was met with too many shouts to decipher. It was obvious no one was going anywhere anytime soon. He pulled into the parking lot outside the fence and decided he'd run in, say hello to Savannah, and tell her he'd catch up with her later at their father's ranch. The last thing he needed was to deal with this type of headache.

He heard his sister's voice and swiftly scanned the crowd. If anyone was giving her a hard time, he'd set them straight. Savannah was standing with her body out of a limousine's sunroof, shouting who knew what as the media hollered questions at Connor through the slightly open tinted limousine window.

Treat leaned against the entrance to the gate, crossed one foot over the other, and watched his little sister in action. Her long auburn hair looked like fire against her serious more-green-than-hazel eyes. She'd inherited their mother's spitfire personality and was the only one to have their mother's coloring, while he and his brothers took after their dark-haired father.

Savannah's gaze shifted in his direction, and her scowl morphed into an excited smile as she hoisted herself through the sunroof like she climbed mountains for a living.

Treat pushed away from the fence and headed toward his sister in full protective mode. She might be tough, but those media animals pushing their way forward could easily injure her. He plowed through the crowd. His six-foot-six frame naturally commanded more space, and the sea of paparazzi parted for him. He gently persuaded the few that remained in his path with a domineering stare—a stare he hadn't needed to rely upon since Savannah was a teenager, when he and his brothers had spent countless hours keeping horny boys away from their precious sister.

He reached up and caught Savannah as she jumped down from the roof of the limo. He spun her around and, as he lowered her to the ground, his eyes landed on a woman standing at the front of the line of cars waving her hands. Her dark hair was pulled back in a ponytail, her red-framed glasses perched on her perky nose. She looked fierce and beautiful, and Treat's breath caught in his throat. *Max.*

MAX ARMSTRONG STOOD beside her car waving her hands, hoping to create a long enough break in the excitement to gain control of the crowd. Chaz Crew, Max's boss and founder of the Indie Film Festival, had created so much buzz over the past few years that they were expecting more than forty thousand attendees. The festival grounds covered one hundred acres a few blocks from Main Street and boasted five new theaters, restaurants, gift shops, and a high-class hotel. Hotels in neighboring towns were booked a full year in advance of the festival. Whether there were twenty thousand or fifty thousand attendees, Max was ready. She'd been handling the festival sponsors and logistics for almost eight years, and nothing could throw her off her game. Not even the ruckus between the celeb's entourage and the media, which was creating a tornado of confusion.

Photographers surrounded Connor Dean's limousine and the two accompanying SUVs. Max should have known this might happen. Dean was a local actor turned millionaire whose reputation had exploded since they'd booked him ten months earlier. She'd been wrong to think the Hulk-like security guards could manage a little drama. Shouts and threats were tossed around like candy to children, and no one was making any headway. *What on earth is that woman doing with her body halfway out of the sunroof on that limo? And what is she shouting? Legal jargon?*

The heck with this. It was time for Plan B. She climbed onto the roof of her car, which she'd strategically parked in front of the first SUV. *This* was why she wore jeans and her usual festival T-shirt. Because crazy shit happened at festivals.

With a quick flip of a switch on the control panel on her belt, she turned on the intercom mounted above the gate. "Okay, the show is over." Her voice boomed from the loudspeakers. "Let's give Mr. Dean some space to continue driving through. He'll be signing autographs and answering questions after his appearance." She scanned the area, her gaze landing on a man towering above the crowd with a gorgeous woman in his arms. He spun the woman to the side and his face came into view.

Max froze.

Treat?

Her pulse soared, and the butterflies in her stomach she thought she'd annihilated weeks ago swarmed to life with a vengeance. She had worked with Treat's assistant, Scarlet, for months coordinating logistics for Chaz's double wedding, which had taken place at Treat's Nassau resort. The other groom in the wedding was Treat's cousin, Blake Carter. She'd dealt with Treat so many times over the phone that he'd become the object of her late-night fantasies. But even her fantasies hadn't prepared her for meeting the impossibly tall, darkly handsome god that was Treat Braden, with his seductive voice and the way every inch of him screamed of adrenaline-pumping, heart-fluttering masculinity. She'd thought herself unflappable, but Treat had proved her wrong.

Her entire body heated up just thinking about the magical evening they'd spent in each other's arms. She could still feel his eager arousal pressed against her as they danced, still taste his warm, sensuous lips, and she could still see him gazing at her as though she were the only woman on earth. He hadn't even pushed when, after hours of dancing and walking on the beach, kissing like they'd been lovers forever, she'd turned down his offer to return to his suite and extend their evening into morning. Seeing him now, she had a hard time reconciling that incredibly romantic, thoughtful man with the arrogant one who had blown her off the next morning. Sure, she'd been in the same clothes she'd worn the night before, and yes, she'd been out for the remainder of that evening with a man named Justin, but Treat's assumption about what they'd done pissed her off. And the look he'd given her was too reminiscent of the painful relationship she'd escaped years earlier to chase him down and explain. She had every right to do whatever she wanted to do with whomever she wanted, without judgment. Even if she hadn't done anything at all.

She shouldn't care what he thought.

But she did, and that hurt because that awful look he'd given her was in such stark contrast to the impeccable manners he'd otherwise exuded, holding doors, thinking of the needs of her and his other guests before himself, taking extra steps to ensure that every little detail of his cousin's wedding had been taken care of. The truth was, she'd fallen hard for Treat within a few hours of being with him. But Max knew she shouldn't let those feelings sway her resolve. She'd been mistreated, demeaned, and judged by a previous boyfriend, and she swore she'd never go down that road again—not even for too-sexy-for-his-own-good Treat Braden.

She stumbled backward. One of the security guards reached for her across the roof of the car, and she grabbed his arm, finding her footing.

"Max! You okay?"

The security guard's voice wrenched her back to the ensuing chaos. She tore her eyes from Treat and whoever the woman was that he was holding as if she meant everything in the world to him and tried to blink away the unexpected sting of hurt slicing through her.

"Clear a path or you'll be removed from the premises for

the rest of the festival." Even she could hear the difference in her voice, the weakness. Her gaze darted back to Treat, who was staring at her with an incredulous expression. Suddenly painfully aware of her jeans and T-shirt, the ponytail in her hair—and how she must look like a crazy woman standing on top of the car—she clambered down to the ground as the crowd surprisingly obeyed her orders and began to dissipate. Threats of eviction usually worked.

She turned off the intercom and fumbled for her keys. Treat was heading her way, but she didn't want to speak to him, couldn't speak to him, after the way he'd looked at her.

"Max," he called.

His rich, deep voice was enough to make her body ache. She cursed under her breath as she started the car and navigated around the crowd. She glanced in her rearview mirror. Treat stood alone in his dark suit, staring after her, while his beautiful companion looked on with a confused expression on her face. Max's hands trembled as she grasped the steering wheel tighter and drove away.

To continue reading, buy
LOVERS AT HEART, REIMAGINED

Watermelon Jam

1 three-pound seedless watermelon*

2 1.75-ounce packages of powdered pectin

8 cups white cane sugar

2 tablespoons lemon juice

Before starting the jam, boil the jars and lids in large saucepan so when you fill them they won't break from the heat of the jam. Scoop out three pounds of seedless watermelon and place in blender. Finely chop the watermelon so that there are still small chunks. Place the watermelon in an 8-quart saucepan and bring to a boil; then add the pectin slowly. Keep stirring so that nothing sticks to the bottom. Bring it back to a boil and add the sugar very slowly so that you don't drop the temperature of the mix too fast. Bring back to a boil for 1 minute and then fill your (already hot) jars. After filling the jars, turn them upside down for 5 minutes and then back upright. This will seal the jars. This recipe will fill 10 eight-ounce mason jars.

*It might take a large watermelon to get three pounds of fruit, so look for the largest one you can find.

AVAILABLE from www.AlsBackwoodsBerrie.com, Amazon, and other retailers.

MORE BOOKS BY MELISSA FOSTER

LOVE IN BLOOM SERIES

SNOW SISTERS

Sisters in Love

Sisters in Bloom

Sisters in White

THE BRADENS at Weston

Lovers at Heart, Reimagined

Destined for Love

Friendship on Fire

Sea of Love

Bursting with Love

Hearts at Play

THE BRADENS at Trusty

Taken by Love

Fated for Love

Romancing My Love

Flirting with Love

Dreaming of Love

Crashing into Love

THE BRADENS at Peaceful Harbor

Healed by Love

Surrender My Love

River of Love

Crushing on Love
Whisper of Love
Thrill of Love

THE BRADENS & MONTGOMERYS at Pleasant Hill – Oak Falls

Embracing Her Heart
Anything For Love
Trails of Love
Wild, Crazy Hearts
Making You Mine
Searching For Love

THE BRADEN NOVELLAS

Promise My Love
Our New Love
Daring Her Love
Story of Love
Love at Last
A Very Braden Christmas

THE REMINGTONS

Game of Love
Stroke of Love
Flames of Love
Slope of Love
Read, Write, Love
Touched by Love

SEASIDE SUMMERS

Seaside Dreams

Seaside Hearts

Seaside Sunsets

Seaside Secrets

Seaside Nights

Seaside Embrace

Seaside Lovers

Seaside Whispers

Seaside Serenade

BAYSIDE SUMMERS

Bayside Desires

Bayside Passions

Bayside Heat

Bayside Escape

Bayside Romance

Bayside Fantasies

THE RYDERS

Seized by Love

Claimed by Love

Chased by Love

Rescued by Love

Swept Into Love

THE WHISKEYS: DARK KNIGHTS AT PEACEFUL HARBOR

Tru Blue

Truly, Madly, Whiskey
Driving Whiskey Wild
Wicked Whiskey Love
Mad About Moon
Taming My Whiskey
The Gritty Truth

SUGAR LAKE
The Real Thing
Only for You
Love Like Ours
Finding My Girl

HARMONY POINTE
Call Her Mine
This is Love
She Loves Me

THE WICKEDS: DARK KNIGHTS AT BAYSIDE
A Little Bit Wicked
Wicked Aftermath

WILD BOYS AFTER DARK (Billionaires After Dark)
Logan
Heath
Jackson
Cooper

BAD BOYS AFTER DARK (Billionaires After Dark)

Mick

Dylan

Carson

Brett

HARBORSIDE NIGHTS SERIES

Includes characters from the Love in Bloom series

Catching Cassidy

Discovering Delilah

Tempting Tristan

More Books by Melissa

Chasing Amanda (mystery/suspense)

Come Back to Me (mystery/suspense)

Have No Shame (historical fiction/romance)

Love, Lies & Mystery (3-book bundle)

Megan's Way (literary fiction)

Traces of Kara (psychological thriller)

Where Petals Fall (suspense)

ACKNOWLEDGMENTS

Spending summers on the Cape for what seems like forever has brought a whole new level of enjoyment when writing. With each book, I get to revisit my favorite place on earth and bring it to life for you. I hope you enjoy the antics of the Seaside crew, and to answer many readers' questions, the Seaside community is a fictional one. Any similarities between the Seaside community in the series and real Cape communities are coincidental.

I'd like to thank Charles "Bud" Dougherty for helping me with all things boat related. Thank you for sharing your insurmountable knowledge and your excitement for nautical life. As always, you are a joy to chat with. I have taken fictional liberties in my story. Any and all errors are my own.

Tremendous gratitude to my editorial team: Kristen Weber, Penina Lopez, Jenna Bagnini, Juliette Hill, Marlene Engel, and my last set of eyes, Lynn Mullan. You are patient, funny, kind, and a pleasure to work with. Thank you, Natasha Brown, for creating the perfect covers for the Seaside Series and bringing my imagery to life, and thank you, Clare Ayala, for your endless patience and expertise when formatting my material.

And a special thanks goes to Al Chisholm of Al's Backwoods Berries, my partner in the creation of Luscious Leanna's Sweet Treats and the best damn jam maker around. If you're in Wellfleet during the summer, you can find Al and Luscious Leanna's Sweet Treats at the flea market, or visit his website noted on the recipe page in this book. Luscious Leanna's Sweet Treats are also available on Amazon.

Last but never least, thank you to my supportive husband and family, who encourage me in every way and make my writing possible.

www.MelissaFoster.com

Melissa Foster is a *New York Times* and *USA Today* bestselling and award-winning author. Her books have been recommended by *USA Today's* book blog, *Hagerstown* magazine, *The Patriot*, and several other print venues. Melissa has painted and donated several murals to the Hospital for Sick Children in Washington, DC.

Visit Melissa on her website or chat with her on social media. Melissa enjoys discussing her books with book clubs and reader groups and welcomes an invitation to your event. Melissa's books are available through most online retailers in paperback, digital, and audio formats.

Melissa also writes sweet romance under the pen name, Addison Cole.

Made in the USA
Coppell, TX
21 February 2020

16049334R00208